TEARS
IN THE
GRASS

Lynda A. Archer

TEARS IN THE GRASS

a novel

DUNDURN
TORONTO

Editor: Allison Hirst
Design: Jennifer Gallinger
Cover Design: Laura Boyle
Image credits: arinahabich/123RF.com
Printer: Webcom

Library and Archives Canada Cataloguing in Publication

Archer, Lynda A., author
        Tears in the grass / Lynda A. Archer.

Issued in print and electronic formats.
ISBN 978-1-4597-3211-7 (paperback).--ISBN 978-1-4597-3212-4 (pdf).--ISBN 978-1-4597-3213-1 (epub)

        1. Native peoples--Canada--Residential schools--Fiction. I. Title.

PS8601.R38T43 2016   C813'.6   C2015-904916-4
                                                   C2015-904917-2

1   2   3   4   5   20   19   18   17   16

We acknowledge the support of the **Canada Council for the Arts** and the **Ontario Arts Council** for our publishing program. We also acknowledge the financial support of the **Government of Canada** through the **Canada Book Fund** and **Livres Canada Books,** and the **Government of Ontario** through the **Ontario Book Publishing Tax Credit** and the **Ontario Media Development Corporation.**

Care has been taken to trace the ownership of copyright material used in this book. The author and the publisher welcome any information enabling them to rectify any references or credits in subsequent editions.

— *J. Kirk Howard, President*

The publisher is not responsible for websites or their content unless they are owned by the publisher.

Printed and bound in Canada.

VISIT US AT
Dundurn.com | @dundurnpress | Facebook.com/dundurnpress | Pinterest.com/dundurnpress

Dundurn
3 Church Street, Suite 500
Toronto, Ontario, Canada
M5E 1M2

For my sons,
Joshua and Tobiah

I watch the child struggle. Trying to make her mouth do what her father's mouth has done. Lips pressed together to make buh. *Upper teeth grazed over the lower lip with a puff of air to give* fuh. *And finally the rounded lips for* lo.

Buffalo.

I like to see the word spoken even though it isn't correct.

I'm a bison. Buffalo or bison, it matters little. As with others who have come here, the word seemed to mean nothing to the girl, even after her father said the Mounties made huge coats from my hide, the Indians pemmican from my flesh.

They've moved on now, on to the next gallery. I've never seen it but I can guess from the comments — the large brown eyes, how gracefully they run — that it's a deer. I've always been in this gallery. Along with a rabbit that never ceases to crouch in the long grasses. Grasses that are brittle and unscented, not moist and sweet smelling like those I was raised on.

The child's stumbling lips stir memories of calves in the springtime.

Swaying bodies. Crumbling legs. Then sprawled on the ground.

There is nothing about calves in the plaque that hangs beside my gallery. Through countless recitations I've come to know what is written there:

Bison (*Bison bison*). Weight ranges from 800 to 1,500 pounds. Largest land mammal on the North American continent. Roamed in the Plains regions — Saskatchewan, Alberta, Montana, South Dakota, Kansas. At its zenith is estimated to have numbered in the millions. Of great importance to Plains Indians.

Some who come to the museum give barely a glance in my direction. Some of the younger ones run their tongues over my glass, draw their fingers through the wetness.

Why do they come? Do they come to remember? Or is it new memories they seek?

Do they want to know that in my life, before this museum, I fathered many calves?

It wasn't easy to get with a cow. If she wasn't ready for you she'd push and shove, turn away, or drop onto her belly or knees. My loud voice and fearsome challenges of the younger bulls were of no consequence. The cow decided when she'd be mounted. Once she did, it was a quick affair. Always the wolves were lurking. And there were other cows to be attended to if the herd was to remain strong.

Through the dark prairie winter the cows swelled up with the next generation.

If the winter wasn't too harsh, in the spring many calves, slippery and wet, dropped onto the earth.

Every year it was the same. Until it stopped.

Until the hunting was relentless.

Why do they come?

There was one person, an old Indian woman, with whom it was different.

When she visited, my glass seemed to disappear.

The buffalo are strange animals; sometimes they are so stupid and infatuated that a man may walk up to them in full sight on the open prairie, and even shoot several of their number before the rest will think it is necessary to retreat. Again at another moment they will be so shy and wary, that in order to approach them the utmost skill, experience and judgment are necessary.

— Francis Parkman, *Buffalo Hunt*, 1849

1

Wrinkled moccasins scraping over a painted plywood floor that rarely felt the scratch of a broom, Elinor shuffled to the kitchen and banged the kettle onto the stove. A shiver, unfettered by flannel pajamas and thick sweater, sped the length of her thin body. She loved autumn. For the abundance of the harvest and the raft of colours and tones that the Earth's plants brought forth. And she hated autumn. Autumn ushered in the cold, and for that, autumn could not be forgiven.

She dropped two tea bags into the brown crockery teapot and headed for her rocker.

The old chair was the only piece of furniture her mother had owned. Her mother had found the chair on the prairie, sprawled on its side, dusted in prairie silt and strewn with a spider's webbing. The spider, its abdomen bulging with a white egg sac, was larger than any her mother had seen. After the egg sac broke open and the mass of squirming creatures scurried onto the ground, disappearing amongst the grasses, Elinor's mother tied a rope around the rocker and dragged it back to their camp. She knew that where Spider had taken up residence and given birth would be a place of creativity and stories.

Elinor eased her stiff body into the rocker. Tugging at her socks, she wondered what the temperature had gotten to in the night.

At first her mother had been frightened by the rocker, the way it rolled back and forth but didn't go anywhere. Theirs was the only tipi with such a contraption. For a long while no one went near the chair except Elinor's mother and Elinor's baby sister, who knew no fear. Over time everyone in the camp came to have a look. And some — there were always those who sought a bit of excitement and risk — chose to sit in the rocker and experience its ride.

Elinor — in those days she was called Red Sky in the Morning — was the only one who saw that the rocker could move of its own accord. It happened in winter, when the nights were long and the moon in its fullness showered light through the smoke hole at the top of the tipi. The creaking came first. *Squeerk. Squeerk. Squeerk.* Then Elinor saw them: babies, tiny children, old men and young women. They spoke in words she didn't understand. Sometimes the voices were joyous, filled with mirth and laughter; other times there was sadness and crying. Years later when Elinor remembered those times, she'd recognize the sounds as English and German, then French, and finally Cree, Saulteaux, and Assiniboine.

Elinor urged her body out of the rocker. Using two hands to steady her movement, she spilled hot water over the tea bags. She took milk from the fridge and the sugar bowl from the cupboard. Leaning against the counter, waiting for the tea to brew — she liked it strong so the flavour clung to her tongue — she studied the rocker. An invisible patina, layers of her life, covered the chair's surface. Sweat and grease from the palms of her father, husband, and brothers. Jam and candy from her children's fingers, tears from their sorrows. And salt, oil, and flour — a remembrance from the years when she made the bannock.

She squeezed the tea bags against the side of the pot, filled a cup two-thirds full, leaving space for lots of milk and two heaping teaspoons of sugar.

She returned to the rocker.

The tea burned her tongue but she didn't mind. She liked the graze of the hot liquid slipping down her throat, plunking into her belly. She smiled at the sound of the honking. Honking. Honking. Loud and louder. Then soft and softer.

Canada geese. Black-necked birds that cleaved the skies in a *V*.

The rocker faced east, overlooking the valley. When Alice, Elinor's granddaughter, was in high school, she'd researched the geological history of the valley. Although Elinor had listened intently to Alice's enthusiastic recitation of all the facts she had accumulated, Elinor remembered none of it.

Elinor was acquainted with the valley in ways that would never get into a school textbook. She knew the valley's steepest flanks, its hidden portals, the calm waters where ducks nested. She knew that the grasses faded by summer to shades of biscuit, buff, and tan and that the oval leaves of the saskatoon bush curled to burnt orange. She knew the strong blow of the wind and how it whispered when the moon rose. She knew, without the aid of her eyes, the best places to hunt rabbit, quail, and gopher, where strawberries, wild onion, saskatoon berries, and the healing herbs were most prolific.

She knew … she knew …

Elinor drained the mug of the last drop of tea. She rolled her lips together and licked the sweetness from them. And as it was wont to do these days, her mind rolled over to another time in her life.

That school had been a betrayal of the valley's past. The white frame building stood in the middle of the valley like a canker, sucking life from all that entered its doors. When the thing burned down a few years ago, Elinor was surprised by the relief that had come to her. She tried to remember the silly song that she'd made up for herself during the difficult times, something with colours, red berries, and egg yolk. It frustrated her how stories and experiences that had been so important at one time couldn't be retrieved from her mind, while other things, memories that she wanted to be free of, remained permanently stuck, entrenched like a badger in its hole.

The outhouse was the one place to which she could escape at that school. Out of sight, the lock on her side of the door, she'd watch the shadows of tree branches jump on the walls or a long-legged spider amble the width of the little building. Even though her cottage had indoor plumbing, she still used the outhouse from time to time. Especially in the summers she enjoyed the warm, close space that held the smells of rotting wood, lye, shit, and pee.

Elinor shivered and tugged the crocheted shawl around her shoulders. It had been a gift from her sister, Lillian, for her last birthday. She stared at the black iron stove in the corner of the room and told herself she should make a fire. If Joseph was alive he would have done that already.

Over the nine decades of her life she had not forgotten her first day at that school. It was autumn and a short time after her people had moved onto the reserves. She was ten, maybe eleven. Long after the rattling boards and squeaking wooden spokes of her father's horse-drawn wagon had disappeared into the first dip of the trail, she'd cried. Like the creeks in springtime, the tears had gushed from her eyes. Still her father didn't look back.

Within minutes of her father's departure she was stripped of her clothing, scrubbed with a harsh brush, soap and cold water, until every inch of her body throbbed. The hair cutting followed. The yellow planks of the pine flooring disappeared beneath the swirls and clumps of black hair. A White Neck, the name they gave to the nuns, wielded scissors like a farmer with a scythe in a field of weeds. How cold her ears had been that day. The entire time she was at that school they never got warm.

Never cut the hair again, Elinor muttered, bringing a match to a sprig of sweetgrass. Most mornings she smudged. Leaning forward, she cupped her hands and scooped the sweet smoke toward her.

To her eyes so she might see more clearly ...
To her ears so she listened with greater wisdom ...
To her mouth so her lips would speak with truthfulness ...
In the four directions.

She gave thanks to the Creator for the Earth, the waters, the sky, and all creatures and plants. And for those who were choosing to build on the land, she asked that they thank the creatures who would lose their homes. If it was a day when she planned to paint — those came less often now — she thanked the Creator for the gift of being able to create, to put to paper in colour and shape her experiences of the Earth, images from inside her head, and sentiments and textures, feelings, from the depths of her heart.

She pressed together her shrunken lips. No teeth. Still in the glass by her bed. That would be an advantage of one of those homes. Someone would fetch her dentures.

Louise, her daughter, thought Elinor should be in a home, one of those places where a young girl made tea and brought it to you. She wouldn't need to worry about anything, Louise said. But Elinor didn't worry now; she imagined she'd worry more in one of those places. Besides, one of those homes wouldn't want an old Cree woman. Politicians weren't interested in helping Indians to live longer. Her people had signed Treaty Four in 1874. It was now 1967, or '68, she couldn't keep track. It had taken almost a hundred years, until 1960, for her people to get the vote. That was how much the government cared for her people.

One of those homes might take her sister, Lillian. She was fussier about her house, her clothing, her entire life. As far as Elinor knew, Lillian didn't smoke or burn the herbs.

Some days Elinor longed to be back on the reserve. But after Joseph's death she couldn't bear it. Even though her friends, women she had grown up with, begged her to stay on. And when John, Louise's husband, told her about the cottage, she knew it was all she needed.

She yawned. The past few weeks, awakened by voices, faces she couldn't bring into focus, she'd not slept well. The voices urged her to speak, to get on with the telling of what for so long she had kept to herself. But what she must speak of required a receptacle, a vessel, just as the seeds she planted needed moist and warm earth before they would sprout.

Perhaps her daughter was ready now.

She took up the book that was never far from her, the same book she'd been reading for twenty years. Others read the Bible every day; she read Charles Dickens. *Great Expectations.* The book was missing a couple of pages; those that remained were dry and yellowed. Her sister, Lillian, had passed on the book, said she didn't like it much, found it too hard to follow. Given that the two sisters often differed (at least back then) on anything from politics to clothes to what type of soap to buy, Elinor figured she might find the book interesting. And she did. The descriptions of the mist, marshes, fog, and damp of the English countryside fascinated her. As did the array of people Dickens spread over his pages. Some were rough and harsh, even cruel. Others were gentle and gener- ous. There were tidy and proper folks and others who were mangy and dirty, flea-infested. Pip, who told the story, was an orphan, and that being so, he claimed a special place in her heart.

Where was her magnifying glass? Under the book. She with- drew the duck feather she used as a bookmark and settled in. Five minutes later she was asleep.

2

Elinor gazed at the hairy brute. Stocky, broad-chested, head as big as a boulder — a handsome fellow despite his circumstances. From the far reaches of her mind her father's voice, slow and sonorous, spoke of a time when the plains were dark with grazing, roaming, rutting walnut-brown bison. She'd met *paskwâwi-mostos* in her dreams; in her wakefulness the smell of his long hair, the sound of his thick breathing lingered.

He was still a grand creature, despite being housed behind glass, doused in artificial light. Although she preferred the real thing, at least this fellow wasn't going anywhere. Probably her own legs couldn't travel much farther than his. She was grateful for the assistance of the town's postmistress, who lent her car and son to drive Elinor into the city. Without Jeremy's assistance, she wasn't sure she would have made it from the parking lot to the basement of the museum. The Museum of Natural History; she saw nothing natural about a stuffed creature behind glass. Better that he had been able to return to the earth at a pace decided by his own body, the worms, wolves and vultures.

Big Brown. That's what I'll call you. I hope that's acceptable. It's a pleasure to be with you. I had no idea you were here, Big Brown. Red Sky in the Morning was the name that was first given to me; a red star burned in the sky while mother laboured. I was born in the springtime, in the valley. In that school they named me Elinor; they did more than change my name in that place. But we won't speak of that now, Big Brown.

She took out her pencil and flipped open her sketch pad. She made a few bold strokes and a half-dozen ovals of different sizes to represent the different areas of the body: Head. Torso. Hips. Shoulders and legs.

Working in small strokes, moving outward from the top and centre, Elinor sketched the oval perimeter of the head. She went down one side to the beard then did the same on the other side. She put crosses to mark the place for the eyes; she'd work on them last. She stared at the neck. Massive and thick, far shorter than the necks of deer, horses, and antelope, it was barely discernible between the head and shoulders. Given the size of the head, how could it be otherwise? She marked out the bulge of the right shoulder and sketched a line down to the knee.

When her fingers started to cramp, she put down her pencil, stretched out her fingers, and squeezed them into a fist. She repeated the movements two or three times. She couldn't work as long as she used to. In her prime she'd keep at the work for ten or twelve hours a day, several days running. Now she had good and bad days. Some days she worked standing up, other days she'd sit. She stepped back to get a different perspective. Spotting the rabbit crouched in the corner of the gallery, she muttered its name: "*Wâposos, wâposos.*"

She moved closer to the gallery, then back. She looked at what she'd drawn, then to the bison, then back to her drawing. She shook her head.

Proportions aren't right, Big Brown. Head needs to be larger, neck thicker.

She told herself this picture would take some time.

She dropped into her chair. Her eyelids flickered then slid downward.

The tail of the bison twitched.

3

Louise had always loved Mary. Not that she would say that to Mary. Theirs was not the kind of relationship in which one discussed feelings about the other. Most of the time Louise didn't put the two words — *Mary* and *love* — in the same sentence, even though Mary took up a large part of Louise's heart, as she had for most of her life. Some might say Louise didn't have much of a heart, the things she'd done in her life. But Louise knew she wasn't without heart, she just didn't wear it on her sleeve. Frequently she tipped waitresses a little extra. When she knew a client was barely scraping by, she charged him less than the going rate. For years she'd helped out at the animal shelter on holiday weekends, cleaning out pens, brushing matted fur from decrepit, scabby cats, bathing flea-ridden dogs.

Light streamed from an east-facing window into Mary's living room, a room that was cluttered with old newspapers, Eaton's and seed catalogues from years ago, a loom that Mary threatened to get rid of, folded laundry, and bags of wool. Louise sank into the navy blue armchair, her long legs stretched before her. She wore black linen pants, a white blouse, and a pale blue cardigan. Her physique was well-rounded, heavier around the hips than she'd like. She kept her black hair short, hoping to mitigate the advance of the greys and whites.

Mary was a short, thin, and wiry woman. Her thick salt-and-pepper hair was pulled back and tied with a piece of string. Swaddled in a bulky red sweater buttoned to her chin and brown pants stained with grease and oil and bits of food, she sat on the maroon corduroy couch, her feet drawn beneath her. On the floor sat her ochre deerskin moccasins. The stitching around the toes was giving way, but she'd never toss them; they had been a gift from Louise.

Mary had never told Louise her age. Louise guessed there were five or six years between them. Mary, the older of the two, was probably sixty-six or sixty-seven years old.

"So, tell me again," Louise asked, trying to suppress a smile, "how exactly did you manage to scrape almost every inch of your face and arms? You look like you've just stepped out of a boxing ring."

Mary threw a ball of wool at Louise.

The two had met in town almost fifty years ago, the early 1920s, just after the First World War. Although a heady time for many, it hadn't been that way for them. Both runaways, they were keening for a better life. At least that's what they told each other. Mary had been in town for six or eight months, although initially she'd told Louise she was born there. They lied to each other a lot in those days, as they lied to everyone.

Mary wound a strand of blue wool over the end of her knitting needle. Knitting, she said, kept her fingers limber. The needles clicked over each other. The few things she knew how to knit — scarves, socks, mitts — she gave to her sons and grand-children as birthday gifts.

Neither woman spoke for a time. It was often that way between them. Just to be in the other's company was sufficient. Like a couple of old cats who shared the same house, knew of the other's presence, but found little reason or need to interact.

The simplicity of her time with Mary was a respite for Louise, a retreat from her busy life as a lawyer. As much as she enjoyed the intellectual gymnastics, took satisfaction from seeing fairness and justice achieved, it had kept her from her family, from herself, from a good night's sleep. But her chronic restlessness and discontent she knew came from a deeper place. Elinor said Louise was like a porcupine, prickly, but if approached carefully, the barbs were kept in check. Louise knew about the barbs; they'd come into existence those first months after she'd left the reserve. Over the years they'd dulled and were slower to emerge. But they were still there, and often necessary in her law practice.

"So, what brings you out this time?" Mary asked, peering over the top of her glasses.

"You, my dear," Louise said. "It's always you."

Mary laughed. "After all these years you still think you can pull that lawyerly stuff with me. Well, I'll humour you. And while I'm doing that, why don't you open that bottle of wine you brought? Hope it's better than the last one you dragged out here."

"And which one was that?" Louise asked.

"That French one. *La Belle* something or other. *Rouge* or *blanc*."

"That's not saying much," Louise said. "You don't remember."

"It will come to me."

Louise searched for the corkscrew. She couldn't assume from one visit to the next where things were kept in Mary's house. And it was useless to ask; Mary's housekeeping was erratic. She didn't live by the dictum *A place for everything, and everything in its place*. Mary lived alone, and as best as Louise could tell, never minded having to search for things. Louise preferred the direct route to what she wanted; all the detours in Mary's house frustrated her. She sighed as she closed one drawer and opened another.

"It's in the drawer to the left of the stove," Mary said.

"Already checked that one."

"Maybe on the back porch, then."

Louise stepped out onto the porch, and the scent of warm earth wafted toward her. When she visited Mary at the height of summer, the fields that surrounded her house were golden with ripening wheat. A yellow-breasted meadowlark flew from the fence post at the bottom of the garden. In the middle of the weathered table constructed from half a wooden door sat the corkscrew, a cork still on the end of it.

Louise and Mary didn't meet regularly, as in every two weeks or three months, or the third Sunday or first Monday of the month. But in the past four decades they had managed to get together two or three times a year. They couldn't *not* get together. Their visits were a necessary reaffirmation, although never spoken about, of what they had shared, what they had done, more than forty years earlier. Mary rarely initiated these visits. Perhaps she was less fearful; she had less to lose than Louise.

What propelled Louise to contact Mary, she did not understand. She didn't care or try to understand. She wasn't one for that kind of reflection. It might be something in the news: A man lost in dense forest, found days later half-dead. A calf that had strayed from its mother, strangled in barbed-wire fencing. Or a black woman in the Deep South raped by a gang of white youths. Or it could be a change in the weather, something as simple as that. Whatever the event, it left a ping, an irritation at the back of Louise's mind. A day or two later she'd call Mary. If it wasn't a story in the news it was the dream, the same dream Louise had had for years. Two girls on the prairie running and chasing each other in the bright sun, their play interrupted by strong winds, dark clouds, then they are running, running to hide from the storm. Always Louise awoke in a sweat, a sense of choking, being choked, finding her own hands around her neck. That day or the following one, she'd call Mary.

Back inside, Louise twisted the foil from the wine bottle and took two tumblers from the cupboard. She only brought French wines for Mary. That's all she'd drink. Homage to Mary's dead father, who was French and beat Mary's mother, a Cree Indian, until Mary threw a knife in his thigh, told him to never do it again, and ran from the house.

"What are you doing in there?" Mary called. "Planting the grape vines?"

They took their wine to the front porch. In the distance, like a mirage, grain elevators rose up like pyramids, and beyond, not visible to the women, the low skyline of Regina, where the two had met. Mary asked if Louise remembered the day they'd met. Louise said it was etched in her mind like leaf imprints in pre-historic stone.

She had come into town to shop and had almost been run down by a truck. She'd not seen it because she was looking at Mary standing outside the café: white shirt, dark skirt, braids down her back.

"I was convinced you were a woman from the reserve."

Mary shook her head, said that wasn't her first recollection. She went to the edge of the porch. "Damned gophers. Look at him, sitting up there in the middle of my garden like a thistle in a patch of pansies." She crept down the stairs, found a stone, and hurled it at the tawny rodent, missing his head by an inch. "You little bugger," she said, "you're lucky I didn't have my slingshot."

"Used to be a time Indians were grateful for the little bits of meat that could be found on a gopher's bones," Louise said.

"Yeah, in the last century," Mary said.

"They didn't taste so bad. Just too little meat for a family of five," Louise said.

The weathered wicker chair, ready for retirement, complained as Mary returned to it.

"We don't have the same memory," Mary said. She told Louise she saw her for the first time when she came into the café with Mrs. Scott and the two children. "The two brats," Mary added. Everyone but Louise had ice cream. That irritated Mary even though she'd seen that kind of thing before. What bothered Mary more was the way Louise was acting. Whenever the cook called out an order, the door banged, or somebody laughed loudly, Louise jumped, her eyes bugged out like a fish's.

"I thought you were going to bolt right out of there. You'd settle down for a bit, stare at the boy, then there'd be another crash from the kitchen, a customer would shout or drop a knife, and you'd practically leap out of your chair. There was nothing I could do."

The boy, Mary said, was a cute kid. Three or four years old, yellow hair, big brown eyes, he was making a mess, slurping his ice cream, spilling it on the table, down the front of his shirt. The girl, whom she wanted to swat, kept taking ice cream from her brother's bowl. He cried and pleaded with his mother to make her stop. Mrs. Scott grabbed Louise's arm, hissed something at her. Louise didn't answer or do anything. Mary figured Louise's English wasn't too good. Finally, Mrs. Scott yanked the ice cream from both of the kids, pulled a handkerchief from her bag, wiped down the boy, and glared at Louise.

"I felt sorry for you. I asked the cook if he knew the woman, where she came from. He didn't. I was so worried for you," Mary said. "I'm not sure why. Maybe you reminded me of myself a couple of years earlier."

Mary sucked the dregs from the bottom of her glass.

"I don't remember any of that," Louise said. "Must've been just after I'd left the rez. I was grateful they had taken me in, fed me, given me a place to sleep."

"You mean that dirty cot in that shed without any heat, cracks between the boards big enough for a rat to get through? You would have frozen to death that first winter if I hadn't dragged you into town. You didn't want to come, though, did you?"

Louise swirled her wine, watched the legs of red liquid slip to the bottom of her glass. Mary loved to reminisce; Louise did not. There was much Louise wanted to forget, much that was better left alone. That other world, the world she had run from, she almost never thought or spoke of. Except with Mary. No one but Mary knew the details of Louise's time with the Scotts. No one but Mary knew how Louise had longed to go back to the reserve, how she hated the work in the café — slinging coffee, eggs, and pork pies, washing floors, fending off crude remarks and pinches from cocky male customers, white males.

"No, I didn't want to come with you."

"Why?"

"Fear, maybe."

"Fear of what? You'd never have gone to law school if you'd stayed with them. You would have been the one scrubbing those kids' clothes as they went off to law school. What were you afraid of? You'd already done the hardest thing, which was to leave the reserve."

They never spoke of it. What they, well, mostly Louise, had done. Louise wondered if Mary had forgotten. In Louise's mind, the hardest thing, and far worse thing, had not been leaving the reserve.

Long summer days. The heat of a prairie sun seeping into my back, shoulders, and rump.

Fields of grasses that flowed beyond the limits of my vision.

The company and comfort of countless others of my kind.

That is some of what I knew before I came into this museum.

There are other memories, passed down from ancestors, which are less pleasant.

Trainloads of humans, sometimes we called them two-leggeds, brought to hunt us. White-faced men, jeering, yelling, shooting, and blasting at bison, over and over and over, until the poor animals were falling to the ground like leaves from a tree in a fall windstorm.

In this museum I still watch two-leggeds.

Why do they come?

The Indian woman came again. Sometimes she draws. Sometimes she only talks. Or she's quiet. This last time I saw the change in her eyes. I've seen that look in the cows after they've lost a calf.

So, finally I determined that as the hide was not to be got off, I would content myself with the tongue, which I hoped to get out of its head somehow in the course of an hour or two.

Falling to work again, I ultimately succeeded in getting out the lingual member. To this trophy I added the tail, which I cut off as an additional evidence that I had positively slain a buffalo.

— "In the Buffalo Country," George Brewerton,
Harper's Weekly, September 1862

4

From the assortment she kept on her dresser, Elinor reached for the photograph of the six of them — she and Joseph, with Louise, Charlie, Le Roy, and Philip — posing in front of the Ferris wheel. An odd place for the picture, since none of them had ridden on the twirling contraption. Joseph wouldn't permit it. He said if the Creator had meant for humans to be spinning in circles above the ground he would have given them wings or more legs and arms. In addition, Joseph thought the ride would be boring. You didn't go anywhere; the view wasn't any better than what he could see every day. He didn't want to stare at a bald head or peer down the throat of a screaming teenager.

Elinor had no idea how she'd gotten the photograph. At that time they didn't own a camera. She squinted at the picture. Was it even their family? Yes. It was the only photo she had of all of them.

There had been other children, never photographed. She'd had twelve pregnancies. Two slid from her body within weeks of Joseph's seed swimming into her womb. Others stayed until legs and arms were formed before tearing away from her body. Her mother told her it was for the best. Either the baby was weak, a cripple, or its death was intended as a sign that something bad was going to happen in the world. Better not to come to this place. Of course, her mother was right. Two babies came early and died within days of their births. After both deaths a sickness swept through the reserve. Like a starving animal the disease ravaged the camp. Ten, fifteen died. Those who survived were left sickly and weak for months.

For years those children who had passed over to the other side stayed near Elinor. She'd hear them rustling in the bushes, see them near the fire, feel them brushing against her face when she walked over the prairie. She was never alone.

She placed her finger on Philip's chest. Immediately, as if she'd touched a coal in the fire, the sadness shot up her arm and into her throat. He had just turned three; she didn't know it would be his last photograph. He'd died just a few months before the end of the Great War. Louise was eleven and already a bold child; maybe she had to be. Conditions on the reserve were bad. So many were sick and there were no doctors to see them, no money for medicines. There was not enough to eat; a couple of gophers didn't go far in a family of five.

Elinor wished Joseph hadn't gone before her. It wasn't supposed to be like that. Some might take comfort that he was there waiting for her, but she wasn't one of them. Especially now she needed him. Finally, she was going to speak about what she had kept secret for so long. Why had she waited so long to tell him? It seemed she had just decided to do so and then he was dead. What did that mean?

She didn't want to think of that time. She shoved it from her mind and thought about the good times on the rez, Joseph and his fires behind the house. The two of them poking sticks into the coals. Laughing about the guy who'd bought a horse that ran fast as the wind but as soon as it was hitched to a wagon wouldn't move. They remembered the days when ducks, deer, and rabbit were so plentiful the hunters never came back empty-handed. And although they preferred not to, sometimes they talked about the drinking, the fights, the stupid accidents with guns and knives, and the children who died before they were five. Joseph would fuss over her. Until the day that he died, he sang to her and made jokes. They'd giggle about the old times, when they had had more energy for wandering over each other's bodies.

Elinor returned the photograph to its place, closed her eyes, and gripped the corner of the dresser. How was she to tell Alice about the child? Her child. A child she'd not seen in decades.

She knew she was putting it off. Reminiscing and telling dreams were easier. Despite the number of years that had passed, the torment had not diminished. The memory oozed like a wound that would not close despite repeated ministrations. Now, before she went into the ground, she wanted a scab for that misfortune — or miracle, more and more she thought of it that way — in her life. She wanted the suffering to shrivel and new growth to sprout.

The windows clattered; the walls shivered, and Elinor knew that wind had passed by.

She shuffled to the spare bedroom, which smelled of linseed oil and dust, paints and graphite. Tubes of acrylic, boxes of watercolours, sketch pads, paint palettes, and the bottoms of plastic jugs bulging with brushes cluttered the table. In the absence of recent creative initiatives, it had become more like a storage room than an artist's studio.

The painting she'd started in the spring — the view of the west of the valley — was on the easel. She'd aspired to something different from what those men had done in the earlier 1900s. What were their names? *Bill? Jeffrey? Kennedy?* It didn't matter. She wanted a work that showed the presence of the Creator and the multitude of life on the land. She envisioned sweeps and curves of brilliant yellow, cinnamon, and sage green. Embedded within the colours would be wings of hawk, ears of deer and badger, wolf snouts, red triangles of wild strawberry, and the piercing ebony eyes of pickerel, perch, and snake. Here and there, subtly, there'd be a breast, a thigh, a portal, soft and moist.

She stepped back from the painting. What was there had blurred. The colours were less vibrant. There was more in her mind than on the canvas. Probably Louise was right. If she wasn't so stubborn she'd go to a doctor and get the cataracts removed. But why couldn't she make paintings of the valley as seen through the creamy opaque lens of a cataract? Why should it be any less valid than what was seen through the transparency of a healthy eye?

She hissed. What had she come for? Not for painting. She scanned the room and moved toward the trunk. It was as old as she was and almost as tall. Its vaulted lid reminded her of a womb ripe with child. She rubbed a finger over the metal stripping blotched with rust, then jabbed the key at the lock. After a few tries she got the alignment right, but then the key would not turn. She couldn't remember the last time she had opened the trunk. Probably years ago. Joseph had such strong hands. She smiled at the memory of his calloused fingers stroking her body. She drew all her strength into her fist and banged the top of the chest. Immediately, the pain shot through her wrist and up to her elbow. *Jefferys* — that was the name of one of those painters. C.W. Jefferys. An Englishman, he'd come out in the early 1900s, painted hundreds of scenes of the Qu'Appelle. Very skilled, she knew, but not to her taste. She liked more colour. And never had she done a painting without an animal, a fish, a bird. She should have given the chest the boot, not the hand. There would be a bruise. Unlike other bruises that frequently and mysteriously appeared on her body, at least she'd know the origin of this one.

Reluctantly, the lock's internal workings gave way. She lifted the lid. A musty smell imbued with scents of smoked leather, pine, and sage drifted forth. Digging like a dog, she pushed aside blankets, sheets, two pairs of beaded moccasins — one small, the other large — an embroidered vest, and flannel jacket. She burrowed to the bottom until her fingers scratched at the stiff paper. It had been years since she'd looked at the photograph. She started to pull it from the envelope, but hesitated. She should wait for Alice. No. She would look at it now. For so long she'd wanted no one to see the child. She feared someone would find the picture. Sometimes she thought she should burn it, but had never been able to.

Hands shaking, she slipped the photograph from the envelope. So beautiful and peaceful, that pudgy-cheeked, black-haired infant. Her eyes sparkled and smiled. Elinor could see herself in that face.

"Time to come home, child," she whispered.

Back in her bedroom, Elinor shoved the envelope in the top drawer of her dresser beneath her underwear and socks. None of her socks were anything like the ones Swift Eyes wore. All the times Swift Eyes had gotten herself into trouble because of her socks. Rainbow socks that her mother had knit. Swift Eyes made colours fly and dance. Even in the principal's office she could do that.

Elinor eased herself onto the edge of her bed and clasped her hands together. The images and sounds from the day she, then named Red Sky in the Morning, and Swift Eyes had snuck into the principal's office filled her mind.

They had been sweeping and washing the floors in the front hall. They were always cleaning and cooking and tidying at that school. Swift Eyes had stopped; her broom lay at her feet. Hovering at the open door of the principal's room, she hissed at Red Sky and beckoned for her to come.

Red Sky had never seen a place like the principal's office. An enormous desk filled half the room. There were chairs made from leather. A couch puffy like clouds. The shelves were crammed with books with gold letters on the covers. The carpets had more colours than her mother's bead collection. In the paintings, white-haired women wore dresses as large as tipis and men in red jackets and shiny black boots that went as high as their knees rode huge horses with flared nostrils and sad eyes.

Swift Eyes, in her search for shiny coins, left every drawer on the desk hanging open. Red Sky went for the writing stick that lay on the top of the desk. She yanked off the cap with her teeth and sniffed at the pen's inky smell. The golden nib, releasing its blue liquid erratically, scratched at the white paper as Red Sky printed the letters of her name. *E-L-I-N-O-R.* The writing excited her, more so than she would permit in her teacher's presence. She raised her head and looked into the eyes of the naked man on the cross. *Had he smiled at her?*

Struggling to remember how to form the letters and the order they must go in, she printed more words — *tree, water, dog, boy, girl.* When she looked again to the cross, she saw her own father, smiling and nodding. Surprise and joy tingled the length of her body. Then came the ache that had been in her heart since he had left her in this place. Even though her father had told her he would return, she feared she would never see him again. She feared she would never go home. It was beyond her understanding why he'd left her at the school.

Her father's face faded, and through her tears came a mass of brown — hairy, furry wisps of brown. Black-brown, tan-brown, ruddy red calf-brown. Buffalo eyes deeper than the waters in the middle of the lake sucked her into them.

Tom. Tom. Tom. White drum speaking.

Faster.

Tomtomtomtom.

Chanting voices. Stomping feet. Eagle feathers and antelope skirts bounce and jiggle. On and on into the late hours of the night the dancers leap as high as the flames of the fires.

The dancing and singing comes closer. The image of the brown furry head, despite her begging for it to stay, fades. The smell of the animal's dung lingers, mingling with a girl's voice that sings about fast waters and silver fish.

Swift Eyes, her bony knees vibrating above the red and green stripes of her socks, shook the coins in her clasped hands to a rhythm of her own creation. Feet stomping, coins jingling, bending and turning, Swift Eyes was in her own world. Red Sky shushed her friend. Swift Eyes shook the coins harder, laughed louder, and tossed the shiny money into the air. The coins, as if held by invisible threads, hung suspended long enough for Red Sky to determine that their sound, despite her best efforts to lunge after them, would not be muffled by the soft carpet. Hitting the pine flooring, they were like hard rain on a tipi.

Red Sky's fear surged into anger. It had been a mistake to come into the principal's office. If they were caught …

Barely had the clatter of metal on wood stopped when Swift Eyes scooped the coins back up into her hands and resumed her dancing. Both things — dancing and singing in their own language — were forbidden at the school.

Red Sky commanded herself to leave, sensing at the same time that it was too late. Laughter had started to climb up her throat. She swallowed hard and glanced at the door, nervous and certain that a White Neck would burst in. The vibration in her throat grew stronger. She bit on her fists. The giggle burst from the depths of her belly, over her tongue and out from her lips. Giggles and more giggles tumbled forth. Her eyes were wet with the fullness of her feeling. Her body convulsed with laughter at her friend's antics, at the thrill of writing at the principal's desk, reading his books, and sitting on his couch.

As if fueled by her friend's mirth, Swift Eyes stomped harder and faster while her eyes, fearless, looked to a faraway place. As Red Sky envisioned White Necks filling the room, Swift Eyes flung her head back, let out a *whoop*, and sent the coins into flight again. Pennies, glistening coppers, bounced and rolled and twirled.

Red Sky rushed to Swift Eyes and threw her arms around her. Clinging to her brave and silly friend, she didn't care that the embrace wasn't returned. Neither was it resisted. For a moment, it was only the two of them, two children, two Indian children.

Elinor awoke in a fluster from her musings. Where was the photograph? What had she done with it? Alice was coming the next day. She surveyed the room and decided she must have put the thing in her dresser; there was little other furniture in the room that would suit for hiding things.

She pulled open the top drawer, pawed through her underwear and socks until her fingers scraped on the thick paper. She removed the envelope, kissed it, pressed it to her chest, then returned it to the drawer.

5

Louise slipped the wooden hanger into the shoulders of her grey blazer, hung the jacket on the back of her door. She did up the three black buttons, straightened the collar, and picked a hair from it. The jacket, purchased at Eaton's, was a favourite and she'd wear it as long as she could. The inside lining had begun to fray and she told herself she must take it to a seamstress. She stepped back from the jacket, undid the top buttons on her white shirt, and allowed herself a fleeting thought that she'd been at this lawyering business for almost three decades.

She'd been lucky to get where she had. Barely a week went by without a story, a news item that reminded her of that: A drunken Indian collapsed on the railway tracks. Indian children left alone at home, a fire, two of the four dead. More and more Indian youth coming off the reserves into the cities. She did what she could — financial donations, pro bono work for Indians charged with robbery and violence — but it was never enough.

She leaned toward the mirror and drew a brush through her thick hair. She twirled the tube of lipstick from its sheath, applied the vermilion colour to her lips, and grinned. Better, she thought as she wiped a dot of lipstick from her tooth. It was a ritual she'd established for herself in an effort to shed the stress that inevitably came after being at court.

She settled into her leather chair and rolled it up to her desk. The desk, probably once used in a post office or printing shop, was a huge oak thing with countless drawers and compartments of all sizes. When it arrived at her office she'd wondered what had compelled her to buy it; it wasn't especially handsome.

She'd found the desk at a country auction house eons ago during a Sunday drive with John and Alice, who was seven at the time. The auction house, a rambling grey building the size of a barn, seemed to appear out of nowhere. The sign on the door said Auctions Every Friday Night. All that remained in the dusty cavernous space that smelled of cigarette smoke and engine oil were a few pressback chairs, a Singer treadle sewing machine, and the large desk, as if it had been calling out, waiting for Louise.

They waited for someone to appear, but no one ever did.

John wrote his name and phone number on a blank page he took from the back of his poetry book. He left the note on the desk beneath a stone. Two weeks later a man called. He spoke in quick bursts and cleared his throat often. He told John he was glad to be rid of the thing. Farmers didn't want desks; they wanted chairs and tables, dressers, cooking pots and tools, guns and machinery. They could have the desk, the man said, delivery included, for twenty bucks.

Louise pulled out the bottom left drawer in the group of nine small drawers and scooped out a couple of Scotch mints; they had been her father's favourite candy. These ones were hard and stale, the centres no longer soft. She spit out the candy and tossed it in the garbage. She flipped through a pile of telephone messages, pausing at one from a reporter with the local newspaper. She wasn't averse to giving interviews; there were times when she enjoyed them, but this one she was going to skip. She slid the pink paper to the edge of her desk for her secretary.

When she'd agreed to act for the Llewellyn brothers, Barry and Elmer, and their project, a year-round amusement complex, she'd assumed everything would be straightforward. Search the title, prepare the usual documents, and send a statement to her clients. There had been no mention of a burial site in the northeast quadrant. She wasn't sure that the farmers who sold the land to her clients were as ignorant about the burial site as they pretended to be. It created a dilemma for her. While she had never presented herself as one who only represented Indians, she didn't feel comfortable advocating against them, either. She'd wait a little, see how the case unfolded. She still might be the best person for the Llewellyns, better able than most of her colleagues to understand their opponents' position.

She yanked papers from her briefcase and reviewed the notes she'd made in court; she was scheduled to return the next morning. It was a sad case of a mother who risked losing custody of her child because she was trying to make ends meet. She'd been doing two jobs, working all day and half the night, and had fallen asleep in the middle of the day from exhaustion. Her three-year-old daughter had slipped out of the house and was hit by a car, left with a broken tibia and several cracked ribs. The father, a drug addict who claimed he was clean, had a steady job. He said he was better able to parent the child and was fighting for full custody. The mother had needed to work two jobs because, until then, the father hadn't given her a penny to help with his daughter.

Due to cross-examine the father the next morning, Louise reviewed his affidavits, picked through her notes from his testimony that morning. She wouldn't want the man to look after her cat. He'd spruced himself up to appear in court. His lawyer, whom Louise thought was a scumbag, had asked the father nothing about his history of drug use. For Louise that was a clue that the man's drug addiction was a bigger problem than they were letting on. And there was another matter that didn't sit right with Louise. The mother was Cree; the father British, or Irish. No one spoke about the white bias. But she'd seen it too many times.

She swivelled her chair around. Facing the floor-to-ceiling bookshelves crammed with thick black volumes of Saskatchewan legal statutes, journals, and reports from the Law Society, she contemplated the pine bookends on the lowest shelf. They had been made by her son, Andrew, while he was in high school. In the shape of a horse head. He'd won a prize for them. Slumped next to the bookends sat a tattered stuffed animal, Catherine's grey rabbit, Henrietta. She took the toy from the shelf, stroked the floppy ears, poked a finger into the spot where the right eye had been. She suddenly realized she had nothing from Alice's childhood; she must rectify that.

She cranked her head back so she could see the wrinkled black-and-white photograph of her father that resided on the uppermost shelf. A head-and-shoulders shot, the photo was taken in front of her house a year or two before he died. He was a handsome man, her father. His was a kind and welcoming face — large, gentle eyes, thin lips, and high cheekbones, a nose that didn't draw attention. He wore a white shirt, black vest, and a baseball cap with the Toronto Maple Leafs emblem. Her father loved hockey; he thought it was the most exciting game. And he loved to skate. Wherever there was a patch of ice, her father skated. It didn't matter if it was a pond, a creek, or a puddle in the middle of a wheat field. She regretted that she'd not allowed him into her life when her children were younger. For certain he would have had them in skates, watched over them while they took their first strides, cajoled them back up after they fell.

Beside the photograph of her father she had placed his gifts to her when she was called to the Bar: a smooth black pebble and an eagle feather.

She left her desk, as she often did near the end of the day, and stood before the expanse of windows that faced northwest. The mid-afternoon traffic rushed up the wide and uncurving length of Albert Street. At the perimeter of the city, the roadway intersected with the highway that joined Regina to the city of Saskatoon, a two- to three-hour drive away. Louise knew the route of Highway 11 well. The frequently empty road pushed straight north past farmers' fields, through the Qu'Appelle Valley, and parallel to the banks of the Arm River. A certain grid road east of the highway went to the segment of the valley where she'd spent her childhood.

In the more than four decades since she'd left the rez, she'd returned only twice: when her grandmother died, when her grandfather died. Both visits — even though friends and family had grinned and embraced her, brought out tea and cookies, offered their beds for her to stay the night — she'd been uncomfortable, plagued by a sense of betrayal. Not their betrayal of her, but her betrayal of them. Even if she had wanted to go back to the reserve, visit more regularly, reconnect with those who had stayed, she couldn't figure out how to do it. Her life seemed so different from that of the people who had remained on the reserve. She assumed, perhaps incorrectly, that no one would want to know what she had become. And she had forgotten who they were. For a person who parlayed words, she was at a loss, didn't know what to ask of others, couldn't imagine what to share of herself. The chasm between the two worlds seemed impassable; she could find no bridge to span the gap.

Years later she'd realize how complicated she had made the whole thing, how guilt had immobilized her, interfered with simple conversation. In truth, her cousins and aunties relished the notion of having a lawyer in the family. They yearned to know more of her life; they wanted to see photographs of her children. All she'd needed to have asked them was how they had been, what stories they might tell of her grandparents.

6

The truck dashed down over the biscuit-coloured slopes of the valley and Alice's fingers curled tighter around the steering wheel. This part of the drive always gave her a thrill. The Qu'Appelle Valley, and at its base the river that calls *katepwewi-sipiy*. She sped through the riverbed flats — green-headed mallards paddled around bulrushes and long water grasses — and up over the lip of the valley into an oceanic expanse of prairie.

It was a land that ran uninterrupted, save the occasional weathered grain storage shed or white clapboard farmhouse, until it reached the horizon; a land that she could see to the limits of her vision in every increment of direction, for three hundred and sixty degrees.

The cerulean sky flowed into the earth and the land into the sky.

She was on her way to her gran's, accompanied by flashes of excitement and fragments of memory that reverberated in her body. Two nights ago she'd stayed late, very late, at Wanda's. Wanda lived in Regina, where Alice taught school. Wanda had wanted Alice to stay the night, but Alice lived in the valley not far from her gran's. It wasn't the first time Wanda had tried to convince Alice to spend the night. Wanda said it was stupid for Alice to leave the city at midnight, one or two in the morning, when she had to return five or six hours later. While Wanda's reasoning was unassailable, for Alice a decision to spend the night in a woman's bed was less about convenience and more about stepping closer to who she was, who she'd always been.

She signalled her turn, geared down, and left the highway. Twenty minutes on grid roads and she was at her grandmother's.

She knocked twice, waited a few seconds, then tried the doorknob. The door opened. Of course it opened. Despite repeated reminders, her gran always left her door unlocked. It wasn't forgetfulness. And maybe her grandmother was right and there was no need for it. All were welcome in her home and to what little she had there. And if there was a fire, her gran said, it would be easier for her to get out. She laughed at the notion that a fire would stand by, blowing down its own flames, suppressing its heat while she, Elinor, fumbled with the lock on the door.

Diminutive beneath the mass of white hair that flowed almost to her buttocks, Elinor beckoned for Alice to come. Alice kneeled beside the rocker and followed the knobby finger pointing toward the window and the deer that stepped through the long grass.

As if he knew they were watching, the animal stopped and turned toward them.

Elinor dropped her arm and leaned forward.

The deer flicked his tail. His tongue, the colour of mulberry, encircled his mouth. Then he was gone, engulfed by the bushes.

They sat in silence.

Alice marvelled at the animal's jagged expanse of antlers. She'd counted at least three prongs. She stroked her gran's hand, aware of its coolness, the purple blotches, and the advancing translucency of the skin.

"The deer, *apisi-mosos*, have always fed our people," Elinor said, "all over the planet. Elk, reindeer, and caribou. Moose." Elinor licked her lips. "Make some tea, honey."

Alice took mugs from the cupboard, milk and margarine from the refrigerator. She asked her grandmother what she had been eating the past few days. With the exception of salt, pepper, a bag of sugar, and a couple of cans of fruit and soup, the cupboards were empty. The fridge wasn't much different: a quarter of a bottle of milk, a half-loaf of bread, margarine, two eggs, and one apple. The butcher's white tape was still intact on the package of sliced ham Alice had left a few days earlier.

"Food is of little concern," Elinor said. "I know in my body my time is coming. Some things must be told before I leave."

"Are you trying to hasten your departure by starving yourself? What things?"

Alice smoothed margarine then sprinkled sugar over a slice of bread. She cut off the crusts and shoved the pieces into her mouth. The plate of yellow, quartered bread she placed on her gran's lap.

"Things from the past," Elinor said. She chewed awkwardly, dentures clicking. For so many years, she'd thought it was better left unsaid, no point stirring up the anthill. Finally, she realized her thinking was faulty. She looked around for someone to tell but found no one. She'd been waiting for someone to come forward. But no one was going to ask her. She must look into their eyes, watch their actions, and decide who was ready to listen.

"It's not about living in the past," Elinor said, "staying back there. But each generation must know of the past so they can pass it on to the next. So you can pass it on to your children."

Alice pulled the footstool near her grandmother. She'd given little thought to children of her own.

A mouse, grey and tremulous, appeared at the corner of the kitchen cupboards, scurried along the base, and disappeared into an opening that Alice couldn't see. The creature could expect a safe journey through her gran's cupboards, where no mousetraps or poison were used. And the same was true for the spiders. Whereas another might whisk away a clump of white fuzz in the corner of a ceiling, or swat at a grand expanse of intricate webbing between the posts on the porch, her gran spoke of respecting all life forms, learning to live alongside one and other.

"Some days I think my head will burst for all the chattering inside." Elinor slurped her tea then clicked her tongue and lips together. "Did you put sugar in?"

"Yes. Can't you taste it?"

Elinor took another swallow. "Barely. I think you skimped on it. Listen. Do you hear that?"

Alice had heard nothing. But she accepted that her grandmother was in communication with the spirits of other life forms. Humans were not the only ones who had something to say: trees wept, waters chuckled, animals whispered, and there were little people who swam in the marshes and lived where the saskatoon bushes grew.

Elinor closed her eyes and started to rock.

Alice knew the rocking would get more vigorous. The first time her gran had gone into one of these states, Alice had been frightened, wondering if Elinor was having a seizure, a stroke. She'd asked if she should call a doctor. "What for?" her gran had snapped. "What would a doctor know about visions, matters of the heart, communications from other times and other creatures?" He'd tell her she was nuts and want to pass electricity through her head. What was the sense of that? She didn't want to become a light bulb. Then she was angry. Rattling on in Cree, words that Alice didn't know. The only word that came through was her mother's name, *Louise*.

A jolt passed through Elinor's body and she jerked upright. Her mug rolled from her lap. A trickle of tea disappeared into the rug.

"When I was a child," Elinor said, "the second or third night in the tipi, after we had moved onto the reserve, I had a dream."

The dream, Elinor said, went on for many nights, each night continuing from the one before. Her pony came to her in the dream. He had died — halfway through the long journey from the west to the lands they'd been given in the treaty. In the dream she wept when she saw him. He willed her to climb on his back. They travelled for many days, every few days in a different direction.

In the south, Elinor said, at the bottom of a dry, sandy valley, a snake, its back brilliant in stripes of yellow and red, grinned. Tongue flashing, black eyes challenging, it struck, biting the horse on the front leg. The pony fell down instantly. For seven days and seven nights he lay still. Elinor stroked his face and brought him water and sweet grasses. She thought she'd lose him again. Her heart ached. On the fifth day, when she was getting weak from hunger, a rabbit came. She killed him and left tobacco in gratitude. Saskatoon bushes dripping with berries shot forth from the earth.

The morning of the eighth day, the pony shook his head, pushed himself up, and faced the throbbing bulge of the red sun. He told Elinor to climb on his back. At first he only walked. As the sun got higher in the sky he gathered speed until he was galloping faster than he had ever gone. Elinor shoved her fingers into the long hairs of his mane and clung fiercely. She dug her knees into his belly; she feared she'd fall off, so fast was he moving.

"I held on," Elinor said, "hard. With every muscle in my body." Elinor rocked gently.

Beyond the confines of the cottage, dark clouds were assembling.

"Life goes faster and faster," Elinor said. "You have to hold on. You don't know when Snake will attack and how long the poison will stay. Wrap your legs around something warm and strong. Take care of it even when it seems it might desert you." She closed her eyes and nodded for a time.

"Our people," Elinor continued, "have stopped holding on. So many have let go of what has spirit in its belly. Drinking and fighting, leaving the children on their own. Too many stupid deaths. Like a river, our people must claim their own course. Only a river decides how it will flow; only the wind knows when and how strong it will blow. We must remember and give thanks for all that the Creator has given."

Elinor leaned toward Alice, within an inch of her face. "There are other voices, other things that must be told. They tear at the inside of my head like Hawk at a snake or mouse. All we have are our stories. And the land. All this time spent in this place, and what's left? Puffs of air that make up words and stories. Does your mother speak *nêhiyawêwin*?"

"I've never heard her."

Elinor shook her head. "She can. That was her first language. Her grandmother held her in this chair and spoke only *nêhiyawêwin* to her. It makes me sad."

She rocked and hummed a song in Cree that Alice didn't know.

"A language," Elinor said, "is like an animal. It breathes and moves its own way. Like an animal, a language watches and tells others what only it can see. What the crow sees and chooses to speak of is different from that of the wolf and the frog. But each creature has valuable things to say. Just like an animal, once a language is destroyed, there is no getting it back." Elinor laughed. "There's another way that words are like animals. Do you know?"

Alice shook her head. "No idea."

Elinor pinched her granddaughter's forearm. "Words can bite and words can lick and soothe, just like the teeth and tongue of an animal. We were forbidden in that school to speak our Indian languages. Those who were caught had their mouths filled with soap or bound shut. The binding was so tight it left a mark for all to see. The mark lasted for hours, sometimes days. Many gave up the words they'd learned from their parents. A few persisted. Slowly, the feeling crept in that there was something wrong with how we talked."

"Some of my students speak their own languages. Cree, Saulteaux," Alice said. "I wish I knew what they were saying."

"You should learn." Elinor rubbed her lips together, bit at the bottom one for a few seconds. "Has she ever told you her name?"

"Who?"

"Your mother."

"No."

"She was called Prickly Bush with Many Flowers. She was born when the wild roses were in bloom. Maybe because the winter had been mild, the bushes were covered in blooms, the air filled with their scent. She was a beautiful baby." Elinor stared into the distance. Baby. There was another baby that was also beautiful. She'd promised herself that today she would speak of her, remove the plug from her mouth.

"And Louise ... that name came from Louis Riel."

Riel, Elinor said, had patted the top of her head when she was a young girl. For years, Elinor said, whenever she got scared she'd remember that hand on the top of her head and feel calmer.

"I'm tired now. I need to rest. Only for a short time." She squeezed Alice's hand. "Don't leave. I have something to show you when I get up."

Alice drew the shawl around her gran's shoulders and tucked it beneath thighs and knees that had the scrawny architecture of a grasshopper leg. She had students taller and heavier. In one movement she could sweep her grandmother into her arms and cradle her like a baby.

She hugged her gran, lingering in the musty smell of tobacco and the softness of her hair.

On the porch, Alice swept away cobwebs and leaves. Sloppy raindrops slapped onto the steps then broke into little droplets. Dark clouds hung over the valley. Alice wondered what her gran needed to tell her and why she didn't get on with it. Then she was swept away by memories of Wanda. It seemed she was always thinking of Wanda. In the grocery store, during recess at school, for sure during the drive between her house in the valley and the city.

They'd met at the lumber store, waiting in line to pay. Alice was buying sandpaper, Wanda a tin of wood stain. When Alice got to her truck, Wanda was sitting on the front bumper. A week later they were in bed, crawling over each other's body like ants after sugar.

In high school, when Alice's friends were swooning over lanky baseball players and football hulks, Alice was secretly following the ups and downs of cute, ponytailed cheerleaders or suppressing a crush on one of the tanned and muscled participants in the girls' high jump. There was always one she found especially attractive: a girl with a crooked grin, thick thighs, and firm butt, who moved over the bar in the high jump in the slow, sleek manner of a jaguar.

Alice told no one of her urges. She was bereft of words to describe the throbbing and tingling that happened in her body during overnights, when she was camping, whenever she shared the same bed with one or two friends. Although uncomfortable with these sensations, they also excited her. The warmth of a taut back could do it, or a head of hair swung in her face. A squishy bum cheek or a nipple was the worst. The heat that came off those places even though they were covered in flannel pajamas or cotton nighties made her blush. Sometimes the nightie rose high and there'd be the patch of hair and the mound, thinner or plumper than her own. She wanted to touch that place, see if her friend's gave the same pleasure as her own.

She told herself it was hormones and she'd grow out of it, but she hadn't.

The sound of her gran hacking and coughing — she wished she'd smoke less — drew her back into the house. She crept to the bedroom and peered through the half-open doorway. Although there were no curtains, the room was almost dark from the huge saskatoon berry shrub that was plastered against the window. Her gran was quiet now, the quilt pulled over her head.

Her gran seemed nervous and fidgety today, not like her usual self, one who didn't hold back on what she wanted to say. Alice didn't mind that, but she knew her mother hated it.

Elinor heard Alice's footsteps and pulled the quilt over her head. How could it be so difficult, this speaking about a child, a lost child, her child? It wasn't as if she, Elinor, had done anything wrong. But whenever she thought that, the *should-haves* rushed in like vultures after a dead crow. She *should have* pushed the child's father from her body; she *should have* run harder, faster, longer. She *should have* told her parents, Joseph, anybody, right away. She *should have* started looking for Bright Eyes sooner.

She flung the covers off, sat on the edge of the bed to gather her courage, then shuffled to her dresser. She pulled the envelope from beneath her socks and shoved it in her pocket.

The rain had stopped; the clouds were on the move. There were patches of water on the porch, and although it hadn't rained long, it was enough to settle the prairie dust for a day or two. Elinor loved the scent of the soil and grasses after a rain, as if the Creator had wiped away the film of dirt and stink, made everything fresh and clean. She wished the news she had for Alice was like that.

Alice was strolling through the garden, bending down every once in a while to tug out a weed. It wasn't fair, Elinor thought, that she was going to send her granddaughter away with such worry on her mind. She was a good girl. And a good teacher; her students were lucky to have her. She bought books and clothes, games for poor children at Christmas. She took apples and bread, cookies for those who arrived at school with empty stomachs. And she never used the strap to get children to behave. Elinor chuckled. But Alice had been a handful for Louise. She didn't want to read books, do puzzles, or sew. She wanted toy guns and she wanted to ride her bike and chase around the neighbourhood with her brother and his friends, playing cowboys and Indians. It was always a battle to get her into a dress or skirt.

Gripping the banister with both hands, Elinor crept down the three steps and made her way to her willow chair, which sat in the corner of the garden. Alice came over and squatted beside her. The sun, trailing a swath of magenta and orange, dropped behind the hills. The air was beginning to cool. House sparrows in the bushes chirped frantically in the final hour of daylight.

"When I was a child, we saw *apisi-mosos* almost every day," Elinor said, "sometimes four or five together. In the spring there were fawns, lots of fawns. Sticking close to their mothers, they'd move as one. We'd have great feasts. Now, those who hunt for the sport of it, for the antlers, leave the carcasses, with red meat clinging to the bones, rotting in the woods. Bring me some tulip bulbs next time. Lillian says they like tulips in the spring."

"How is Aunt Lillian?"

"She calls me when she's got nothing better to do."

"Maybe she calls because she's your sister." Alice watched her granny's knobby fingers fumble over the cigarette case.

"You're right. The past few months she's been calling every Thursday morning. I've caught myself looking forward to it. We talk about the old times — *ôyê*. I think she misses the old days, too. Damn thing." She handed the cigarette case to Alice.

Alice pinched the bottom half into itself and pulled back the lid. Like a box of crayons or pastels, the pearly-white cigarettes, their papers twirled at each end, lay snuggled in a tight row.

"That young fellow from the village still rolling for you?"

"You mean Jeremy? Yup. Faithful as the seasons."

Elinor took two short puffs of her cigarette then started to cough. She hacked and spit through a billow of smoke. As soon as the expectorations had settled she took another drag.

"I needed that before I could begin," Elinor said. "You won't forget the tulip bulbs. Red ones. Lots of them. We'll plant them together. Red ones for fire; red ones for red people." Elinor patted Alice's shoulder.

They sat in the afterglow, the exuberant chatter of the sparrows eclipsed by the darkness that hovered in the wings of the day.

Alice, shivering, did up the buttons on her sweater. "Let's go in."

"There's lots of time for that." Elinor had a distant look in her eyes. "When I was ten ... or eleven, it's not important ... my father took me to that school, the white man's school at the end of the valley." She took a long drag on her cigarette. "Three or four years I was there. It seemed like a lifetime."

A single star shone in the cobalt sky. A breeze, carrying the scent of the river, sighed through the bushes.

"A child came there," her gran said, "warm and brown-skinned, born in the darkness. No rejoicing and singing. No ceremony for finding a name. I called her Bright Eyes. And then she was gone." Elinor dropped her butt at her feet, where it joined a community of paper fragments.

"Never have I not been able to hear her cry. Hers is the loudest of all those that have passed on. She calls for me to bring her home." Elinor, her eyes bursting from their sockets, turned toward Alice. "I want you to find her. Bring her back to her family."

"Pardon?"

"You heard me. Bring her back. That's simple enough."

"Let's go in," Alice said. She held the cane before her gran and reached out to help her get up.

Elinor swatted away Alice's arms and threw down the cane. "Are you listening? I want you to find that child."

"I don't know what child you're talking about."

"Your mother's sister. Your aunt. My daughter. I was raped in that damned school."

Alice's stomach clenched; a chill passed the length of her body. Her gran was a child. Surely it wasn't true. She picked up the cigarette case, which had slipped from Elinor's lap. They needed to get inside. Suddenly, it was cold; Alice was shivering.

Straining, her body wavering, Elinor pushed herself up. Semi-vertical, she brought her face within an inch of her grand-daughter's. "You must find her before I die. You must bring her home."

Elinor swept aside Alice's extended arm and turned toward the house.

Forcing her own legs and feet to move, trying to dispel the spinning in her head, Alice followed closely behind her gran. She wondered if her mother knew about the baby. Maybe she did and had dismissed it as another of Elinor's stories.

"And no, your mother doesn't know. I could never speak to her about this. It has fallen to you. I curse myself for my cowardliness in not speaking of it sooner. I only hope it's not too late."

Alice settled Elinor into her rocker and went to make tea. *The child could be dead. Certainly very old*, she thought.

When Alice returned with the tray, Elinor fumbled in her pocket, withdrew the envelope, and shoved it at her granddaughter.

"Open it."

The wrinkled and faded black-and-white photograph of the fat-cheeked, black-haired somnolent infant bore a strong resemblance to Elinor.

"She's beautiful," Alice whispered.

Elinor smiled at the picture. She muttered words in Cree. Words Alice had heard many times. They spoke of thanksgiving and gratitude. "That's all I have of her. And my memories." Elinor kissed the photograph. "I want to know she's all right. I could have kept her. I could have taken her home; it would have made no difference to Mother and Father. But they — at the school — they didn't let me. Within hours of her coming from my body, they took her. A few weeks later, the photograph was in my cupboard."

Elinor took a swallow of tea then shoved her mug at Alice. "Something stronger is required. Whisky. In the bottom drawer of my dresser."

Alice found two flasks of Johnnie Walker, like eggs in a nest, snuggled into her gran's sweaters. Alice poured the amber liquid into her gran's cup and then, at Elinor's insistence, put an ounce into her own cup. She wasn't a whisky drinker. Elinor raised her cup, squinted, and grinned. "To your success in bringing Bright Eyes back to her people."

"To Bright Eyes," Alice said, trying to sound enthusiastic, trying to counter the thoughts that insisted the child had died years ago.

"She's alive. I know she has done something fine with her life," Elinor said. "I'm tired now. Help me to bed."

Elinor shed layers of clothing until she was down to a sleeveless T-shirt and underwear that fell straight from her waist, no buttocks to round them out. Breasts flat to her chest, hip bones protruding, flabby grey-purple muscle jiggling on the undersides of her arms, she was as she described herself: skin hanging from bone.

Alice threw back the sheet, blanket, and the quilt worn thin at the edges from years of being grasped and tugged. She plumped up the pillow. As soon as Elinor's head was on the pillow, she closed her eyes. Alice stroked back the white hair and kissed her gran's cheek. So still was the face, so minimal was the rise and fall in the tiny chest, her grandmother could have been dead.

Elinor's eyes snapped open. "Talk to Lillian," she said. "And leave the lamp on."

Alice folded her gran's shawl over the back of the rocker, set the bottle of whisky on the counter, and rinsed out the mugs. Lillian, five or six years younger than Elinor, lived in Saskatoon. When they were children, Alice and her brother, Andrew, spent most of the visits there chasing each other around the playground, playing cowboys and Indians. Her sister, Catherine, read books. Alice was always the Indian, always getting handcuffed or jailed. Inevitably, the jailor nodded off and she broke out, or was freed by an Indian friend, her brother, who soon found the role of warden dull.

Lillian tried with candies, gifts, and questions about friends and school and hobbies, but Alice had never liked her. Probably she and Andrew, in the wisdom of children, had decided that their aunt was a witch and not to be liked because she told them not to interrupt adults while they were talking. *Wash your hands before dinner. Stop teasing the dog.* All benign, innocuous requests that any aunt might make of a niece and nephew.

Elinor was snoring softly when Alice checked on her. In the dim yellow light, her wrinkled face had the appearance of an ancient boulder.

Who would want an Indian baby in those days? Probably she'd been killed. That would have been easy enough. There were stories about Indian families taking in illegitimate white babies in those days, but not the reverse.

The wipers struggled to keep up with the deluge splattering over the windshield; the pounding and rattling on the hood and roof of the truck was as loud as a drum band. In the darkness and wet, the road, barely visible, was long and lonely. Alice pulled to the side of the road. She was shivering even though it wasn't cold.

It was too late to go into the city. She wanted Wanda. She wanted to snuggle against her back and thighs, to feel the squeeze of her strong arms around her chest, her fingers grasping the fullness of Alice's breasts. She yearned to hear Wanda's laughter, even her delight in teasing Alice about her lust and silliness in the bedroom. Mostly, she wanted Wanda to tell her everything was going to be all right. Even though she knew it wasn't. She'd only known her gran to be a feisty woman. Now there was desperation and urgency. As if there was a deadline. There was a dead line, a rupture in the family line, which might not get reconnected before Gran died.

And what would her mother make of it? Would this news bring Gran and her mother closer together? Or widen the rift between them?

She was here today.

That Indian woman. There were long intervals when she was quiet, busy with the drawing. Other times she talked. Talked to me. Called me Big Brown. Or paskwâwi-mostos. *I struggled to find ways — twitching my tail, groaning, blinking — to tell her I'm listening. I think she knows.*

No creature, she said, was as important to her people as the bison. No part was wasted when a bison was taken. All flesh and organs were eaten, blood drunk. The hair was twisted into rope, gathered into clumps for pillows. The hides were used for tipis, moccasins, and robes. Horns became spoons and cups and toys; bones were carved into shovels and pipes, knives and war clubs. Stomachs, bladders, and scrotums served as containers for water or foods.

Bison were much-revered, she said. The Sun Dance gave recognition to that.

She snapped her pencil in two.

It was impossible, she said, to talk to her daughter about these matters.

The burden had been passed on to her granddaughter.

I swished my tail as she moved away.

7

Alice slipped into her parents' back garden. The scent of vinegar and sweet apple wafted toward her from the yellow and red orbs rotting beneath the crabapple tree. In the pond, white cartilaginous mouths at the water's surface made rippling rings and faint popping sounds like the first drops of rain. From the garden she entered the house and the kitchen. One of her mother's six budgies chirped. Her mother adored the birds; Alice joked that she took better care of the birds than she did of her children. She bought them fancy foods, fed them fruit twice a week, cleaned their cage every Saturday morning, and played music for them. Vivaldi and Chopin to calm them, Spanish guitar and Herb Alpert's Tijuana Brass to get them chirping.

Her father, squatting outside the bathroom, was holding the door between his knees. A tall white-haired man, he wore a baggy yellow T-shirt and khaki shorts. His legs were tanned and slightly bowed; a Tensor bandage encircled his left knee. Avid hiker, gardener, and Mr. Fix-It that her father was, Alice was used to seeing Band-Aids, Tensors, and supports on his fingers, wrists, and knees.

"Why don't you get a locksmith to look at that thing?" Alice asked.

"It's not that complicated. I can do it."

"You'll get stuck in there one of these days," Alice said.

"Get stuck where?" Louise asked, coming into the room. She was bundled in a white terry-cloth robe, her hair wet from a shower.

John laid the door lock, screws, and screwdriver on the counter. The vacant space in the side of the door yawned into the room. He said he'd get the door back together in a few days after he got a part from the hardware store.

"Honey, we all know your few days will slip into weeks," Louise said.

John said he was no more of a slacker about these things than Louise. He reminded her that a bag of birdseed had occupied the kitchen counter for four days before she'd put the thing in the cupboard. "And then, of course, there are the legal journals."

Louise rolled her eyes at Alice. "You can see some things never change. Did we have a date for dinner and I've forgotten?"

Alice dropped her keys into her purse. "We need to talk … about Gran."

"Is she ill?" Louise asked. She grabbed the kettle from the stove, filled it with water.

"Not exactly. But kind of."

"What does that mean?" Louise asked.

"We need to sit down. And have a talk."

"Is there time for tea?" Louise asked.

Alice shrugged. "If you like."

"Why are you being so mysterious?" Louise asked.

Alice pulled a chair from the table, a long pine table with six high-backed chairs that she had grown up with. She ran her finger over the black *C* that had been burned into the finish; her brother had placed a hot cast-iron frying pan on that spot. Alice sucked in a long breath.

"Just tell me she's all right?" Louise said.

"I guess it depends how you define all right. She hasn't had a heart attack or a stroke, but—"

"Jesus, Alice, spit it out."

Alice leapt up, clenched fists at her side. "Maybe I'll write you a letter. Sometimes you are so thick. Aren't you picking up that what I need to tell you isn't easy to talk about? Not for me, anyway. Maybe it will be for you. Maybe you'll be out on the street telling neighbours, strangers, judges … your budgies. But it isn't that way for me. I've been dragging this around for three days because this is the soonest I could get here. And I wasn't going to tell you about it over the phone."

"I'm sorry," Louise said. She tugged the tie around her robe tighter and said she was going to get dressed and would be back in a jiffy.

John washed his hands, squeezed Alice's shoulder, and suggested the two of them go into the living room.

John switched on the corner lamp. The white light spilled a cone of warmth. There was a fireplace of natural grey and brown stone, a cream-coloured couch strewn with bright cushions, and two worn black leather armchairs, each with a footstool. The walls were filled with art, mostly work by local Saskatchewan artists, including some of Elinor's prairie and valley scenes. But there was also some brightly coloured abstract modern that Louise knew her mother hated.

Alice dropped into one of the armchairs. Most of the time she found her parents' living room a comfortable space, but not that night. She crossed and uncrossed her legs, shoved her fingers through her hair, and undid the buttons on her sweater. She'd heard her mother come down the stairs and now she was in the kitchen fussing with the tea. Why did she need to bother with tea?

Her father, ever the one to placate and defuse, asked how

Alice was getting on in her new school. She said she liked most of her colleagues; every school had its pain in the neck. She had a good group of students, although a couple of kids, Indian kids, were proving a challenge. In the past she had discussed her difficult students with her father; he'd been teaching for more than thirty years. He loved the profession and seemed to have a way with angry parents and disobedient students.

"What's going on with them?" John asked.

"The usual, I suppose. Often late, homework lost …"

"Okay, here we are." Louise swept into the room with a tray on which sat a teapot under a cozy, teacups, and a plate of hermit cookies. She slid the tray onto the coffee table and sat down on the couch.

"So, what's going on?" Louise asked as she lifted the teapot.

"Something you'd never imagine in a hundred years," Alice said. She sat forward in her chair. "You know that Gran, like most of her generation, went to that residential school. Well, she got pregnant while she was there. And … and … she had a child."

Louise finished pouring the second cup of tea and sat down the teapot. "A child? You're sure about this? She often gets mixed up these days, forgets where she puts things."

"Not this time. I am quite certain she was not confused. She was extremely clear. And adamant."

"She can be adamant one day and forget what she said the next."

Alice wanted to scream, but breathed in and out slowly, searching for how to respond to her mother.

"Someone had his way with her? Is that what you're saying?" John asked. "She would have been young."

Louise stared at the blue-and-white quilted tea cozy. One side had a brown blotch the shape of a lemon; the bottom edge had begun to fray. She handed a cup of tea to John. She offered the second cup to Alice.

"All these years," Louise said, "and she never said anything. Did she tell Grandpa?"

"I don't know."

John took off his glasses, folded in one shank and then the other.

From the radio in the kitchen came news of the Olympics in Mexico City. Six thousand white doves released in the opening ceremonies. Then a story about a South African doctor, Christian Barnard, who had completed the world's first heart transplant.

"It was a girl," Alice said. "One of the nuns took her when she was a few hours old. Gran wants to see her. Before she dies."

"Before the child, the woman, dies? Or before Gran dies?"

"Before Gran dies."

"But the woman could be dead also, don't you think?" Louise said.

"I've thought about that, but Gran doesn't think so. She's convinced the woman is still alive."

John stirred sugar into his tea. Louise grimaced as John slurped the first swallow. Alice blew on her tea.

"Who would do such a thing?" John said. "Surely he's dead now. I hope he died a horrible death. Might he have had other children? Did Elinor say his name?"

Alice shook her head. "No. I've barely slept the last three nights thinking about this."

"Did your grandmother have any idea where to look for this person?" Louise asked.

"She suggested I talk to Lillian," Alice said. "They were at the same school together."

"Lillian has never said anything about Mom having another child."

"And Elinor. How is she?" John asked.

"I think she's relieved she told me. But she's desperate to find this woman."

Louise stared into her cup, took a sip, and set it on the coffee table. "Leave it with me. I don't have any brilliant ideas at the moment."

Alice pushed herself up out of the armchair. She shoved her hands in her pockets, then remembered she'd put her keys in her purse. She said it was late and she had papers to mark for the next day.

"Will you be all right?" John asked.

"Don't have much choice, do I?"

"Get some sleep," John said. He gave Alice a hug.

At the door Louise gripped Alice on the shoulder. "We'll figure something out. Let's talk in a couple of days."

"I've got work to do myself," John said, when Louise returned to the living room. "But I think I'm kind of in shock. I've never heard of anything like this."

Louise shook her head. "I don't know. I'm stunned, doubtful that it happened."

"You were in one of those schools, weren't you?" John asked.

"Yes, for a while. I kept my head down, then I ran away. Some of the nuns were mean, others were kind. I never heard of anything like this." She stacked the cups into each other.

John squeezed and massaged the knee that had the Tensor band around it. He undid the metal clips at the end and wound the brown elastic cloth from his leg. He slumped back onto the couch. "I can't get my head around this. Imagine if someone had whipped Catherine out of your arms within minutes of her leaving your body. And you never saw her again. Ever. I'd kill someone, I would." He leapt up. "Let's go for a walk. I'll not sleep for a while after this."

"Oh, John. I've got files to review."

"They'll wait." He held out his hand. "Just to the corner and back."

Hands clasped, they strolled along the sidewalk. Two houses away from their house a blue tricycle sat, abandoned, in the middle of the sidewalk. John plopped it at the foot of the family's driveway. There were five children, and their trikes and wagons were frequently left on the sidewalk or on a neighbour's driveway or lawn.

"Were we that bad when our kids were younger?" Louise asked.

"Don't think so. I think Jane is a little overwhelmed with the lot of them, and Randy being out of town so much."

Louise laughed. "Little and overwhelmed can't go in the same sentence. Overwhelmed is overwhelmed."

"Okay, Mrs. Lawyer. I think our daughter was overwhelmed by your mother's news."

"Yes. I think she was. I wish Mom had talked to me."

"Maybe your mother had more hope that her granddaughter, more than her daughter, might actually do something."

As much as Louise didn't like what John had said, she knew there was truth in it.

At the corner they crossed to the other side of the street. John waved to an elderly man sitting on his porch.

"Maybe this is your chance," John said.

"Chance for what?"

"To make amends. Your mother is not going to be around forever."

Now she was irritated. She didn't want to think about her mother's death. And she didn't want to think that not only had her mother been raped, but there had been a child. And the child had been taken from her. It just got worse. "Is this walk making you feel better?" Louise asked. "Because it's not for me."

"Don't get cranky on me," John said.

He looked up and down the street. Still holding hands, they scurried across to their house.

Inside, John told Louise not to think about it anymore that night.

"I'm going to bed. Are you coming?" he said.

"Soon. I need to tend to the birds."

Louise nestled her extended finger at the base of the bird's chest. Its cool grey fingers curled around her own. She withdrew her hand from the cage, brought the turquoise budgie to her mouth, and kissed its beak. "Hey, Buddy. How are you? Need some fresh seed?" The bird, with the slightest movement of its crusty beak and knobby grey tongue, nibbled at Louise's upper lip. Louise stroked the bird's chest. "Such a pretty boy." She placed her hand on her shoulder and the bird hopped on. She removed the water tube and feed dishes from the cage.

She worried about Alice. Although her anger came forth readily, her daughter wasn't inclined to speak of her sadness or fears. There had been an incident in high school. Alice's reaction had been over the top. Louise didn't know what to do with her. A high school friend, the two had been inseparable, had died from a rare cancer. Alice had refused to go to school. She spent hours riding her bike around the neighbourhood, and when she wasn't doing that, she made paper airplanes and threw them into the door, the wall, the big maple in the backyard. Hundreds of crashed planes. Then she made a fire and burned them all. Louise wanted Alice to go to the doctor, but Alice refused. "How can a doctor help?" she'd shouted at Louise. "Doctors couldn't save Emma."

Finally, it had been Elinor who was able to soothe Alice. She told her that Emma would always be nearby. That she must listen for her in the wind, in the rivers, and call to her in the stars.

Louise wanted the news about Elinor's child to be a figment of her mother's imagination. However, she did know those kind of things happened. She'd had her own experience. She refused to think about that now.

That her mother had gone to Alice was hurtful, but she knew why. Her mother thought Louise wouldn't believe her, that she would do nothing.

She spilled yellow seed into the bird's dish, filled the tube with water, and clamped it back on the side of the cage. She needed to make notes, see things in front of her. She grabbed a pad of paper and sat at the table.

1. The man who raped Elinor. Who was he? Did he have relatives he might have told about the baby?
2. Teachers, priests, nuns, the cook, the gardener, anyone who worked at the school. DEAD. But had they left stories, secrets with relatives, friends?
3. Get church records. Lists of students at the school.
4. Access fed gov't records for Indian Affairs.
5. Vital statistics. Provincial registry of births and deaths.

It would take months to follow up on these options.

She could run ads in some newspapers. But she had no name for the child. Alice said her mother called her Bright Eyes, but that wouldn't be the name the woman had gone by. She jotted down a draft: *Saskatchewan Indian woman seeks child, a girl, who was taken from her as an infant. Child was born in residential school in southern Saskatchewan in the early 1890s. Anyone who attended the school, who was involved with or worked at the school, who is related to people from that school. Anyone with any information at all, please contact Louise Preston at ...*

She slapped the table. Who was she fooling? No one would come forward. No one would give a damn about an Indian baby. She scribbled out what she had written. She would have to find other ways.

Her mother had never, ever spoken about her time in residential school. Had others? She didn't know. She and her mother were not so different. Neither had wanted to talk about certain things in their past. Louise didn't have the fond memories of high school that John had. Or that her own children had.

She drew the cover over the birdcage, wished the birds a goodnight. Elinor hated that Louise kept birds in a cage. Louise had found her mother with the cage door open, encouraging the birds to come out. They needed to fly, she argued, even if it was only around the kitchen.

The screen door squeaked as she pulled it open. The sound seemed louder in the darkness, the quiet still of midnight. Moving slowly, picking her way down the steps, then along the garden path, she marvelled that her mother, whom she'd always known to be a purveyor of truth and honesty, had kept this secret for so many decades. How had she managed? What had kept her from speaking out?

Oh, Louise, stop being a ninny. She spoke into the darkness. *You know how it's done.* She had her own secret that she'd kept for her entire life. A secret she intended never to speak of.

Even though in her work she pursued the truth, truth in the service of justice, she was convinced that everyone lied, everyone kept secrets. Ministers, priests, judges, plumbers, and teachers. Shopkeepers, bus drivers, and politicians. Young children, teenagers, grandparents, parents, aunts and uncles, cousins. It was a given. Everyone had a secret. Dogs hid their bones, squirrels buried their nuts. Birds tucked away treasures. The issue was not that people lied and kept confidences. What was more interesting to Louise was why people gave up their secrets. That was her job as a lawyer — to find out how to unlock the vault of secrets of the accused. Or her own client. To find the key to the vault.

Thin clouds slithered over the half-full moon. A dog a few blocks away barked into the advancing night. More clouds, more darkness, save a shard of white light along the fence from the street light. She'd try. She'd try damned hard to find this child. But she was not hopeful.

8

Leaning heavily on the white hickory stick Alice had given her when her arthritis got bad, Elinor crept outside. The last time she'd gone without the cane, she'd fallen. Her left hip and thigh had swollen up like a melon; the bruised area had been a palette of colour, first the deep purple-blue of a plum and then the white-violet of a grape's interior. Only when the pale yellow came did she know her body had almost completed its repairs.

A breeze off the waters, pregnant with autumnal moistness, wrapped itself around her. She wished River a good day and gave thanks to the Creator for the clear waters, the fishes and ducks that it nurtured. River was so much older than she, yet he continued his smooth movements without the need of a cane. She thanked the valley for its unchanging beauty. Even with her eyes closed, she knew the forms that were there. Just as her fingers knew, and would always know, the softness of the skin of her babies.

She inched across the front of her yard.

In her worst moments, she thought it was entirely her fault that Louise had shunned all that was Indian. Louise being the oldest, although not her first-born (too many babies had been lost before her), she had borne the brunt of Elinor's unhappiness and the malaise of their people that followed so many years in that place, that *kiskinwahâmêtowikamik*. She could still see that teacher, his face uglier than a badger's. Fat purple lips, crooked teeth, eyebrows and moustache wilder than the wind. She had never forgotten those nights he'd taken her to the principal's office. No one knew how he crawled over her body, pushing himself inside her until she thought her heart would be shoved out of her mouth.

Mihkominak. Mihkominak. Red berries. Red berries.

She'd say the words over and over and over. Until he left. Until her breathing slowed. Until her heart stopped racing.

She gripped the fork handle, steadied herself, and pushed the tool into the earth. The fork slipped easily into the sandy soil. She loved her garden. Clumps of earth crumbling into her palm, silken soil slipping through her fingers. The joy of discovering one morning that the earth had given birth, uppity shoots of onion, soft hairs of carrot, bold leaves of bean and pea. She supposed she could thank that school for teaching her how to garden; that was not something her mother would have shown her. In the summers when she was home with her parents, the stench of his mouth, the weight of his body surged into her mind. Some nights it was if he was there in the bed with her. She'd shove the pillow into her mouth to silence her weeping.

She lifted another clod of earth, heavier than the previous perhaps, and within seconds of doing so, the difficulty breathing and light-headedness came. She willed her body to the bent willow chair on the edge of the garden.

When her breathing had steadied she took the slim blue metal case and the box of wooden matches from the pocket of her sweater. She struggled to pry open the metal box; some days her hands worked like a dog's paws. Finally the lid came free and she took out a cigarette.

Roll-your-owns, that's all she'd ever smoked. She hated filters. The tobacco in the uncut stuff was fresher. Her withered lips held a trembling pucker around the thin cigarette. She fumbled to get hold of a match. Finally, the long flame bit at the twisted paper end. She smoked only outside; if she nodded off in the garden there was only herself to be burned down. A strand of smoke swirled before her then drifted upward. She leaned back into her chair. She still enjoyed a good smoke. That would be another problem with moving in with her daughter or taking an apartment in the city — she wouldn't have Jeremy to roll smokes for her. Every few days he'd come by, check her supply, then roll ten or fifteen. He told her to call him when she needed more, but she'd never had to; he always showed up when there were only two or three left. She took a couple of short puffs. If Louise was there she'd be rolling her eyes. At least she'd stopped giving her the speech about smoking being bad for her health. She wondered what her daughter and granddaughter were doing to find Bright Eyes. Five days. That's how long it had been since she told Alice. Louise was coming to see her in a day or two.

A twig snapped. Then short, quick blasts of breath. She stilled herself. There was no need to turn; he was beside her, and if she chose to, she could touch the muscled flank, stroke the soft ear.

"You've been away," she said. "You had me worried. Other gardens more to your liking?"

As if heeding her words, the animal, a full-grown male, ten or twelve hands high, lowered its head and snapped off a marigold. When the sounds of mastication, the crunching of orange petals, was replaced by the clunk of a single swallow, she extended her hand. The animal blinked but made no attempt to leave as she drew her fingers through the thick, short hairs of the taut hip, hairs like those she had scraped from a skin outside her parents' tipi. It was that muscle, rock-hard, almost devoid of fat, that enabled the almost effortless bounding across fields and flight over low fences. It had been years since she'd had a venison steak.

The buck stomped a front hoof, snorted, then gracefully (perhaps he'd sensed the old woman's gustatory fantasies), without haste, raised one slender leg after another. At the underbrush he ducked his head and disappeared from Elinor's view.

Leaves crunched, twigs cracked. Then silence.

Drowsily, Elinor brought the cigarette to her lips and sucked hard on the cooling ember. The cigarette glowed red, the paper curled and shrank into itself. The thin smoke tasted the musky trail of the animal.

Humans named them rubbing stones. We bison had no name for them.

But we cherished those rusty-grey boulders stranded on the prairie. So soothing. To rub my hip, or scratch my head on a craggy point, or drag the entirety of my body over the unflinching hardness. Many springs I shed my winter coat at the base of a rubbing stone.

The Indian woman barely spoke last time she was here. Nor did she draw. She sat in her chair and rocked. Some of the time she sang. I was reminded of the cows at those times.

The sound they made when their calves had been lost or taken.

Their crying began with the first light of day and continued until long after the moon had risen.

A sound like no other, it spread through the herd and over the prairie like a fog. Thick, impossible to escape, the sound touched every stone, spear of grass, creature with ears.

The wailing of the cows told the land and the sky that their calves were not returning.

Not ever.

9

Stroking her fingers over the dryness of the thin brown envelope, Elinor watched the white-edged ripples on the water; the wind was up. Louise had called a few hours ago. She was full of questions, most of which Elinor did not know how to answer. No, she did not remember the names of the teachers. She didn't know if there had been a doctor at the birth. Finally, she'd shouted at Louise that more than seventy years had gone by. Some days she didn't remember her own name. She heard the impatience in her daughter's voice. Louise was used to getting information out of people, but the two of them were not in a courtroom.

She should never have let that nun take the child. What was she thinking? She had let her first child be taken by the same people who had been stealing Indian children for years, making parents bring them to those schools. Or arriving on their doorsteps to drag them away. No discussion about this with the chiefs or elders. It was the law of the land. The white man's law, not Indian law.

She'd never forget the words the nun said to her. *I'll wash her up, make her nice and clean, and be back in a few minutes.* She had patted Elinor's left shoulder. *You rest. You've had a long labour.*

Elinor grunted. Her real labour, her lifelong pain, started the moment she let the nun take her baby.

Elinor squeezed her left shoulder, pulled down her night-gown to have a look. There was never anything to be seen. At least nothing that another person would see, but she always saw it. The imprint of a hand … *his* hand. She'd always had problems with that shoulder. It ached and ached. Some years were better than others, but it never seemed as strong as her right shoulder.

She did rest after the nun left with her child; she fell asleep for hours. She shouldn't have done that, but the labour had been long and hard. She was tired and weak. She'd called and called for her mother, but she never came. Elinor had wanted to go outside, to walk in the garden, through the trees, but they kept her in that room, in that bed. It was not the way she'd seen her mother give birth to her babies. No one took her mother's babies away after they were born; she kept them tied to her body; they went everywhere she went.

Elinor slipped the photograph from the envelope, drew her finger around the head, over the plump cheeks. How could she not have told Joseph about her? Such a kind, gentle man. He would have told her to find her, bring her home. So many times she had promised herself she would tell him. After the first snowfall. When the wild strawberries came into bloom. The next full moon. The next time a hawk flew over the camp. But she never did.

And then to have Louise run away. She thought her heart would break open. When Louise left she was the same age Elinor had been when she birthed Bright Eyes. For weeks Elinor had lived in fear that the same would happen to Louise. Some white man would have his way with her. Or worse, she'd get her-self killed. Settlers were flooding into the west from England, Scotland, Germany, and other countries she'd never heard of. They were filling up the land with farms and stores and churches.

After the Great War, white people had money. Indians had hardly enough to buy food.

She kissed the photograph and returned it to the envelope.

The house shook with a gust of wind, and then slivers of rain were sliding down the windows.

She wiped the tears from her eyes. And what would Louise say about this? Why was she worrying about that? Her own mother would not have been worrying about what Elinor might think about her. It used to be that the younger looked after the older, cooked and cleaned for them, listened to the stories, respected what they knew. But so many of those ways had changed, gone the way of the bison. So many of their people were drinking, beating on their wives. Young mothers were feeding their babies from bottles instead of their breasts. How could some formula concocted in a factory be as good for a baby as a mother's milk? All her babies had sucked from her breasts.

One thing had not changed: her yearning to find her first-born daughter. That had not diminished. It remained as large as that bison in the museum. Neither had her love for Louise changed, even though it was easy for them to bicker and disagree. It was because they were so alike. Both strong-headed. Long before Louise had run from the reserve, she, Elinor, had run from that school. So many times had she done that. Others stayed on, living in fear or letting their heads get filled up with all the white people's ideas, but she had always resisted. Even when others were getting strapped or their mouths bound for speaking in their own languages, she continued to speak *nêhiyawêwin*. She'd whisper the words into her pillow; sing the songs beneath her breath in the outhouse, in the garden, when she was hanging the clothes on the line.

Never did she let go of her language.

10

Louise rubbed her hands briskly together in an effort to ward off the chill of her mother's cottage. She wondered if her mother's hands, bent and thin, clasped in her lap, were also cold.

Elinor, slumped in her rocker, a blanket bundled around her, wore thick socks that rose halfway up her calves. Maybe it was time, Louise thought. Maybe Alice was right. Her mother should be in town, closer to doctors, in a place that was warmer than this shell of a house. A few months ago when Louise had driven out on a whim, her mother wasn't in her cottage. Louise, thinking she'd gone to the water, expecting her to appear out of the bushes, had waited on the porch. Eventually, Elinor came around the side of the house. Louise didn't ask; she knew her mother had come from the outhouse. When she reminded Elinor that she had indoor plumbing, her mother said she found the little building a comfort.

"Don't you find it cold in here?" Louise asked.

"No," Elinor said. "I wear warm things."

There was a limit to how much clothing she was prepared to wear inside, Louise thought.

"How about a fire?" Louise asked.

"That would be nice," Elinor said. "When your father was alive, he started one at the end of August and kept it going until the springtime." She rolled her lips together. "Do you remember those winters on the reserve?"

"I don't like thinking about them, but I remember them," Louise said. Mostly, she remembered the cold: Freezing drafts around the windows and beneath the door. A film of snow on the floor if the wind had been especially strong. Frozen tea at the bottom of mugs. She tired of turnip and gopher meat; some days there wasn't even that.

She crumpled newspaper and shoved it into the sooty cavity of the stove. "Got any kindling?" There were a few birch logs near the stove but nothing smaller.

"On the porch," Elinor said. "It wasn't all bad on the reserve. At least everyone was together. Sure, some had their problems, but we had community and that gave its own heat."

Not the kind of heat she liked, Louise thought as she grabbed a handful of twigs and a few pieces of split wood from the pile on the porch. A daddy-long-legs, exposed by her shifting the wood, picked its way back into obscurity. She wasn't convinced there was much of a community. What kind of community could there be with so much misery? Her mother wouldn't see it that way. She'd not dispute the suffering, but she wouldn't get stuck there. She'd remember the laughter, the jokes, the dancing and drumming and costumes at the powwows. And those who were able helping out those less capable, knowing that at any moment their places might be reversed.

"I'll get John to bring more wood," Louise said. She criss-crossed twigs on top of the newspaper then struck a match and held it in a fold of the paper. The tiny flame quivered and smoked then went out. It was the same with the next match she struck. Louise fussed with the paper, spreading it open, tearing smaller strips. This time the fire took hold. Once the kindling had caught, she laid the split wood on top and moved a couple of logs near.

"Whatever happened to Blanche? What was her last name?" Louise asked.

"Horsetree," Elinor said.

Louise and Blanche had been close friends. They'd play cards for hours and hours or take long walks in the woods when Blanche could spare some time from helping her mother. Louise had wanted Blanche to go with her when she left the reserve. Maybe she wouldn't have been lonely for so long if she'd had Blanche. But Blanche wouldn't leave her mother; she wouldn't leave her mother to care for her seven sisters and brothers on her own. Blanche wasn't as restless and as unhappy as Louise.

"Do you see her? Or her mother?" Louise asked.

"Pretty hard to do that," Elinor said.

Flames roared through the kindling. Louise positioned a log in the midst of the fire and closed the door of the stove.

"Is she sick?"

"No. Not really."

"Did they move? You lost touch?"

"You didn't hear?" Elinor asked.

"Hear what?"

Elinor pushed the blanket from her shoulders. "Five years ago, they were all killed in a fire. Someone left a pot of oil on the stove. Only one who survived was the younger brother, Willie. He was away at a hockey game."

"Was it in the news? I never heard a thing about it."

"It was in the Indian news," Elinor said.

The Indian news. Louise arranged lettuce and slices of tomato on bread. She put extra mayonnaise and pepper on her mother's sandwich. It would have been front page news in the Indian community. In the standard news, there might have been a single paragraph, at the bottom of a page, near the end of the newspaper. If that.

"That's awful," Louise said, pulling up a chair beside her mother's rocker.

"It was a terrible thing. They found the bodies in their beds. Smoke must have got to them before they realized there was a fire. Poor Willie, only eleven. He went crazy. He'd been such a good kid, a really good hockey player. Well, he quit that, refused to go to school, and wouldn't work. His auntie didn't know what to do with him. I don't know what's happened to the boy. Another lost one."

Elinor's dentures clicked as she chewed.

They gazed at the valley. Clouds moved in and out of the sun's rays; dark blotches appeared on the floor of the cottage then disappeared. White light jiggled on the walls; the room was bright, then grey, then bright again.

Louise wished her mother would say something about Bright Eyes. She should be the one to begin the conversation, but she wouldn't. It would be up to Louise.

"Should I make tea?" Louise asked. "Are you going to eat the rest?" Her mother had eaten half the sandwich.

Elinor shook her head. "Any news yet?"

"News of?" Louise asked.

"The child, of course. I don't care about anything else right now. I can't bear to listen to anything more about that Vietnam War. Although I think it's a horrid thing. And shooting Martin Luther King. What is wrong with people?"

Louise said Alice was going to talk to Lillian. And they were trying to get a list of students who'd been at the school when Elinor was there. She said it would help a great deal if they knew Bright Eyes' adult name. She stacked up the dishes, put them in the sink, filled the sink with water, then came back to her mother. "I hate to ask you this, but do you remember his name? The father's name?"

Elinor began to rock and muttered words Louise did not understand.

"I'm not understanding you," Louise said.

"Red berries. Red berries," Elinor said. "That's what I said to myself when he was doing it to me. I've worked very hard to forget his name, the smell of his breath, the feel of his fingers ..." She rocked harder.

Louise sat beside her mother and took hold of her hand. "Are you sure you want to do this, Mom? It's been so long ..."

Elinor yanked her hand from Louise's. "How can you think that, let alone ask it? Of course I want to do this! I have to do this before I die."

A hawk soared over the river. Shrubs swayed and shook in the wind. Some reached over to touch the water.

"Did Daddy know?" She didn't look at her mother as she spoke the question.

Elinor shoved a finger along her bottom denture. "I couldn't tell him. I was too ashamed."

Louise hesitated. She stacked the magazines on her mother's table, swept her hand over the surface to take away the dust and cigarette ashes. "You never told me," Louise said.

Elinor muttered in Cree. Words Louise didn't know. "No. You didn't want to hear. At least that's what I told myself for a long time. Maybe that wasn't fair."

"I was stupid. Mean. Only thinking of myself."

"Perhaps it was for the best. Perhaps the Creator knew another might care for her better. But she's been away too long." She turned toward Louise; her eyes were moist but they weren't heavy with sadness. "I know it's a lot to ask. I know you are busy with your work, important work. Have I ever told you you've made a good thing of your life? But I must see her before I die."

Louise saw no point in saying it was such a long shot. She might have to reconsider the idea of running an ad in the local, or even national, newspapers. She needed names of teachers, those who worked at the school. They'd be dead. But perhaps they had spoken to a relative.

"I know you think it's impossible," Elinor said, "like chasing after fluffs of milkweed in a windstorm. But she *is* alive and she is ready to come home. She has always wanted that. It's my fault. I have not given her a clear enough message to return."

"Alice said you have a photograph. Can I see it?"

"It's in there." Elinor pointed toward the bedroom. "In my dresser, under the socks."

Louise turned toward the bedroom.

"Wait. Why are you so shocked about this?"

"It's disturbing. That such an awful thing happened to you."

"Lots of disturbing things happened to lots of our people. We've been silent too long."

"You really think she'll be alive?" Louise asked.

"Why not? Somebody took you in, put food in your belly."

"I suppose."

"Who was she?" Elinor asked. "I can't figure whether I should thank her for caring for you. Or curse her for stealing my daughter."

"She's dead. Can I get the photo now?"

"She's not just my child. She's also your sister. Remember that."

Elinor pulled the blanket over her legs. She believed her expectations were great, but not impossible.

11

Elinor tried to wiggle her finger under the flap of the envelope, cursing when the paper would not come unstuck. She got a knife, shoved it into the crack at the end of the flap, and tore at the paper. She pulled out the contents. It was rare that she got a letter, and this was a thick one.

Dear Ellie, it began. No one but her sister called her that; she didn't like it much.

> *I phoned several times. You didn't answer so here I am writing you a letter. I hope you read it. How are you? I am well enough but my hip bothers me more than I would like.*
>
> *I had a lovely visit with Alice the other week. It's been so long. I was surprised to hear from her but she said you told her to call. That was even more of a surprise.*
>
> *Why is she not yet married? Such a lovely girl. Her students are lucky to have her.*
>
> *She brought me a pair of rolled beeswax candles. I told her you had kept bees on the reserve for a while. You got lots of honey but the bees kept swarming.*

We talked a lot about you. Alice was keen to hear all my stories. I told her you were always feisty and independent. And bossy. I remember you being so bossy. We'd go berry picking. It was all business to you. We had to pick so many berries before we went back. I just wanted to lie in the sun, glut myself with strawberries, raspberries or whatever it was we had gone after.

Alice told me about her teaching, that she had lots of Indian students and how hard it was to keep them interested. I remembered the summers when we were home from that school. You'd get into the worst moods. I wondered what they were teaching you. Mother and Father had no idea what to do with you. It was years before I realized how hard it must have been for them. I went to that school, too, but it didn't have the same effect on me. Not that there weren't hard times.

You tried so hard to look after me when you were at school. You were never like that at home. And boy, you hated that one teacher. What was his name? You made me promise never to get myself alone in a room with him. You kept pinching me until I promised. Was he the one? The one who made you pregnant? How did I not know you were pregnant? You were very good at hiding it.

Elinor turned from the letter and rubbed her eyes. Had she made a mistake telling Alice to talk to Lillian? She lit a cigarette, sucked in a few puffs, stared at the black cast-iron pot on the stove. Alice had left it; it was full of beef stew. She was a good girl. All of Louise's children had turned out very well. Better than her own kids. She mustn't think that way. Le Roy fell apart after Joseph's death. Charlie was a good man; she didn't see him much. He'd chosen a simple life way north in the bush. She should have spoken out sooner. All those years lost. Why had she not gone looking sooner?

She picked up the letter again.

Elinor, I told Alice there were good times too. Always cousins to play with. Somebody to give you a hug. An auntie or grandparent to tell you a story or sing a song. We'd walk in the valley, look for wild onion, rosehips for tea. Sometimes the wind blew so hard you'd think you'd never get back to the camp. Remember the time we found that dead coyote, crawling with maggots, half its belly eaten away? You poked a stick at it and a cloud of flies flew up from it.

But it was hard on the rez too. So many starving, sick, freezing in the winter months. They expected us to farm, but what did Mama and Papa, or anyone know about farming in those days? That was not a fast way to get food compared to hunting and finding what was growing on the land. Some years there was nothing from our gardens. Grasshoppers ate it all. Or there was no rain and the plants shrivelled up and died. Every tool they gave us was stamped with Dept. of Indian Affairs. What were we? The hired help?

After I got away from the rez, I didn't pay attention to my Indian sisters and brothers for a long time. I'm not proud of that. I suppose I got comfortable. My life with Leonard seemed so far away from all that. What could I do for those taking drugs, drinking until they fell down? And then there was that business with the girl from Sandy Point last spring. Did you hear about that, Ellie?

Elinor flung the letter across the table. Yes, she'd heard about that poor child. She didn't want to think about it again. The story cut too close to the bone for her. A fourteen-year-old raped by a pack of hoodlums. Poor child. She shouldn't have died, but because of her diabetes and missing her medicines.... The fools dropped her miles from her reserve when they were finished with her.

Elinor shuffled to the kitchen. There were mouse droppings on the counter, but Elinor's eyesight being what it was, she didn't see them. She filled the kettle with water, plunked it on the stove, and turned away, forgetting to turn on the element. She returned to Lillian's letter; it was the size of a small book. That's why she didn't always answer her phone, because Lillian would talk on and on for hours.

Elinor, I couldn't talk to Leonard about the girl. He'd say she shouldn't have been walking by herself. He'd say lots of Indian girls her age are on the streets selling their bodies to pay for their alcohol. Of course, he'd never ask why they are doing that. They never used to. The only good that came out of that poor girl's tragedy was that I got past my fear. I got mad. Damned mad.

Alice asked about that kiskinwahamatow-ikamik. I didn't want to talk about it. I think that's how it is for most who went there. Even though the building burned down. Some still won't go near the place. Most have wanted to forget that time. But it's like a burr on a sock. You barely know it's there; it won't fall off of its own accord. You have to yank it away.

Alice asked me if I knew about your child. I told her I only found out after you stopped going to that school. I still remember the day you told me. Do you remember that, Ellie?

It was early spring, fall maybe. Yes, fall. The sun stayed low in the sky. We walked fast to keep warm, shoulders hunched up, hands shoved in our pockets. We'd gone into town to get a few things. A woman came into the store. She had a young child, three or four years old, long black hair, olive complexion. You kept staring and staring at the girl. You had always been one to study things, to pay attention to the shadows and brightness in the light, how the colours changed through the course of the day. But this was different. It was a look like a cat gets when it sees a bird it might be able to catch. I hissed at you to stop but you kept on. Fortunately the woman didn't notice or there would have been trouble.

When you started to move toward the child I grabbed your wrist and squeezed as hard as I could. I wanted to hurt you, anything to distract your attention. It worked. You got very bossy and told me to hurry up. Usually you were a careful shopper but this time you grabbed anything. You didn't even count the change. As soon as we were

*out of the store you were walking so fast I could
hardly keep up. We had the groceries to carry. I
said I wasn't hurrying.*

*We were barely ten minutes from the store
when you stopped and fell down on the side of the
road. You wrapped your arms around yourself
and started rocking and moaning. Like you had a
stomach ache. I had no idea what was happening.
I didn't want anyone to see you. I pulled at you to
get up, to hold on to whatever it was until we got
home. But you wouldn't budge. A couple of cars
slowed down. I waved at them to keep going. You
were wailing and curled up in the grass. Finally,
you sat up, swiped the tears from your face, and
told me everything that had happened to you. At
first I thought you were lying. You liked to make
up stories, remember? But you'd been crying so
hard; I'd never seen you like that. I knew it was
the truth. Probably I hoped it wasn't. You made
me swear not to tell Mother and Father. We never
talked about it again.*

Elinor pushed the letter away. She wanted to burn it. It was
too hard, all this remembering. That's why the Creator enabled
people to forget. But even as she thought that, she knew it was
better that the stories from the past be given to the next generation. It had always been that way; it was one of the things that
kept her people strong.

She went to the stove; the kettle was cold as ice. She snatched
the letter from the table.

Thankfully, there was only one page left.

Elinor, Alice said you want her to find that child. Are you CRAZY? How will she do that? All the people who knew about it are pretty much dead. It's been SEVEN decades. She asked me if I knew who the father was. You never told me, Elinor, but I have a pretty good idea who it was. He'll be dead, too.

I know Alice was disappointed that I couldn't give her names or places to look. It's a very TALL order, Elinor. I'm not sure it's fair that you are asking it of her. Especially since it's so long ago. Can't you let it go? Pray for your child, pass on your love through the stars, the fire, and wind, but asking your granddaughter to go on such a chase? And what does Louise say about it?

Oh, I don't want to sound so harsh. I did tell her I would ask around, but I am not hopeful.

Miwasin, miwasin. It was so good that she came.

And Elinor, PICK UP THE PHONE next time I call.

Love,
your sister, Lillian

Elinor folded the letter back into its envelope.

Damned Lillian and her capital letters, trying to tell her things she already knew.

She would find Bright Eyes.

Someone always knew; someone would have told.

Secrets are like pods of the milkweed. They always burst open.

I will never forget the first time I saw a hill of bones.

The thing was mammoth. Even with my weak eyesight — bison have weak eyes — I was able to see the mound from a great distance.

My first instinct was to run from it, but I crept closer. The hill spanned the width of many wallows. Standing on one side of it, I couldn't see to the other side. The height was far greater than the largest bull or rubbing stone.

When the wind picked up, the bones rattled and clanked, whistled and wailed.

Smaller bones were swept onto the ground with stronger gusts of wind.

I stood at one end and tried to hold my head high.

Naked and pure white.

Countless bones.

Skulls.

Shoulders and ribs. Thighs and ankles.

Bison bones. A herd of bison baking in the prairie sun.

12

Elinor flipped to a fresh page in her sketch pad. The drawing wasn't going well. The constancy of lighting in the museum and the absence of movement from Big Brown were helpful, but only to a point. She'd never had a calling to paint teapots, houseplants, or bowls of fruit. The closest she'd got to that kind of work was a watercolour of saskatoon berries. She'd started with a branch of the berries, glistening blue and purple in the late afternoon sun. Very soon her images from within took over: Small hands reaching for the berries. Cheeks bulging with the sweet fruit. Bent fingers pressing the ripe orbs into dried meat.

The absence of life in *paskwâwi-mostos* had an effect on her work.

Big Brown. Lillian, my sister, sent me a long letter. Alice was probably still on the highway when she started writing. Otherwise, I don't think she would have remembered all the things they talked about. She told me they had a lovely visit and then she was cranky, asking why I hadn't spoken up sooner about the child. And what was I thinking, asking my granddaughter to find her after all these years? I didn't have a good answer for her, Big Brown. It's like asking the wind why it blows hard one day and soft the next. That was how it was. Like the principal at the school asking why Swift Eyes and I had gone into his office. Over and over, before he brought the belt to Swift Eyes' palms, and then mine, he asked why she had taken the money. What answer would suit? Elinor chuckled. *Because it was shiny. Because it sounded like rain on a tipi. Because we wanted to see the picture of Queen Victoria.*

Then Lillian said she was sorry. She remembered me telling her about the child after our trip to the store. She said I'd been so upset that day. She said I kept staring at this young girl in the shop, how she had to grab me before I got myself into trouble. I had for-gotten that, Big Brown. How could I have forgotten something like that? Makes me wonder what else I have forgotten.

Elinor laughed. *I'll never know that, will I, Big Brown? But I'll not forget you. There will be drawings to remind me.*

Elinor dragged her chair closer to the gallery. Working in short, careful strokes, she drew the beard, hair by hair. She remembered the dry thickness of the hair on the blankets her mother had made. When she felt a tingling on the crown of her head, she stopped her work to look around. No one. The last time she'd been at the museum, there had been a group of children on a school trip. Some had been polite and curious to see what she was doing. One girl wanted to know why she was drawing the bison. Why not a horse or a dog?

The sensation on Elinor's head grew stronger. As if a hand or a bowl was being pushed downward. She rubbed her hand over her head. Only hair.

Her eyes were tired. It took more effort to move the pencil over the paper.

Steadying herself with her cane, she moved closer to the gal-lery. She was tempted to press her face to the glass. It was obvious by the smudge marks that many had already done so. Keeping her eyes on *paskwâwi-mostos*, she shifted a few inches to the left and then to the right. It was going to be hard to do the eyes, so lifeless were the glass orbs. Probably, if she searched, she'd find two or three bison living in a zoo or a game farm. Two or three. Hundreds of thousands reduced to a handful; the thought enraged her. She wouldn't be able to draw or paint those animals. Creatures standing dead, that's what they would be.

Jeremy had brought her into the city. Where was he? She wanted to go home.

She stepped back from the gallery. Now what? Her eyes were playing a trick on her? Had the bison's tail moved?

She dropped onto her chair. A chill ran the length of her spine. Whether the tail moved, or she *thought* it moved, wasn't the point. It was a sign. Something she needed to attend to. If there were spirits in boulders, trees, rivers, grasses, why not in this creature? She must revise her opinions about museums; maybe they held more than she had accorded to them. Maybe she needed to listen more closely, look more carefully.

She leaned forward. "I'll be back, big fellow," she said.

She looked for a further movement of the tail. None came.

Instead a rumble, a deep, throaty groan.

13

Alice, short of breath and a stitch in her right side, caught up to Wanda at the back of the legislative buildings. Wanda, her cheeks red, curly black hair wet with sweat, was staring up at the sandstone building. The muscles in Wanda's thighs and calves bulged; her entire body was firm and taut from years of running. Although she was almost flat-chested, Alice could still make out her nipples through her damp T-shirt.

"Where did they get all the stone?" Wanda asked. "This is the plains, not the Canadian Shield. It's like a pyramid in the middle of the desert."

"It's Tyndall stone, quarried in Manitoba." Alice laughed.

"What's so funny?" Wanda said.

"I'm remembering a class tour of the building a few months ago," Alice said. She leaned forward in a stretch, touching her toes. Before she met Wanda she'd not done much running. Occasionally, she'd gone hiking and canoeing with friends, but she wasn't a fanatic about it like Wanda. As they talked, Wanda was running on the spot.

"One of my students, Daniel, is a bit of an egghead. He got obsessed with the fossils in the stone. You can find quite a few of them. He wouldn't leave when it was time. He'd been counting, making sketches and notes of the different fossils he'd found.

Trilobites, cephalopods, and brachiopods. Little footprints of history. He was beside himself. Finally, I had to yank his pencil out of his hand and drag him to the bus."

"I don't know how you do it," Wanda said.

"I love it. Although I'm happier with the fourth and fifth grades than I was with the kids in kindergarten and grade one."

"How so?"

"Younger ones always need more looking after. You spend time wiping tears, tying shoelaces. I love to see them grappling with arithmetic and science ideas. Can't imagine you teaching in elementary school."

"Some days I think it might be easier than university. You expect students to get things in on time, do the readings, have some interest in what they're learning. But every class has someone who's full of excuses for why his stuff is late, why he's done a half-assed job. Then he has the nerve to complain about the mark he gets."

Alice grinned. "And you're a paragon of patience."

"When have you seen me impatient?"

"All the time. Hovering over the toaster waiting for it to pop, tapping on the steering wheel when the light's red, at the grocery store waiting to pay for your food."

"Everybody gets impatient at those times. I was a camp counsellor for three summers in upstate New York. I was the one who handled the kids who were homesick, the kids who were afraid to go in the water, burned their fingers in the fire. That takes patience. And, it seems to me, I've been pretty patient with you." She leaned toward Alice, kissed her on the lips, stroked her hair, then ran off.

Alice watched Wanda for a few seconds then turned away. Even as she was aware of the lightness and tingling in her body, she was furious at Wanda. She imagined hundreds of eyes peering from the multitude of windows at the back of the building. Parliamentarians, janitors, tourists, government officials had all left their duties to spy on Alice and Wanda. Newspaper headlines flashed across her mind. *Alice Preston, grade four teacher, kisses woman. Premier calls for her resignation.*

Silvery sunlight bounced from the windows of the legislative buildings. It was impossible to see inside the building; she'd never know if she'd been seen. She ran a few yards then slowed to a brisk walk. She didn't want to catch up to Wanda. Even as her mouth throbbed with the sensation of Wanda's tongue thrusting against her own, she detested what Wanda had done. It was useless to tell Wanda her worries. Whenever she did, Wanda told her she was paranoid. People, Wanda would say, were going about their work, not glued to the windows in case a couple of dykes stopped by. There was more at stake for her, Alice tried to impress upon Wanda. This was her hometown. People knew her; they knew her family. And two years ago a man in the Northwest Territories had been charged with, and found guilty of, homosexuality.

They'd argued before they'd gone out. Wanda had challenged Alice to accept who she was. Yet again Wanda said the words that had become a mantra between the two of them: *Women have been loving women since antiquity. The Greeks knew that. No modern-day politician, parliamentarian, or neighbourhood mechanic is ever going to change that.*

Even Hitler wasn't successful, Wanda added, when she really got going.

Those were the moments when Alice became silent. She didn't think Wanda was wrong. But small-town Saskatchewan was not Greenwich Village. Saskatchewan — while the birthplace of Canadian medicare and socialism — was full of farmers, not artists and beatniks, writers and Jews. If Ross Thatcher, the current premier, had his way, the place would become more conservative, not less. Her father had been furious when Thatcher's party won the last election; health and social services were cut, taxes went up. And the province was "open for business."

Unlike the sociology department, where Wanda worked, which was full of outspoken left-wing radicals, most of the teachers at the elementary level were more concerned with recipes for cookies and salads, which team had won the last football game, and how to deal with a difficult student. She was new to the school. Perhaps in time more important conversations would emerge. At the moment she had no idea from whom those might come, or when.

She spotted Wanda in the distance, running on the spot and waving her arms as she waited for the traffic light to change. As soon as it was green, Wanda tore across the street. Alice wished she had Wanda's courage. Knowing no one in Regina, or Saskatchewan, Wanda Cohen had picked up and left New York for a job at the university. It was her way of protesting the Vietnam War. In New York, Wanda had had a circle of lesbian friends who met weekly to talk books and protests. And dance. Women dancing with women scared Alice. Alice hadn't met other lesbians in Regina, but, within a few weeks of moving to the city, Wanda seemed to know them all. Just as she had picked out Alice.

Wanda was sitting on the front steps of her house, a two-and-a-half-storey white stucco with green trim and attached garage. The front yard was taken up by a sprawling oak. Wanda had taken off her shoes and socks and was picking at her left large toe as Alice walked up the sidewalk.

"Good run?" Wanda asked when Alice got to the steps.

"All right. Yours?"

"Shouldn't have stopped to look at the legislative buildings."

Wanda unlocked the door and Alice charged up the stairs and into the bathroom. She peeled off her sweatpants and shirt and turned on the shower. She was braless, in the midst of stepping out of her underpants when Wanda, breasts bouncing, buck naked, plastic vampire teeth overhanging her lips, burst in.

"Never let your guard down," Wanda said, her voice thick with Transylvanian drawl. "You never know where Dracula is lurking." She nibbled at Alice's neck.

They showered a long time. Long after the sweat and grime had been sloughed from their bodies. Until the bar of pink soap, lodged at the lip of the drain, had turned mushy and slippery. Finally, naked and wet, they dashed to the bedroom.

Standing in the kitchen, the scent of peppermint wafting from her teacup, Alice scanned the white, yellow, and pink papers stuck to Wanda's oak cupboards. There was a reminder of an upcoming meeting of the urban studies section of the sociology department, two flyers announcing protests against the U.S. Army band scheduled to play at a local high school, and an invitation to a bris for the son of one of Wanda's colleagues. A poster announced that Joni Mitchell was singing at the 4th Dimension coffee house, and there was a note in Wanda's handwriting reminding her to send money in support of the Morgentaler abortion clinic in Toronto.

Max did the traditional cat dance. Purring loudly, strolling and turning full circle every few feet, he dragged the length of his body over Alice's calf, then turned to bunt his head against her ankle. He pushed into the massage when she scratched the top of his head. Not usually a cat fancier, so loose, languid, and serene did she feel, she could find even a cat's antics amusing.

Wanda cantered down the stairs and into the kitchen. She dropped a newspaper in front of Alice; one of the headlines was circled. Student protestors in France were being charged and jailed.

"That could be you," Wanda said. "Are they still intent on erecting roller coasters and whirligigs out there?" Local entrepreneurs were planning to build an amusement park on land that was believed to be an Indian burial site. Alice had been attending meetings to plan a protest.

"Seems so. I wish more people showed up at the meetings," Alice said.

Max leapt onto Alice's lap; she pushed him off. Wanda picked up the cat, stroked the length of his back. His tail twitched, then he bit her hand. She tapped his nose, poured him from her arms.

"You sound discouraged," Wanda said.

"Impatient, I guess. The whole thing makes me think about my mother. She doesn't seem to give a damn about it."

"So don't talk to her about it. You're a big girl, aren't you?" Wanda grinned.

Alice spotted an ant shifting back and forth on the lip of the counter. She whisked it onto the floor and shrugged. "It seems logical to talk to her. She's Indian. Both of her parents were Indians. But she's so hard on her own people, like it's all their fault. If you ask my mother, there's nothing good about being Indian. Our time has come and passed. It's so different from how Gran talks. Thank God for my grandmother."

"I don't find the whole idea that strange," Wanda said. "There are Jews who don't tell anybody they're Jewish; they try to pass."

"Pass?"

"You have led a sheltered life, haven't you? They try to pass as Gentile, goyim."

"But why?"

"Oh, Alice. Think about it. You're no different from them. Why don't you want anyone to know you love women, that you prefer sex with a woman over a man?"

"It's none of their business," Alice said.

"And you're afraid. Afraid your mother will be mad, afraid you'll lose your job. You want to pretend that what you and I do together doesn't happen."

Alice didn't want to admit that Wanda was right. She hated to be wrong; she'd always been that way. Her mother would say she was stubborn; her father would say she had strong opinions and that was good.

Wanda pulled a chair from the table, sat backward on it, arms crossed over the top, a leg splayed out on each side. She drew her fingers across the top of Alice's head; Alice hung her head back as Wanda combed her fingers through the foot-and-a-half length of it, jiggling out tangles as she went. Alice recalled the roughness of her gran's thick fingers fumbling with her hair when she was younger, pulling it so tight the roots tingled. Wanda brought the end of the braid over Alice's shoulder, asked her to hold it. She rummaged through a kitchen drawer and pulled out a clump of ribbon. Red, yellow, green, and blue entangled like seaweed thrown up by the tide. She asked Alice which colour she preferred; Alice picked yellow. The yellow ribbon had a couple of knots. Wanda fussed with it for a couple of minutes, then shoved it at Alice. "You do it. I've got no patience."

Alice smiled. The knots were pulled tight but she managed to get a fingernail under a small segment. Gradually, she wiggled the section of ribbon free from itself and handed it back to Wanda.

Wanda stepped back after securing the ribbon around the braid and grinned. "Such a lovely Indian maiden you are."

"Shut up," Alice said.

Wanda pulled Alice from her chair, bowed, then asked if she could have this dance. They waltzed around the kitchen in a clumsy two-step, with Wanda humming the "Tennessee Waltz." When Alice tripped on the cat and the thing shrieked, the moment was lost.

Wanda rummaged in the fridge, finally locating an open can of cat food from behind a jar of sauerkraut. She scooped a couple of spoonfuls of the grey mush into the cat's bowl, pushed the dregs from the spoon, and wiped her fingers on the back of her blue jeans.

Alice watched the cat's tongue. Slender and pink. Lithe. So efficient at swiping every speck of food from around its mouth. Like the nuns at that school. Sweeping away that dark stain from the perfect white world before anyone had a chance to see.

"I've been feeling guilty. And frustrated," Alice said. She drew her braid around to the front of her neck, twirled the end hairs in her fingers.

"With me?" Wanda asked.

Alice laughed. "That would be easy. No. This business with finding my gran's child. I don't see how we'll find her in time. If at all."

"In time for what?"

"Before ... before she dies. I don't like saying the words. I can't imagine my gran not being here."

"So hire a detective. He can work ten hours a day, every day of the week, chasing down leads. And a detective can be pushy where you or your mom may not be able to."

"Not sure Mom will go for that."

"Don't tell her. Do you tell your mother everything? I don't. Well, I can't. She's dead. Has your mother got any better ideas? I think you need a good detective. There's a lot of legwork. Why do you think police forces put ten or twenty guys on a case if it's a vicious murder?"

"Never thought of it."

"They know how many people they're going to have to talk to before somebody gives them a tidbit. If they've got only one guy at it, doing it after his day job — like you and your mom — it ain't going to happen very fast. And clues dry up." Wanda opened and closed several cupboards, finally pulling out a bag of pasta.

"How do you know all this?"

"*Perry Mason*. And my uncle was a cop in NYC. He loved the work. He loved talking about his work. He'd come over, drink coffee, and talk and talk. My father hated when Uncle Saul came, but I loved it."

Her uncle, Wanda said, talked about following a lead, talking to a whole bunch of different people, chasing after it, then nothing. He'd get another hint, go after that person. Nothing. One day, out of the blue, somebody would walk into the precinct. He'd been away on vacation, left the day after the murder. He'd say he saw this guy running across the park at two in the morning.

"My uncle says he gets this dizziness when they're getting closer to the guy. He knows they're close because he gets that. He can't sit still or sleep; he only eats hot dogs and oatmeal. Sometimes it goes on for days. And then they pounce."

"Too bad your uncle doesn't live here."

"I'll bet your mother knows somebody. She's a lawyer."

14

Little whitecaps scurried over the surface of the lake like gophers on a grassy knoll. There had been frost last night, a fine white dusting that covered the planks of Elinor's porch, the grey stones of the driveway, and the ruddy brown twigs of her garden chair. The first few winters on the reserve, when they had little wood for fires, she and her cousins and sister would stay under the bison hides until the sun was higher in the sky. They'd hover over a candle, trying to warm their hands. One time, Elinor's hair caught fire. So many died from disease and hunger. It was their custom to place the dead, wrapped in hides, on platforms above the ground or in the trees. That winter the trees blossomed with dead bodies. Hundreds of blossoms.

"Damn!" Elinor dropped the phone into its cradle and shuffled to her rocking chair. She hated telephones. Speaking in person was better. She used to despise television, said she'd never have one in her house. Until Alice brought her one. She was embarrassed that she was intrigued by the machine's ability to take her from the streets of Regina to Washington, D.C., Victoria, Halifax, or Vietnam with the turn of a knob. She changed the channel when they reported on that war in Vietnam. It disturbed her. Images of parents with a naked child draped over their arms like a carpet. Villages, beautiful fields of rice, bombed and burning. What good did it do anyone to know of those things? She liked very much programs that showed pictures of mountains, rivers, beavers or eagles, wild horses in Alberta. Some of the shows made her laugh. Cooking shows in which a white woman with perfect hair and lovely clothes demonstrated how to slice onions and carrots, how to melt butter in a pan. Where were their aunties and mothers? The shows for the children angered her. Children should be running, chasing, fighting with each other, not watching others do such things.

She jumped at the banging of the door, then the sound of tapping on glass. She pushed herself from her chair and squinted at the kitchen window; she couldn't tell whose face, hands cupped around it, was pressed against the glass.

"Come in," she said. "The door's open."

A tall, lanky youth, sixteen or seventeen, balancing letters and a large, flat package on long arms, shoved open the door.

"Jeremy, it's you," Elinor said. She stood wavering by the kitchen table. "Put it there on the table. It's my new brushes and canvas. Help yourself to some Coke. You know where the glasses are."

She dragged one of the letters toward her. Recognizing the rough, awkward printing, mostly in capital letters, she groaned. "Now what?" She fumbled to tear the end off the envelope.

"Something the matter?" Jeremy gasped after a long guzzle of Coke.

"Oh, probably," she said, struggling to get her fingers inside the end of the envelope. "Can you get the damned thing out?"

Jeremy pulled out a single sheet of notepaper and handed it to her. She didn't want to read it. The very thought tired her. She pushed the letter to the side and asked Jeremy about school.

"It's cool," he said.

"Your mother must be happy."

"Pretty much." He nodded then asked what she was painting.

"Not quite sure yet," she said. Actually, she did know, but didn't want to speak about it. Talking about the work, before or in the middle, tended to interfere with the necessary and mysterious unfolding of the picture she had chosen to make, the story she wanted to tell. She likened the process to the opening of a rose. You never knew how, or why, or when, the first petals separated themselves from the bud, or the pace at which the others would join them. Sure, there were theories about warmth and moisture and hours of sun, but who really knew. Only *Manitow*, the Creator, knew.

Jeremy asked her to show him some of her paintings. Most times she enjoyed Jeremy's visits. Often, they'd have long talks about what he was learning in math, social studies, his plans after graduating from high school. And if she really needed to get somewhere Jeremy would drive her. But now she wanted to see what the letter required of her. She said she was tired and suggested he come back the following day.

"Sure. Or next week, if that's better," he said. He asked about her supply of cigarettes, then left.

Elinor opened the letter, a sheet of stationery from St. Paul's Hospital in Saskatoon. There were only a few words; they sprawled across the centre of the page.

I'M IN HOSPITAL HIT BY CAR
LE ROY

She dropped the letter on the table and looked to the window above the sink. Clouds, their undersides the grey and black of pencil lead, had started to form. Snow clouds. She'd sensed from the recent gatherings of geese and crows that winter would come early this year. No doubt he had been drunk. Probably he hit the car, instead of the car hitting him. His body was so saturated with alcohol his liver probably crunched like a pickle. She didn't blame Louise for banning him from her life. His spectacular rendition of "Jingle Bells," in between coughing jags and crawling through the snow in her front yard, was not what Louise had wanted for her Christmas morning. He was lucky she hadn't called the police and pretended she didn't know him.

Elinor wanted to believe that if Le Roy was in hospital, he wouldn't be able to drink. There wasn't much that he hadn't tried. He wasn't beyond searching out the rubbing alcohol or convincing one of the cleaning staff to smuggle in a mickey or two. She wondered if she should call him. Last time, he'd cried and cried on the phone, promised he'd get off the booze and go for treatment. Three months later the phone rang at four in the morning. It was Le Roy, wanting to sing "Happy Birthday" to her. It wasn't her birthday. Probably he didn't notice that she'd hung up the phone after the first line of the song. She didn't answer when he called back.

She opened the package Jeremy had brought and took out the brushes. She drew the thick, soft bristles over the top of her hand. Bringing the tubes of acrylic within inches of her eyes, she read the names of the colours aloud: "Burnt Sienna. Violet Oxide. Raw Umber." It was like tasting a soup or a sauce, assessing the flavour when she said the names. She'd been extravagant and ordered three larger canvases. Maybe it was foolish; she could be dead the next day. She saw no point in waiting for Death's arrival; that kind of attitude was an invitation. Death was going to have to catch her. That way of thinking probably gave her a little extra time. She believed Death was lazy and would seek out the easy ones first.

Now it was time to paint the buck. If it was a harsh winter, as she predicted, he'd come more often for the carrots, grain, and apples she intended to leave in the garden. She would need to be disciplined, checking frequently at the window for his arrival. It wasn't likely that he would knock first. Only his hoofprints, droppings, and the disappearance of the food would tell her he had been. He would come, of that she was sure. Some would say, make it easy on yourself — take a few photographs and paint from them. While photographs captured an image, they were without breath and movement and odour. She needed all of that to paint. This project, and Big Brown, would occupy her while Alice found her first child.

She held up one of the canvases and envisioned the great creature upon it. He would fill up the entire space with his erect ears, chestnut eyes, ebony nose, muscled shoulders and thighs. She'd never known a fat deer. She saw the grand animal moving across black fields of summer fallow, then into the air — as if he'd sprouted wings — and over the farmer's fence, intended to keep the cattle in and the deer out.

Shuffling to her bedroom, she wished that even for a day she might have the buck's energy and strength to take her to Bright Eyes. It was hard to admit, and she'd not say so to Alice, but she had had thoughts that the child had been killed, smoth- ered within hours of being snatched from her. She had to banish those thoughts. She had to believe that someone had taken care of her daughter, loved the child as if she had come from her own body. *Manitow* would have seen to that.

15

Alice glanced at her gran, hunched forward, hands clasped in her lap, seemingly oblivious to the rattling and bouncing as they passed over a rough patch of road. When they got to the restaurant it would be easier to talk. In the truck, her gran would only get every fifth word. She slowed almost to a stop and swerved around two deep potholes. "Guess the grader hasn't been through in a while," Alice said.

"Nope," her gran said. "They come in the spring, level it out nicely, spread a load of gravel, then forget about us until the next year."

Elinor popped out her lower denture, ran her finger over the toothless gum, then held the finger out to Alice. "What's this?"

"Looks like a raspberry seed," Alice said.

"They don't fit as good as they used to. Stuff keeps getting under them."

They bumped over the railway tracks, passing a grain eleva- tor, a single boxcar huddled next to the maroon-and-grey prairie sentinel. Alice wished she had something hopeful to tell her gran. Her mother was waffling about putting an ad in the news- paper, something about all the nuts they'd have to deal with. She was trying to get access to government and church records. Alice had visited Lillian a few weeks earlier, but had left with nothing firm to grasp onto, no useful leads.

She glanced at her gran.

Elinor stared straight ahead.

They drove another mile or two. On either side of the road, farmers' fields as far as the eye could see. In the middle of the field on her left a grey square building, abandoned, door ajar, a strong lean to the right. She'd spent last night at Wanda's, caressing, being touched in parts of her body she'd never been touched before. She savoured it all, even as she wanted to stop. She longed to be free of her fear, her shame, the idea that what she did with Wanda was wrong.

If anyone ever found out.

Elinor cleared her throat and Alice started.

"It was the government's plan to have us disappear," Elinor said. "Big Bear, Poundmaker, Piapot. They all knew it right from the start." She tapped her middle finger on the dash. "They knew it all." She jabbed her finger toward the windshield. "All this was our land. Now look at it, chopped up into farms and ranches."

They drove past the white chip wagon and the sign for Anderson's Butcher Shop.

"After you have known the kicking of a tiny foot," Elinor said, "the turning of a small body within your own, then the pain of the child passing through your body to enter this world, an indelible memory is created. You can't get rid of it. Not with other children, painting, or prayers. It's like the stain of strawberry juice on a white shirt. No amount of scrubbing, soap, and sunlight takes it away. The colour fades, but it never leaves entirely."

They crossed under the sweeping white arches of the town's only bridge. Now the bridge spanned a stream bed that held only a mere trickle of water contained within a cement spillway. Two or three years ago the river had risen up in the springtime and swollen over its banks.

"It's an ugly thing they've made of it," her gran said, turning to the defeated river. "Why can't humans leave things alone? As if a river needs to be told how to flow."

The Midway Restaurant was small, and the only one in town. The seating was all booths, red leather, each with its own jukebox. The place was half-full. They took a seat and ordered what they usually got: won ton soup, chicken chow mein, steamed rice, and sweet-and-sour spareribs.

Elinor swung her head toward the jukebox. "Your grandfather liked those things. Used to be a Chinese restaurant we went to in north Regina. He'd take a pile of quarters. We'd order tea and fried rice. Those days you got three plays for a quarter. He didn't know most of the songs; he'd start at *A* and keep going until the quarters were gone. He never got past *G*, as I recall. When there was a fast song he'd get silly, ask me if I wanted to dance."

Every time they came to the restaurant, her gran told the same story. With one variation: the alphabet letter changed. Sometimes her grandfather got to *B*, other times it was *H* or *T*. Alice had been keen to tell her gran about the meeting she'd gone to. Fifteen or twenty Indians gathered to talk about how they could stop an amusement park being built. The idea of roller coasters, Ferris wheels, and bumper cars running over an Indian burial ground was not amusing to her people.

Her gran grunted.

"Elders, babies, little kids, they were all there," Alice said. "I'd never been in that kind of group. I don't think Mom had any Indian friends. Well, Mary, but our family never got together with her. I envied those kids at that meeting, running around, laughing, eating cookies, every person there smiling at them."

Elinor licked her lips, rubbed her hands down her skirt. "Your mother has been so stubborn about keeping away from her roots, from her people. And keeping you, Andrew, and Catherine from me and her aunties and cousins. I've never understood why she had to do that." Elinor stared at the table across from them as the waitress delivered platters of hamburgers, french fries, and coleslaw. "Your mother came last week. We talked a little. She has not had an easy time of it. I know she has done and said things she regrets, but she's not figured out how to reclaim her steps." Elinor drew her thumb over her bottom lip. "Do you know what I think?"

"No idea."

"Your mother has her own secret."

"Why do you say that?"

"Just a sense. Hard to explain. She's always so stiff, on guard. Why does she keep visiting that Mary woman? Have you ever talked to her?"

Alice shook her head. "Nope."

"She knows something." Elinor sighed. "Something else I must attend to before I die."

The waitress slid two bowls of steaming soup onto the table. Elinor dropped her spoon on the floor. Alice gave Elinor hers and got up to ask for another. Elinor dipped the spoon into the soup, blew on the spoon, then slurped. She patted at her eyes with her napkin and complained that the soup was too hot. Alice reminded her that she liked it that way.

Elinor loved Chinese food. She sucked at the tiny bones of the spareribs, scooped the thick, dark sauce over her rice, and licked her lips frequently. A spoonful of rice bumped against her upper lip and the sticky white food fell like clumps of wet snow.

"I thought I could forget," Elinor said, "pretend the child didn't happen. For years I told myself I had been blessed with other children, and grandchildren. But one morning I woke up, my head was pounding, the wind was furious, and the word *betrayal* came. To not seek her out was to continue the betrayal."

She shoved a won ton into her mouth and wrestled it into submission. "Even if she's dead, it's still important to know what became of her. Her spirit should know we are looking for her, so it can rest, so we can bury her in our way."

Elinor cracked open a fortune cookie and handed the two pieces to Alice. Alice extracted the narrow rectangle of paper and handed it to her gran.

"You read it. They make the writing so small."

Alice laughed. "It says you will have a long life."

"Take another. I already know that."

Elinor dipped a corner of a sugar cube into her tea. Green liquid seeped into the whiteness almost to her fingers before she put it into her mouth.

Alice snapped open another cookie. She laughed. "Don't kiss an elephant on the lips today."

"Chinese logic," her grandmother said. "Did I tell you about the time your grandfather and I went to the Rockies? It was just before he died; he'd always wanted to see the mountains. We went on the train, got a berth and did it up right. Your grandfather loved having his tea from the silver tea service. Just the way the queen would have done it, he said. You could see your face in it, that's how much someone had scrubbed the thing. It was the same for all the heavy cutlery with the CPR letters on the handles. Canadian Poopy Railway."

"Granny."

"Yes. Canadian Poopy Railway. That's how they brought out the troops. Might have been a different ending for Riel and his followers if they didn't have the railway. They shipped all those police from the east. Police from the east." She giggled. "Besides being the place where the sun rises, that's why the door of your tipi should face east. Police come from the east."

"So, what about your trip with Grandpa?"

"What trip?"

"When you went to the mountains."

Her gran squinted. "When we got a few miles past Calgary and he could see the mountains in the distance, he got more excited than your mother does with those birds of hers. I'd only seen a smile like that when we were a lot younger and we'd just had a good round in bed."

"Granny!"

"What? You think we were never that way?"

"I guess you were."

"You think I was always this old? Your grandfather was very sensitive to what made a woman happy. What was I saying when you interrupted?"

"About the mountains."

"Mountains?"

"You and Grandpa went to the mountains."

"He cried as soon as he saw them. That this Earth not only had the prairie with its big skies but also mountains with cliffs of rock, evergreen trees, and snow-capped peaks that pushed through the clouds." She slumped back into her seat.

"Tired?" Alice asked.

"I miss Joseph. It gives me comfort to think of him. For a long time, our lives weren't easy. The later years were better. He gave up the drink, talked to the young ones about doing the same. He was a good carpenter. There was a lot of respect for his work. We had fun. Bingo. Long walks in the valley. He was the one who stuck by your mother. Never said a bad word about her."

Elinor rolled her lips together. She stared at the pile of grey bones from which she'd sucked every shred of meat.

"I never told him about Bright Eyes." She picked up a bone, then dropped it. "I should have. I should have told him."

"So …" Alice hesitated.

"Why didn't I?"

"Yes."

"The shame stopped me. It was enormous. Shame holds secrets like a banker's vault. Only death does a better job."

16

They bounced over the unpaved grid road, Louise in the driver's seat, Elinor, eyes closed, hands clasped in her lap, seated next to her. She'd hardly said a word during the forty-five-minute trip from the city. There was little gravel left on the road, potholes and hard pan, clumps of grasses and weeds being its prominent features. After a quarter of a mile the road ran out, out onto the prairie. There were no sidewalks or gutters, no separation between the front yards of the houses and the roadway. Kind of like a big camp, except instead of tipis there were houses, cheap houses that would fall over in a good windstorm.

"Looks like we're here," Louise said.

Elinor opened her eyes and pulled her body up straighter from the slump it had assumed most of the trip. "Are you sure this is a good idea?" she asked as they drove slower, deeper into the grouping of small homes. A couple of the houses had fresh coats of paint, a garden in the front yard, a wooden chair or rocker on the porch. Other houses had broken windows, a door bashed in, tires and tools strewn about, a child's headless and limbless doll. At one house the front yard was taken up by a rusted, wheelless car up on blocks.

"Why wouldn't it be?" Louise asked. She rolled down her window and caught a scent of cooked onion and meat. She was transported to another time, a time when she was ten or eleven and her mother was frying gopher.

Elinor pulled her sweater tighter around her body. "Don't like to bother people. I haven't visited in such a long time. They'll think I'm a ghost."

"Which is Rosie's house?" Louise asked.

Elinor leaned forward, squinted, and pointed her knobby finger. "Up there, I think. The one on the left. The one with the stove in the front yard. She might be dead, you know."

"Is there no one else from that time?"

Elinor shook her head. "Maybe. Maybe lots of folks. I can't remember. Did you find a picture from the school? They were always making us stand up straight, look at the camera. What did they do with all those pictures?"

"Alice found some pictures, but not from your time."

A small black dog, missing one ear, ran at the car, barking and leaping against the door. Louise closed her window; she hoped he'd go away before they wanted to get out of the car. She pulled up alongside the stove; three black holes gaped where the elements had been. The door was gone from the oven. Maybe her mother was right, they shouldn't be here. The place, its condition, made her nervous.

"You're sure you don't know his name? Did it come back to you?"

"Who are you talking about?"

"The man, the father of your child?"

"He's called *brute*, *rapist*, I don't know. Why do you keep asking? He never properly introduced himself. What I do remember about the man, you don't want to know."

A barefoot boy, six or seven years old, squatted at the side of the road, scratching in the dirt with a fork. Louise didn't want to think about what her mother had endured. The boy drew circles, then laid pebbles, twigs on the circles. Another recollection from Louise's childhood. Her mother making sketches with a pencil or a hunk of charcoal from the fire. Whereas another might be pleased to have these images bubble up, Louise was not. Best to keep them all suppressed, since there was no way of selecting the good from the bad.

"Do you know what he did at the school? Was he a teacher? The janitor? The gardener?"

Elinor stomped her feet, shoved her hands in the pockets of her sweater. "Why do you persist with all these damned questions?"

"Because sometimes people remember something a few hours later, or the next day. I've seen that so many times in my work. A client will assure me he's told me everything I need to know. Then a week later he remembers something else. And something else." She knew about this from her own life, that's why she worked so hard at not allowing the slightest recollection to creep out. If her mother remembered the guy's name, maybe he had relatives; maybe he had said something to them. Or maybe the nun had killed the child.

She pulled to the side of the road that was barely a road and turned off the ignition.

"Can I stay here?" Elinor asked.

"Mother, I can't do this all on my own." She pulled the rearview mirror toward her, shoved her hair back from her forehead, rubbed a smudge of dirt from her chin. As she pushed the mirror back into position she caught a glimpse of a tall, slight man in a dark blue shirt, his black pants held up by suspenders. He walked quickly down the middle of the road, never getting closer to the car. Louise recognized him: Ian Scott. A clammy cold passed over her even though it was warm in the car. She glanced at the boy squatting by the road; when she looked back to the mirror, the man was gone.

"Oh, isn't that a surprise," Elinor said. "I thought that was how you usually did things."

Louise was startled by her mother's voice. "I guess I've been learning." She put a hand on her mother's. "I think Rosie will be thrilled to see you. You were good friends. She was the one, you said, who had the cot next to yours at the school; she was the one who rocked you to sleep after they took the baby. She's younger than you, you said, so maybe she'll remember more."

Louise desperately hoped the meeting with Rosie would unleash names, stories, recollections in her mother. Memories were as elusive, finicky, and unpredictable as a prairie spring-time. It made no sense to Louise that she recalled what she regarded as useless, unimportant details and events, like the scar in the shape of an *M* above Ian Scott's left eyebrow, the smell of burnt onions in the restaurant she first worked in after she left the reserve, the stupid practical jokes of one of her classmates in law school. Yet important things that she wanted to cherish were gone: the place her son took his first steps, Catherine's first words, Alice's stunning arguments in the cross-city high school debating competition. Was that why two parents were necessary? So at least one parent held onto the memories? John was that parent, not Louise.

"Let's get it over with," Elinor said, yanking at the door handle. "And I need to pee."

They picked their way across the stubbly grass to the pale yellow house that was barely as large as some of the garages in Louise's neighbourhood. They climbed the two steps of the unpainted porch, which stood on concrete blocks. The white door was scuffed with black, red, and brown marks. The pale green curtains were pulled across the windows so it was hard to tell if anyone was home. Louise knocked. She thought she heard music, a violin, singing. No one came to the door. She knocked again, louder. Her mother bent down to scratch the ears of a brown-and-white dog that had joined them on the porch.

"Just open the door," Elinor said. "Either they'll invite us in, or they'll send us away."

Louise knocked again, and when there was still no answer, she turned the knob and pushed open the door. She called out hello, asked if anyone was home.

Elinor pushed by Louise into a room that appeared to serve as kitchen, living space, and sleeping area. There was a small fridge, a two-burner hot plate, a kitchen table with a green Arborite top. On the table a white mug half-full of tea, a plate with orange smears, a knife and fork. The plywood flooring was covered with an oval hooked rug, in the centre of which was depicted a pair of deer.

Elinor crossed the room to a closed door and knocked. "Are you in there, Rosie? It's Elinor. Elinor Greystone." Elinor opened the door a crack, leaned into the room. Although dark, she could make out a double bed with a quilt of many colours, a four-drawer white dresser, a table stacked with clean laundry — towels, shirts, and socks. On the wall to the left of the door were several photographs, all in black frames. Elinor flicked on the light. There was her friend in the photos. Beside the river, in the bingo hall, in front of the white church. Grinning in the midst of several young children — her grandchildren, Elinor assumed. Rosie was just as she remembered her. Round face, keen eyes. Short and stout, white hair tied back in a ponytail. Elinor took one of the photographs from the wall.

"I think we should go," Louise said.

"Hold on to this," Elinor said, shoving the photograph at Louise. "I still need to pee bad." Elinor shuffled down the hallway to the door at the end. She pulled on the knob and it banged onto the floor.

"Mom," Louise hissed.

"It's broken," Elinor said. "It was broken before I got here. I'll go out the front. Come to think, there's probably an outhouse."

Louise placed the photograph on the table and picked up the knob. It was dented. Either it was a really cheap doorknob or something had smashed into it with great force. She tried to return it to the door, but it wouldn't stay. She set it on the floor. She noticed, and her mother had not, that the entire perimeter of the door was taped up with grey duct tape. Nobody was going through that door. She returned to the main room and the photograph her mother had handed her. She could see why it interested her mother. Standing in front of a long, two-storey building were three rows of Indian children, flanked by a priest and a couple of nuns. Was this the school her mother had gone to? Louise looked closely at each child, wondering if one was her mother. No one was smiling, but in those days no one did smile in photographs. Beyond that observation, she thought the children were all the same. She could shuffle them about and the picture wouldn't change. Everyone wore a white shirt and dark pants or skirt. They all stood stiff and straight with a vacant, distant look in their eyes. She wondered what each child was thinking at that moment. Surely there were one or two who had thoughts before the photographic moment. Thoughts of mothers and fathers, dancing around a fire, eating rabbit, listening to stories.

She took the photograph near the window where the light was better and looked at each child one at a time. Was there even one child who wasn't looking straight ahead? Even one whose eyes were closed or looking down? She liked to think that she would have been that child. Or her mother. Or Alice. As much as the two of them bickered, she was glad her daughter could stand up for herself. She smiled. At the periphery, the child closest to the priest — his head was twisted slightly, his eyes turned down. She wondered what had become of him. That photograph demonstrated why she had made the choices she had — run from the rez, lived with Evelyn McKellar, gone to law school, married John. So if she ever had children, they would not look like these children.

She slid the photograph onto the table. Where was her mother? Had she fallen down or fallen asleep, gone back to the car? She'd hate for Louise to come looking for her, but if she wasn't back in the house in another five minutes, Louise would do just that. And where was Rosie? Louise rubbed a chunk of dirt from the toe of her shoe. How embarrassing it would be if Rosie returned and Louise was here on her own.

Restless, she paced the small space, counting her steps. She estimated the living room and kitchen area weren't much more than ten by ten. On an upturned wooden crate next to the armchair, a few feet from the television, were an ashtray and a pair of knitting needles, a ball of red wool. The couch was covered with a blanket that had been thrown back, as if someone had been sleeping there. She heard voices from outside and crept to the window, moved the curtain a few inches. Two children, about six or seven. One child was struggling with a bucket of water that was sloshing over the edge; the other child dragged a couple of planks. She was about to sit down on one of the kitchen chairs when she remembered the bag of food in the car.

Elinor drew up her skirt, fumbling to get her underwear pulled down while shoving her skirt to one side, finally getting herself settled on the firm, cold bench with barely a second to spare. *Ahhhh …* the wonderful relief of the pee spilling from her body. She marvelled she'd not wet her pants, so intense was the urge. On occasion, at home, she'd had an accident getting from her garden to the house or even her outhouse. She'd told no one about that. Louise would be dragging her off to the doctor for tests; she didn't need that.

She'd stay on for a few moments, even as she imagined her daughter pacing about in Rosie's house. Maybe Rosie would arrive before Elinor. It would be good for Louise to have a chat with Rosie on her own. She looked up to the crack of light and blue sky that came through the boards near the roof. She'd never painted an outhouse, inside or out. Perhaps she should, if for no other reason than to bug her daughter. Would she hang one of those outhouse pictures in her lovely living room? *Such nasty thoughts,* she told herself. Louise was trying to be helpful, as best she could.

Forgetting where she was, she sucked in a long breath and immediately regretted it. Hacking and puffing, she hurried to get her underwear pulled up, her skirt straightened. She patted the wall to her right, thanked the building for doing a good job. Imagine, she thought, as she pushed open the door, imagine a world without outhouses. Well, there had been that kind of world when people lived in tipis, and it worked out just fine.

She noticed Louise at the car as she came along the side of the house. Surely she'd not leave without her, without saying goodbye. Elinor quickened her pace for a few steps, then slowed when she saw Louise step back from the car with the bag of food they had brought.

They returned to the house together, Louise saying if Rosie didn't come home soon, they would come another day.

"She's always home," Elinor said, as they returned to the house. "Nobody on the rez goes anywhere. She'll be back in a few minutes. I don't want to drive out here again." She took the photograph from the table. "I want to see if I can find myself in here." She sat down on the couch and held the photograph inches from her eyes.

This is not right, Louise thought. They shouldn't be poking around like this. She tolerated it only because something — a name, a picture — might jog her mother's memory.

Elinor, intent on the photograph, moved her finger from one child to the next. Sometimes she smiled, other times it was a grimace or a shake of her head. She set the photograph on her lap and leaned back on the couch.

Louise heard voices from outside. She said she'd hang up the picture. Swiping tears from her cheek, Elinor clung to the photograph, then shoved it at Louise saying she hadn't found herself in it.

"It's hopeless. I recognize some of the faces, even remember some of the nonsense this one or that one got up to, but the names are gone." She grabbed the picture back from Louise, peered at it again. "See here. See that man standing off to the side by the lilac bush? Maybe that was him." She shook her head. "But I'm not sure. This whole idea is crazy. Why didn't you and Alice tell me that? Why let me hope?" She lifted the photograph up in the air as if she might smash it to the floor. Just as Louise grabbed for it, the door opened.

A short, stout woman, dressed in a maroon skirt, white shirt, and blue sweater, her thick white hair in a single braid, came into the room. Her right hand shaking with a slight tremor, she cradled a package the size of a shoebox wrapped in brown paper. If she was startled, frightened, she didn't show it. She stared at Elinor, glanced at Louise, then back to Elinor. Then she grinned, a large smile that revealed two missing teeth on the top left.

"Elinor? Elinor … is it you?" She spoke in Cree for a few sentences. Elinor nodded, then laughed.

Rosie sat on the couch next to Elinor, grabbed Elinor's hands and squeezed. "So good to see you, old friend. How long has it been? Why do you never come visit? Shall I make tea?"

Elinor patted Rosie's hand. She said they'd brought cookies and fruit and Louise could make tea while they caught up.

Elinor and Rosie chattered in Cree. Louise only got every tenth word — *Grandchildren. Summer berries. Somebody had died. The reservation. Sickness.* The kettle boiled, then a harsh whistle. Rosie pointed at the cupboard to the left of the sink, said the tea was in there. The teapot, a brown crockery one like Elinor's, sat on the windowsill above the sink. There were mouse droppings in the corner of the ledge. Through the window Louise watched two dogs, nose to nose, front legs braced, in a tug of war over a chunk of leather. The larger dog risked a gulp, securing a better grip, then, shaking his head, he wrenched the contested object (it looked like a sleeve from a leather jacket) from the smaller dog and ran off. A few feet away he dropped the prize to lick and sniff it, then snatched it up as the other dog charged at him.

Elinor and Rosie studied the photograph.

"Where did you get this?" Elinor asked. "Why do you keep it on your wall with your family?"

Rosie laughed and said Johnny had found it in a second-hand store, in a box with a bunch of other old photographs, tools, and canning jars. She said he was so excited to find his mother. She laughed again. "In a box of junk. He wasn't sure if it was me. And neither was I."

Louise was enjoying Rosie. Rosie's laughter was infectious; her face crinkled and wrinkled, her body jiggled when she laughed.

Rosie went to the fridge and pulled out a large chunk of chocolate cake. She said it was left over from her granddaughter's eighth birthday party two days ago. The tremor in her right hand worsened as she sliced the cake; she brought her left hand to her wrist to steady the hand. She said she'd seen three different doctors and none of them could explain why her hand shook the way that it did. Some days were worse than others; today was a good day. She pulled out a jar of jam from the fridge, knives and spoons from the drawer next to the sink.

"Why do I keep that picture on my wall?" Rosie asked, standing by the table, cutlery clutched in her hand. "You probably think I'm nuts. Lots would. They'd want to burn the thing, stomp on it with heavy boots."

Elinor eased herself from the couch, shuffled to the table.

Rosie said she kept the photograph to remind herself. Never again. Every Tuesday, she said, she played bingo. Every Wednesday she wrote letters to the band council, the town's mayor, provincial and federal officials. The minister of Indian Affairs. She said she told them what was happening on the reserve. She shook her head. "Mostly I tell them about what's not happening."

Louise took the photograph to the table. Between bites of cake and cracker spread thick with saskatoon berry jam, Rosie stabbed her finger at the children in the photograph. Frankie read English words before anyone else in the class. George was the slowest at digging up potatoes and carrots. Margaret lost the end of a finger chopping onions. There was blood everywhere. How could such a tiny finger have so much blood in it? Frank ran away. Almost every week he did it. So many times he'd run. Each time everyone cheered when they heard he was gone again.

Elinor had cake crumbs stuck to her top lip. As Rosie remembered, Elinor seemed to slip away and into herself. Her eyelids flickered, her head drooped. *She's not going to talk about the child*, Louise thought. Louise tried to get her mother's attention, but she wouldn't look at her. Louise stared at the photograph, the man standing in the bushes, slightly out of focus, wide suspenders stretched over his thick body, probably thirty or forty years old. Had he married? Did he have other children? Certainly the man was dead now, but sometimes on their deathbeds people confessed, gave up secrets they'd held onto all their lives.

Louise thought of her friend Mary. They needed to talk about what they'd done. In more than four decades they'd never spoken of it. What if Mary died first and felt compelled to confess, cleanse herself of ill deeds before she died? Even if she didn't say Louise's name, it would be easy enough to track her down.

Louise's father had slipped into unconsciousness within minutes of Louise getting to the hospital. She knew now it was her grief, but for months she'd been angry with her mother that she'd not called Louise sooner, had not called for an ambulance. All that time lost, blood oozing from her father's body, as Elinor had struggled to get Joseph to the hospital after the car had broken down. So pale he was, only a whisper for a voice. Yet, as always, a steadiness as he smiled at her, thanked her for coming, patted her hand, asked her to take care of her mother. Her father had died more than fifteen years ago. She still missed him so much. On every anniversary of his death, she visited his grave, said a prayer, left a swatch of tobacco. She had always gone alone. She could see now that was a mistake. She should have taken her children, her mother. There could have been a celebration, a meal afterward.

Louise pointed to the man standing in the bushes. "Do you know anything about this guy, Rosie?"

Elinor jerked awake.

Rosie leaned closer to look at the photograph, pulled back and shook her head, then leaned forward again. She rubbed a finger over the glass and the man as if that action would bring him into greater focus. Or obliterate him.

Rosie said she woke sometimes in the night and the room was filled with a terrible smell like rotting meat. "Like the stink of a mouse that's been dead in the cupboard for two weeks. Awful.

"It comes from this picture," Rosie said. "I take it outside, leave it there for a few days, burn sweetgrass in the house. I should send the picture back to the store where Johnny got it. But that's me there, too. So I keep it."

She jabbed at the man. "I want to say he's the one." She turned to Elinor, placed a hand on hers. "But I don't know if he was. I have to say the truth. I don't know. But I remember you had a child in that place. And they took her away." Rosie jabbed at the two nuns in the picture. She jabbed so hard Louise thought she might break the glass. Rosie turned the picture upside down. The back of the picture was covered in brown cardboard, with tiny nails to hold it in place every few inches. There was a brown stain that looked like tea in the bottom left corner. The Scotch tape was dry and peeling. Rosie grabbed the picture, leapt up, opened the door, and threw it out.

The sound of glass shattering. A crow calling. The scent of smoke from a fire coming in through the open door.

"I should have done that a long time ago," Rosie said, turning from the door. "Some things from the past are better thrown out."

Louise wished it was that simple.

17

"The Skaters' Waltz," loud and scratchy, blared forth from the speakers, bounced off the bleachers, and reverberated amongst the girders of the arena's ceiling. Alice dropped onto the battered wooden bench, loosened her laces, and rubbed her ankles.

"Look at that pair," her father said, pointing to an elderly couple, she in camel skirt, red sweater, and navy scarf, he in brown pants and tweed jacket. "They move as one. Quite beautiful."

"They are," Alice said.

The music changed to an Elvis Presley love tune and the shouting erupted; *yeahs* from the girls, *boos* from the boys.

Alice told him she'd gone to the church archives office.

"And?"

"Nothing really."

The records custodian, Alice said, with her carefully coiffed grey hair and double-breasted blue suit, reminded her of Greer Garson in the film *Mrs. Miniver*, although she wasn't nearly as beautiful. She had a breathy voice that barely rose above a whisper and one eye that turned inward. They went to a basement room that smelled of rubber and old papers and was crammed with file cabinets, ceiling-high piles of wooden stacking chairs, and huge cardboard boxes marked CHRISTMAS DECORATIONS. The single, bare light bulb made Alice think they weren't likely to find anything smaller than a rain barrel.

"She seemed to have no idea what I was looking for," Alice said. "She explained that most records were kept at the head office in Ottawa, not in the local church." Alice had told her she was there at the behest of her grandmother, who hadn't long to live. She didn't think it hurt to embellish things a little.

"It made me nervous," Alice said, "the idea of having direct contact with something from Gran's school. One of the people who wrote in the records could even be the child's father."

A horn blared. Alice jumped. A voice came over the loudspeaker asking all skaters to leave the ice. Two boys in scruffy sweaters stayed behind until the rink was empty. They raced down the centre of the rink, every inch of their scrawny bodies pushing and surging. They were readying to do it again when an attendant stepped onto the ice.

"There were pages and pages with lists of student names," Alice said. "At the top of each list was the name of the teacher, some preceded by Miss, Mr., others by Sister and occasionally by Father. I wrote down some of the names to see if Gran might remember them."

The large gates that gave access to the hockey players' dressing rooms and equipment-storage areas swung open. The Zamboni, the machine that could do in ten minutes what it took three men to do in ninety minutes, lumbered onto the ice and turned right.

"I keep thinking the child was killed, dumped in a snowdrift, or some unmarked grave on the prairie. It would have been easy enough. In a few weeks the coyotes would have found her. Who's going to believe a kid from a residential school?"

"I don't think that's what happened," her father said.

Alice's eyebrows arched up. "It's such a long shot."

"It is. I still trust Elinor's intuition. I've seen it proved right too many times. Your gran would make a prediction about the weather, or that one of you kids was getting sick, and it pretty much turned out the way she said. She'd say it was going to be a bad year for gophers, grasshoppers, potato beetles. And she was right. She had a sense that your grandfather wouldn't live a long life. Said that to your mother once."

"Surely she's been wrong sometimes," Alice said.

"Oh, probably. I haven't kept a scorecard. But she's so strong about this child I think she's picking up something, from somewhere." He laughed. "From the stars, the way the wind's blowing, how the birds are flying in the fall before they migrate. It's mysterious, but I trust it."

The Zamboni, like a harvester in a wheat field, left a wet swath about five feet wide as it followed the curvature of the rink.

"Your mother has her own perceptiveness, but she doesn't talk about it or use it the way your gran does. Leaving the reserve when she did is a good example. As best as I can tell, it was a horrific time on the reserves."

"Like it's any better now," Alice said.

"Maybe not. Depends who you ask and which rez you're talking about. Some have strong leadership, they're pushing back, getting government to come up with more money, or developing their own sources of revenue. But it's slow."

The horn blared and skaters trickled back onto the ice.

John had loosened his laces and now tugged at the ones on his left skate. In the middle of looping his laces around the boot, he stopped and leaned back. He said he remembered the day Louise had told him she was Indian. He said he'd always had his suspicions but didn't want to ask for fear of getting her mad — she angered easily in those days. They were leaving the library. There had been an article in the newspaper about those who had been killed in the First World War, including men from one of the reserves. She said she didn't understand why they volunteered to fight for a country that treated them so poorly. He asked what she meant, and she blurted out that of course he didn't know about such things and started walking very fast. He chased after her, said he didn't know and that was all the more reason for her to tell him. She started to cry.

"I didn't know what to do. I'd never seen her like that. One of the men killed, she said, was a cousin. Then she told me all of it.

"Her parents weren't dead; they were living, if you could call it that, on a reserve outside of Regina. She had two brothers, Charlie and Le Roy; Philip had died when he was very young. There were aunts and uncles and friends. She missed them. Everyone was poor, but she said they laughed more than the white people she knew. Even so, she said she hated the rez and would never go back.

"I was shocked. I'd never heard anything like that." He laughed, slapped his palms on his thighs. "Shit. What did I know about life? I had some vague sense there was another side of the tracks, but I'd never been there. Some friends talked about what went on in the north end, but I guess I was too cautious." He winked. "Or scared of the back of my mother's hand. You never wanted to get on the wrong side of her. But mostly I was seventeen, eighteen, growing up in a nice family in the south part of the city."

His mother, he said, loved to have her hair done and kept up with the fashions. He'd never seen her without makeup. She did laundry on Mondays, cooked fish on Fridays and roast beef on Sundays. Every week was the same. His father wore a hat, white shirt, and tie to his office; he was a manager in an insurance company. His parents played cards with the Rileys on Friday nights. Every family he knew was the same.

"I asked myself, what I was doing chasing after this girl? My mother would figure out Louise in five minutes." He shook his head, looked out to the rink and the skaters. "Over the years, I've tried to figure out why I didn't run away, right then. Your mother was holding the door wide open. She was practically shoving me through. And if my mother had known the precipice I was standing on, she'd have shouted louder than a fan at a hockey game, jumped up and down, too, ordering me to get the hell out of there. I'm sure there's a poem that captures the whole scenario. I can't think of it at the moment. I'll get back to you on that." He grinned.

"What do you figure kept you there?" Alice asked.

He shook his head. "Who knows. The war had ended a few years earlier, the future seemed full of promise. Maybe it was me finally taking a risk. I'd never been inclined that way. It was my brother who drove my parents nuts — walking the railway bridge at midnight, stealing cheap things from the drugstore, forging notes from my parents to get out of school. Whenever I get that kind of note from a student, I call the parents immediately, check to see if they've actually written it."

Alice grinned at the image of her Uncle William forging notes to teachers, straddling the rails under a full moon. Her father, being a vice-principal, got to deal with all the problem kids. He probably surprised them with what he knew.

"How did I get onto that tangent? The truth is, I adored your mother. I'd never met anyone like her. She was rough, argumentative, brilliant. Clearly a risk-taker, not like most of the girls I'd met. And she had this other side that didn't come out often. If we got out of town, into the country, by a creek, she'd go quiet and still. She'd shush me. A kind of wonderment came over her. She never talked about what was going on with her in those moments. I suspect it was something spiritual. Like the day we saw that grass snake. Every girl or woman I'd known until then was terrified of snakes. Not your mother.

She picked it up, stroked the back of its head, muttered some words, which I now know were Cree, then let it slide off her hand and slither through the grasses." Her father fell silent and drifted off.

Alice thought of her mother with the snake and then with her caged birds, how attentive to them she could be. It was hard to imagine her mother being a runaway, hiding out, living in some shed. How did she do it? She wished they could talk about those times. Her friends' mothers recalled their childhood antics, but never Alice's. It was as if she had never been a child, never had parents, brothers, or sisters. Until her Grandfather Joseph died, they had spent every holiday with her father's family. She didn't meet her gran until she was a teenager.

For years Alice hadn't noticed that her mother never spoke of or acknowledged what was happening to Indians in the province or the country. She started to think differently after she'd been teaching for a few years. So many of the Indian students did poorly. They missed weeks of school at a time, or if they got themselves to school, they arrived late, hungry, schoolbooks lost, homework not done. Lots dropped out by grade eight, if not sooner.

Her father stood up and suggested they do a couple more loops.

"I wish I could feel more optimistic about finding Bright Eyes," Alice said.

"As you said, it's a long shot. That doesn't mean nothing will come of it."

"But we don't have any strong leads. It was such a long time ago. Nothing came of the visit with Gran's friend Rosie."

They reached the ice and both bent down to take the guards from their blades. John said some things didn't happen in a straightforward manner, but more in the way that bees travelled.

"They seem to be flying about in a haphazard manner. And yet, look what they manage to produce."

They waited for a gap in the skaters then stepped onto the ice.

The scattering of snowflakes when they'd arrived at the arena was verging on a blizzard as they left. It was hard to see even across the street. Piles of thick, fluffy flakes made puffy, pointed hats on fence posts and smooth rounds like bread loaves on car roofs. The familiar sounds of winter were everywhere: roaring engines, shovels scraping on cement, the futile spinning whirr of tires on wet snow.

With her skates off, shuffling to her truck, Alice was aware of the flats of her feet, the absence of the tight boot pressing against her toes, the long blade running down the middle of her sole.

The first major snowfall of the season. Alice knew by the thickness and speed at which the flakes were falling that it would continue for hours, leaving two to three feet, or more, before it ceased. The city had been transformed to a sparkling and pristine whiteness. Snowflakes, like autumn leaves, drifted steadily downward. Alice thought of a children's picture book and imagined a kindly and smiling yellow-haired woman looking down on the Earth as she shook silken filaments from a million milkweed pods. Little dots of wet cold, like effervescent bubbles, pricked on Alice's cheeks. She held out her palm, waited for a small jumble of flakes to settle on the cranberry wool of her mitten, then returned the gentle travellers to their companions with a single puff.

She cleared the two-inch accumulation of snow from the headlights and windows. Dry and light as it was, the snow dispersed as easily as a pile of goose down. Inside the truck her father trolled radio stations for weather reports.

Alice swatted the snow from her pants and jacket and hopped into the truck.

"Ten inches by morning," her father said.

Wipers clunking up and down, warm air creeping over the fog on the inside of the windows, the truck inched its way into the line of slow-moving cars.

"I hope Gran's all right," Alice said.

"She's been through lots of winters."

"Yes, but she's older now, and she doesn't always remember to put on the fire."

"So we'll check on her when we get home."

"May not tell us much. She doesn't always answer the phone."

18

Snap, snap, snap. The screen door clapped against its frame. *Wind is strong this morning,* Elinor thought. It was taunting her, grabbing her home and poking its chilly fingers wherever it found a plaything. A gust the size of a bison threw itself against the small building and the entire house shook. Elinor pulled the hook on the screen door and fastened it down. She chuckled. This time she had outwitted Wind.

She wrapped a blanket tightly around herself and dropped into her rocker. The snow was coming so hard she couldn't see across the lake. She could barely see to her garden. The pain in her left shoulder was worse with the cold. She stared at the fire. There was a bit of heat coming from it. Maybe it would last another hour or so.

She looked back to the thick whiteness outside her window. "You don't scare me," she said. "I survived that cyclone in 1912, or 1921, whenever it was." She was sounding like one of those bumper stickers: *I survived the hurricane, I survived the Depression, I survived residential school.* She could obliterate a car's front and back bumpers and probably half of the trunk with all the things she had survived.

Tears rushed into her eyes. *And I have survived the theft of a child.* Not until this moment had she called what was done to her theft. *Kimotiwin.* But *theft* was the proper word. Her body was the one that had nurtured the child's development. Inside her body, the fingers and toes had sprouted, the little heart taken its first beat. The first kicks from the legs, punches from the arms, were made within her womb, not in the barren body of a White Neck. No god had given White Neck the right to take the child from her.

When she figured out why her body was changing in the way that it was, she ran from the school. The child's father, not a father in the church, found her and brought her back.

She ran away again and again.

He brought her back. She hated that she couldn't be certain if the man in Rosie's picture was him. He knew where Bright Eyes had gone. But he was dead. She knew Louise had left Rosie's with great discouragement.

Elinor pulled the blanket more tightly around herself. Was that the phone ringing? Damn thing. Let them call back. Maybe tomorrow she'd pick it up. Too much talking through wires wasn't good for people.

The fear that she had lived with for so long swelled up in her chest.

There were two White Necks the day she laboured. The tiny, young one had been kind. Although the labour was long, the young nun never left Elinor's side. She said prayers and spoke softly, wiped Elinor's face with a cool cloth. At the moment Bright Eyes, wet and slippery, broke free, Elinor thought her body was going to split open. She fought to get up, to sit upright as she'd seen her mother and aunties do. The White Necks pressed her down on the bed.

The young White Neck smiled at Bright Eyes and said how beautiful she was. Bright Eyes was so clever, she smiled back. There was such love in the nun's face. Elinor thought everything was going to be all right. How naive and trusting she had been.

Despite the constant hunger, the slaps and straps, even some dying at that school, she'd always thought things would get better. Nothing she'd seen with her family, on the rez, had prepared her for the harshness she saw at that school.

She wanted her mother and father to see Bright Eyes, their first grandchild. They never did. They would have had no shame from the circumstances of her birth. They'd thank the Creator for such a beautiful child. By then the country was littered with mixed-blood children.

When the older White Neck — they called her Man Face because she had so many hairs on her chin — came, Elinor knew there'd be trouble. Man Face sent the young White Neck away. Elinor clung to Bright Eyes. Even though Man Face smiled and talked sweetly to her baby, Elinor didn't trust her. Her smile was forced. Her voice had the sweetness of a fox at the door of a rabbit hutch.

Man Face asked to hold Bright Eyes. Elinor squeezed Bright Eyes closer to her chest; she wanted to push her back inside her body. She should have refused Man Face's request, run from the school, hid in the coulees, and travelled by night until she got to the reserve. Her parents would have taken the child as their own.

Man Face said she was going to bathe and clothe the infant.

That was the last time Elinor saw her child.

Elinor rocked, a gentle swaying of her body, not sufficient to move the rocker. The sounds that burst from her throat were quieter now, not because her heart was any less broken, only because with age the strength of her muscles and lungs had been diminished.

Her mind grew quiet and she slipped into sleep.

The rocker moved of its own accord. Perhaps it sensed the woman's need to be soothed. With the gentle rocking, Elinor slept more deeply than she had in months. And while she slept, others awoke. They squeezed their bodies around, above, and beside the curled torso of the old woman. They reminded her she was not alone. Each of them, at one time, had been above, on, and beneath that rocker. Some were humans — babies, infants, small children. Others were scaled or winged, furry and four-, eight-, or no-legged. Some created sweetness; others wove webs of great detail, strength, and connectivity. Fingers and wings and paws reached out to Elinor, drawing her deeper and closer into their world. Theirs was a world where all creatures lived in harmony.

Elinor slept on and on.

Outside the snow fell and fell.

If awake, she might have remarked that it had always been curious to her how one colour, white, could bring such beauty. When she painted snow, she mixed white with blue or purple, pink or grey. Nature never had a problem with the mixing of colours.

19

The snow in the yard and on the porch, unmarred by human or animal footprints, was luminescent. The temperature had dropped. The snow, as if alive, squeaked and crunched, lamenting each of Alice's footsteps. Despite her hurried pace and the short distance from her truck to the cottage, the cold seared Alice's forehead and cheeks. By midnight it would be minus thirty degrees. People died of exposure at that temperature, especially if the winds were strong.

Elinor's cottage was dark. Alice tapped at the door. When Elinor didn't answer, Alice let herself in. The cottage was cold. Freezing. Alice swept her palm over the wall, searching for the light switch. Probably her gran hadn't gotten up from her afternoon nap; it had been overcast all day. Dull yellow light spilled over the room. And over the scene that would replay in Alice's mind in the days and weeks to come — Elinor in the rocker, slumped deep, white head almost to her lap. No response to Alice's hand on her shoulder. No groan or complaint at Alice's whispering. "Gran, Gran."

Only stiffness and cold.

And silence.

As quiet as the stones on Elinor's porch.

20

Listening to the whisperings, sensing the warmth and light-ness of her body, Elinor wondered if she had passed over. It hadn't been so bad, the journey, quite smooth and quick. She didn't remember any of it. Where had she been before the Creator had come for her? What was she wearing? Was some-one looking after her garden? What of the deer and rabbits that counted on her snacks?

Now, a glimmer of memory. She'd been in her rocker, watch-ing the snow dancing toward Earth. She'd been thinking of Bright Eyes: the slim, hot fingers clinging to her own, Bright Eyes' breath slight and quick as a bird's tickling at her neck. She could almost taste the musty, warm scent of her womb and its fluids that cov-ered Bright Eyes.

Now she felt the sense of something shifting over her, a darkening, the light occluded, the smell of sweat and perfume. Soap? She cracked open her right eye. Within inches of her face, she saw pale skin, freckles, an arm reaching in, fiddling at something. Then Elinor's arm was being lifted up, a hand on her wrist, a sense of pressure against the side of the bed. Where was she?

She struggled to lift her eyelids. The right snapped open again but the left was more reluctant. Finally, a slit of light came in, enough to see a person in white. The line of red colour at the perimeter of her lips suggested this wasn't the Creator. They were heavy-set, thick lips. Eyes closed, the woman's hand remained on Elinor's wrist, fingers pressing lightly on the inside.

The word *hell* popped into Elinor's mind.

She was in hell.

She might as well have been. She hated hospitals. She swallowed away the tears. The last time she'd been to the hospital she'd wanted to die. What good had the hospital and all its fancy contraptions done? Joseph had died. And Louise hadn't spoken to her for months, as if Joseph's death had been Elinor's fault.

She thought back to that hot summer night. Everyone had their doors and windows open, children were playing hide and seek, laughing and calling, dogs were barking. Radios were playing. There was laughter. She wished it had been a full moon. At least she would have had that to explain what happened that night. But it was a dark night. And it only got darker.

Joseph had made a small fire behind their house. He loved his fires, regardless of the time of year. They were drinking tea sweetened with honey and eating bannock with margarine and strawberry jam. The fire crackled, crickets buzzed in the long grasses. Every once in a while a coyote called. The mosquitoes had been terrible that year, biting and biting like there was no tomorrow. But that night they had gone on vacation. Joseph had been away for two weeks at the Sawchuk farm, putting up fences and corrals for the cattle. He'd returned exhausted but pleased with the money he'd made.

Those days Elinor had been thinking even more of Bright Eyes. Her memories got stirred by a couple of teenage girls on the rez who were pregnant, their bellies growing rounder each week. They weren't going back to school in the fall. She'd promised herself that when Joseph came back from his work, she'd tell him. She'd convinced herself he'd understand; it was she who didn't want to speak of it. She didn't know how anyone ever spoke of such things. She imagined Bright Eyes was a young woman, maybe with children of her own. Hardly a day went by that Elinor didn't think of her, send her blessings when she smudged in the morning, blessings in all directions the smoke drifted.

Joseph was telling Elinor how the farmer kicked his dogs, beat the horses, how unnecessary it was, when they heard men shouting, curse words, coming from the front of their house. She didn't know who the men were, but she could tell they were drunk. She and Joseph waited and listened, Elinor, especially, hoping that the fools would move on because she knew what Joseph would do if they didn't.

Damn, Elinor muttered to herself. What was she doing in hospital? She needed to get out. She had no time to lie about while some fat-lipped nurse held her hand.

When she tried to sit up, her left arm didn't work too well.

Now what was the woman doing? Slipping some stick into Elinor's armpit.

"Stop that," Elinor grunted.

"Did you say something?" the nurse asked.

"I said stop that." Elinor twisted and snatched at her right arm, the one the nurse was involved with. "Where are my clothes? I need to get out of here. I've got things to do."

The nurse withdrew the thermometer from Elinor's armpit, jotted down the reading. She suggested Elinor grab on to her arm and pull herself up so she could fluff her pillow, straighten her sheets.

"I don't want my pillow fluffed. Stop that. Just get my clothes. And where are my puffs?"

"Your what?"

"My ... my ... oh, you know, the fire sticks, for smoking." Elinor allowed her head to sink into the pillow. She was exhausted. How was she going to get out of here? It terrified her. People died in hospitals. It seemed to her more died than got fixed. She closed her eyes.

So long she'd been on her own, all because of those two. Those two and their drink and their stupid argument and fight that Joseph felt compelled to intervene in. She and Joseph were holding hands, watching the fire lick over the birch branches. His hands were so strong, always dry and calloused, three fingertips missing from frostbite.

Such swearing from the drunks, then the threats to hack out a tongue, twist a knife in a gut. Joseph's hand squeezed tighter around hers. His tension siphoned into her arm, over her chest. Then he was heading around the side of the house. For a short man he had a long stride, even with the hitch in his left leg from the time he fell off a horse onto a boulder. She called after him to leave them alone, said they'd stumble into the bushes to sleep it off. But Joseph hated listening to fighting. He didn't want the children to hear it. It scared them and it set a terrible example. She should have gone with him, but he'd done this kind of thing before. She expected he'd be back in a few minutes.

But these two were different. They turned on Joseph.

It was quick and then it was silent.

Only the sound of the crickets, a chorus of crickets, endless, unceasing.

At first she thought the steps were Joseph's, but they didn't have the rhythm of his limp, and they came fast, like a dog after a rabbit.

"It was an accident," he said, "we didn't mean nothin'."

He'd started to cry, told her to come right away, said there'd been a terrible accident. When Elinor came around the house, Joseph was on his back in the middle of the road, blood seeping from his body. She shouted at one of them. She didn't remember their names; she wanted to forget them. She told him to call the chief, to get a car. It would be faster than waiting for an ambulance. They'd just put a man on the moon, but they couldn't get an ambulance out to the reserve unless some white person had had a heart attack.

Somehow they got Joseph moved into the chief's car. Except the damned thing died a half-mile down the road. Cars and trucks were scarce in those days. Nobody had money for gas or tires for cars. Lots still travelled around with horses and buggies. They waited in the car for half the night, it seemed to Elinor, while the chief's son ran to find another car. It was an empty road. No other cars came along. There was only the buzzing of the crickets. Coyotes howling. The scent of sage and soil.

She'd bound an old towel around Joseph's belly, but she could feel it getting wetter and warmer. She'd tried to stay calm for him, but he was the one who held the calm for both of them. He insisted on talking even though she told him to save his energy. Voice weak, barely above a whisper, he remembered the first time he'd noticed her. He'd just turned twenty, she was seventeen. It was early summer. He'd come back from fishing at the river; she was crouched down picking strawberries. He grinned, started to laugh, but it hurt too much. She told him to stop. He was quiet for a moment then told her that before he'd seen her face, he'd seen her behind and thought it was fine, wide enough for babies. Another time she would have swatted him, but this time she wiped the sweat from his forehead.

Finally, she heard the truck; it belonged to the Indian agent. There was a bed and a chair in the back of the pickup, lots of blankets, and a Thermos of tea for Elinor. And that was how they arrived at the hospital. The care went downhill after that.

* * *

Elinor didn't know how long she slept. It was a struggle to get her left eye open and to move her left arm, but with her right eye she saw Alice and Louise at the window, their backs to her. She closed her eyes. She had to decide on a strategy. She could get around Alice, but Louise would be insistent that she stay on in hospital. And after that? She tried to get a sense of what they were plotting.

They weren't talking about her! They were talking about Louise's silly birds, Alice's new winter boots, an accident on the Trans-Canada Highway near Moose Jaw. She needed a smoke. Her body ached for tobacco, the warm, weedy smoke filling her mouth, coursing down her throat into her chest. The thought of it set her off coughing; she struggled to sit up.

"Gran. Gran."

She saw tears in her granddaughter's eyes. And even in her daughter's. Not a good sign. She'd have to act quickly.

She asked them to help her sit up. From her new vantage point, she saw her clothes on hangers (she rarely used the things), slippers beneath them. But where were the smokes? Louise asked how she was feeling. Alice asked if she wanted some tea.

"Never better," Elinor said. She wouldn't tell them about her eye and arm.

Louise said Elinor had had a small stroke. And she was anemic and underweight, probably from poor nutrition. Louise offered Elinor a glass of water. Her dry throat welcomed the cool wetness. She closed her eyes. Never had she felt so tired. She wondered what drugs they'd been pumping into her.

"When can I get out of here? And where are my smokes?" She struggled to push herself higher in the bed.

"You can't smoke in here, Mom."

"That's all the more reason to get out." Her hands were shaky; she was having trouble catching her breath. She didn't want to

die here like Joseph. From another room a scratchy voice calling for a nurse. A few minutes later she heard the banging and
clatter of metal, trays being taken in and out of the food trolley,
smells of onion, tomato, and coffee. Elinor's stomach growled
and she realized how hungry she was. She leaned back.

Alice went in search of tea.

Louise washed Elinor's face and hands with warm, soapy
water, then she brushed her hair. Elinor was soon impatient
with it. Louise was in no hurry. One brush stroke from the top
of Elinor's head through the length of her hair seemed to take
forever. Elinor glanced at Louise and decided to keep her eyes
closed. It was too hard to see the fear and worry in her daughter's eyes, as if this was Elinor's last day on Earth. It had been the
same when Joseph died, except there had been more fury. After
the third brushing that she thought would never cease, Elinor
grabbed the brush from her daughter.

"I am not doing to die, Louise, certainly not today. There are
things to be done."

"Yes, I suppose there are, but when you're better, Mother."
Louise cleared her throat, straightened the sheets on the bed.
She said she and Alice had been thinking about where Elinor
would live after she left the hospital.

"Why would you be talking about that?" Elinor said. "I'm
going home."

"You're too weak. And if Alice hadn't come out to your house
that afternoon ..."

"I'd be dead," Elinor said. "But at least I'd have died in
my own home, looking out to the valley, smelling some good
tobacco, maybe a deer or a gopher stopping by. Sounds pretty
good to me, better than this place with its sheets, stiff as cardboard, reeking of starch. Where did that idea come from?
Starched clothes. Why?"

Louise sighed. "Don't be difficult, Mom. We want you to be safe."

"Don't you remember your father? What did they do for him?"

"I do remember. If you'd called the ambulance ..."

"They wouldn't have come all the way out there. Do they go even now?"

Alice brought a tray with a pot of tea, a bowl of sugar cubes, and a plate of cookies.

Elinor wolfed down two cookies, dropped three sugar cubes in her cup of tea. Licking her lips, she told herself that was all she needed, a good shot of sugar and tea. She poked at the tubing that carried the clear liquid into her body. When she tugged at the tape holding the intravenous needle in place, Alice pulled her hand away.

"The nurse will take that out after you've eaten," Alice said, "or maybe tomorrow."

"I've eaten."

"Only cookies."

"And tea," Elinor said. She wanted rid of all the paraphernalia. A plan for her escape was beginning to form in her mind.

Louise said John would come by after school; he had some new poems Elinor might like, poems about stones by a Chilean poet. Elinor thought she'd hate to miss the poems, but she hoped she'd be gone by then. Although better that she wait until John left; she'd have a bigger chunk of time before anyone noticed she was gone. She knew how to get out of difficult situations; she'd been doing it all her life.

"Any news of Bright Eyes?" she asked. She didn't want to ask, but she needed to know. If they were on the verge of a discovery, she'd hold off.

Alice said the day she found Elinor she was planning to tell her what they'd done, what they were thinking of doing next.

"So …" Elinor asked, "have you found her?"

Even though she had only one eye working at the moment, she could tell from her granddaughter's face that things were not going well. She covered her face with her hands. She would have to do this on her own. She wanted to shake her daughter and granddaughter. They did not understand. If you wanted deer or duck or rabbit on your dinner table, you went out and tracked it down, you didn't hang a sign on your fence post and hope the animal would stop by, jump onto your table, into your soup pot. You went after it, for as long as was necessary, until you got close enough to shoot it and drag it home. Alice said maybe they'd run ads in some newspapers. That wasn't good enough, Elinor said, they needed to talk to people. Lots of people. They needed to stop everything else they were doing.

"Put more ads in more newspapers. Get out to all the reserves," Elinor said. "This is an emergency. Don't you see that?"

A nurse brought a tray with tomato soup, potatoes, green beans, meat loaf, a bun, and a bowl of purple Jell-O. Elinor said that was a lot of food for lunch. Louise told her it was dinner. Elinor wasn't going to tell them she'd lost track of the time and the day.

There was little feeling in the left side of her mouth. Her lips didn't grip the spoon very well. Soup dribbled onto her chest. She pushed the bowl to the back of the tray. The vegetables and meat loaf were bland, but she could manage them. Alice wet a towel with hot water and wiped up the soup.

Louise said Elinor was looking better than she did a few days ago. She gathered up her coat. Elinor wondered how long she'd been in hospital. Louise squeezed Elinor's shoulder, kissed her on the cheek, told her she'd be back at lunchtime the next day.

"You scared me," Alice said after Louise left.

"Well, good. Sometimes it helps to be scared. I'm scared, too. That I'll never get out of here. Let me say that again. Of course

I'll get out of here, but I'd like to be vertical when I depart. Find me some cigarettes; they will speed my recovery."

"Or hasten your departure," Alice said. "No can do."

Elinor swatted at Alice and flopped back on her pillow.

"Don't want your Jell-O?" Alice asked.

"It's purple. Not one of my favourite colours."

"Want to come and live with me for a while, Gran?"

"I want to go home."

"It's winter. You could have frozen to death if I hadn't found you. Your place looked deserted."

"I like it like that. Get that nurse to take this damned thing out of my arm. I'm strong enough. And I need to go to the bathroom."

While Alice went to look for the nurse, Elinor tugged at the tape on her hand. It was difficult; she couldn't get the fingers on her left hand to come together; she supposed that was the stroke. She rubbed at the edges of the tape, gradually curling it away from her skin. It hurt like hell. It would be even harder to get the needle out with her fingers acting the way they were. All the needles they'd shoved into Joseph when they finally got to the hospital. None of them did any good. He died on the operating table. He'd lost too much blood.

She'd wanted to be strong for Louise and Charlie, but she could not stop her tears. At least Louise had John, and Charlie his woods and his buddies along the trapline. Le Roy had no one. He disappeared for days. When he came back his eyes were bloodshot, he couldn't stop shaking; he'd go to Joseph's grave and talk and talk to it as if he expected Joseph to answer. He didn't eat; he didn't sleep.

She tried wiggling the needle. It was thick and long. Pain shot up her arm. She thought she might pass out. She had to get out of this place. It had been too long. The wild roses were blooming the day she'd told Alice of Bright Eyes. Now they were rosehips covered in snow. She'd let herself get too hopeful about what Rosie might remember. It was up to her. She'd not die in this white man's tomb before Bright Eyes had known her mother.

"Hey, hey. What are you doing there?" the nurse said. "You shouldn't be touching that. It will get infected." The nurse swabbed the area with rubbing alcohol, pushed down with a swab of gauze on the needle that lay beneath the skin, and yanked.

"Hell," Elinor shouted. "What do you think you're doing?"

"Just what you asked for," the nurse said. "The pain will stop in a minute. It's worse if I take it out slowly." She pressed a ball of cotton over the needle hole and taped it down. Elinor's arm and hand were covered in bruises.

Elinor caught a glimpse of the snow on the window ledges and rooftops, glistening in the last light of the day. It was winter. She might have to rethink her plan. Or put it off for a few months. She didn't like that idea. She'd find a coat and boots even if she had to steal them. She could withstand cold; nothing had been as cold as that damned school the first few months she was there.

"Did you bring my coat?" Elinor asked.

"When I found you, I was only concerned about getting you to hospital. The ambulance had blankets; it was heated. I'll bring it when you're ready to come out."

Elinor swung the covers away. She waved at her clothes and said she wanted to get dressed. Alice said she'd be more comfortable in her nightgown and that the doctor had not checked her out.

"I don't need a doctor to check me out," Elinor said. "This isn't a prison. Or that school. I can walk out on my own."

"You're too weak," Alice said.

"I'm not. It's from lying around in here. Take me for a walk. I want to be dressed for that. Don't want everybody staring at my bum." She shifted her legs over the side of the bed, hitched her bottom to the edge, then feet on the floor. Her left leg was the same as her left arm and fingers: weak. All the more reason she needed to get moving. Keep moving. She told Alice to bring her clothes. Alice shook her head but knew her gran would not take no for an answer.

Elinor loved the smell of the smoke on her clothing — the long navy blue skirt, the turtleneck T-shirt, and the red sweater that Alice had given her one Christmas. She hoped Alice didn't see the hole at the front, a cigarette burn. There were no shoes. She'd insist that Alice bring them tomorrow. Maybe it was a good idea to rest up a few nights. But too much time in bed and she'd only get weaker.

Alice pulled Elinor's hair back from her face and tucked it under her sweater.

"Are you sure you can do this?" Alice asked. She stood a good foot taller than her gran.

"Of course. All this lying about would make anyone sick or soft as pudding." She tried to take a step, but her left leg wouldn't move so she moved the right one first and dragged the left behind.

Over the next eight days, Elinor gathered her supplies. She walked farther and farther around the hospital, building her strength, preparing herself for what only she could do. Maybe coming so close to death was a sign that she must make haste and that only she, the mother, could find her child. She told herself she could withstand the cold. Hadn't she already done that the day Alice found her? Louise and Alice would say she had almost died; Elinor told herself she had survived.

21

While the nurses were busy gathering up breakfast trays, distracted with dispensing pills and little paper cups of white liquid that tasted like chalk, Elinor, her belly full with porridge, toast and jam, boiled egg and bacon, left. She'd eaten every bit of it. For the past week she'd saved food from each meal, even hanging about the food trolley, taking food off trays that others had left. It was amazing all the food that went uneaten. It wasn't great stuff, but it was good enough. Didn't people want to get out of here? Alice had brought her coat, scarf and mitts, boots, socks and sweaters, cane and smokes. Poor Alice. Elinor had even convinced her to give her money. Elinor said she needed it so she could buy candy in the gift shop, maybe a newspaper to keep up with what was going on in the world.

As far as she could tell, there were only terrible things happening in the world. Mostly, she read the birth notices. Bundles of joy and delight, occasionally a photograph of a wrinkled newborn. She should have had Alice bring her the Dickens book. She missed reading about Pip. He was an inspiration to her. The ways he managed to get himself out of tight spots.

The cold air enveloped her body, pressed onto her mouth and lips, chilled her lungs with each breath. Her eyes watered. For a few seconds everything was blurry until she blinked and swiped away the wetness with her mitt. It was colder than she expected. She pulled her scarf tighter over her head, checked to see that all the buttons on her coat were done up. She walked faster to warm herself, but couldn't persist beyond ten or twenty steps. Even so, she was happy for the freshness of the air. Outside air. Clean air. Not stuffy, dusty, dry air that smelled of pee and poop, soap and starch, medicines, tomato sauce and coffee.

A few blocks from the old university, at the corner of College and Albert, she came upon a square, white stone building with a long, straight sidewalk that led to the entrance. It seemed familiar. What was it? She stared at the bold structure. Had she been in there? A half-block past the building she remembered. How could she forget? That was Big Brown's home. Not much of a home. Pretty pitiful. It had been so long since she had gone there. She yearned to chat with Big Brown about her plan. Just to be near him would give her strength to carry on. But she couldn't risk it. She needed to get to the highway.

She headed south on Albert Street. This trek was taking longer than she thought it would. She was stopping every few minutes to rest and get her breath. Her father would tell her not to think so far ahead. Approaching the bridge with the buff stone pillars and replicas of brown bison heads every few feet, she recalled how much she liked the bridge. Then she remembered that Louise and John lived nearby. They mustn't see her. She must watch for their car, bend over, turn away. Now was not the time to meet her daughter.

She started across the bridge. It wasn't a high bridge, and it had been constructed to accommodate both walkers and cars. The limestone pillars were about eight inches in diameter. The limestone balustrade came to Elinor's chest. Looking to the east, one saw Wascana Lake, frozen and snow-covered. A man-made lake, it had been a make-work project during the Depression years. In the opposite direction was Wascana Creek, a meandering stream that began in the prairie.

Halfway across the bridge Elinor stopped at one of the bison heads, of which there were many, twenty or more. She drew her mittened fingers over the bumpiness of the burly brown head, along the snout, down the throat. Perhaps some would be pleased at this recognition of the great animal, but she wasn't one of them. Better to have honoured the creatures when they roamed freely.

Once she was off the bridge, there were houses on her right and a line of pine trees on her left. The trees afforded some protection to the grounds of the provincial legislature. She strained to see to the end of Albert Street, but it was too far for that. In truth, she had no idea how far it was. Louise would inform her later, and not in a kind manner, that it was a good three miles, if not more.

Elinor was tiring. She spotted a bus stop a half-block ahead with a bench. She'd take a break. It was early in the day.

While it was good to rest her legs and feet, she knew she mustn't stay long. She feared if she gave in to her tiredness she'd not be able to continue. She told herself this would be the worst part of the trek. She placed a mitt over her nose, blew into it for warmth. She tugged her hat lower over her ears. She rummaged in her bag and pulled out the sandwich she'd saved from yesterday's lunch: bologna and mustard. The meat was cold and crunchy in her mouth. It tasted awful but she resisted the urge to spit it out. It was food; her body would make use of it as best it could. She took another bite and pretended she was eating rabbit stew like her mother's, made with carrot, turnip, sage, and onion. Already she felt stronger and more nourished. She took another bite. Pemmican this time. Chewy, a little tough, but food that lasted through the winter and kept her strong.

A siren blared. She shrank into her coat, tightened her scarf around her head. She tensed as a police car approached. Not yet. Surely Louise had not called the police already. The car, almost in front of her, was slowing down. *Damn, Louise.* She turned around, bent over, and searched in her bag. She heard a car door slam shut. She thought she might panic. Steps behind her.

"Excuse me," a man's voice said. "Ma'am?"

She pretended she didn't hear him and continued to search in her bag. A touch on her shoulder. The *ma'am* word again. Then he was standing in front of her.

"Did you see a young fellow in a yellow jacket, red hat, running this way?"

She wanted to laugh. She croaked out a no. He apologized for bothering her and suggested she get inside, a blizzard was on the way. She nodded, listened for the car to pull away. She'd planned to have a smoke but decided she must hurry.

She wondered if she was going in the right direction. Where was the bloody highway? South and east. She looked up to locate the sun. There it was. She was going the right way.

She counted houses. One, two, three, eight, twelve. She counted houses with cars in the driveways, then houses without cars. She counted black cars and silver cars, red cars. She counted fire hydrants. There were too few of them to keep her mind occupied, so she switched to telephone poles. The sun was climbing higher in the sky; there were more cars on the road. She wondered if she should get off this main street, weave her way through the side streets in case Louise was already looking for her. She rejected that idea; she might get lost and it would waste too much energy.

Elinor stopped to rest at another bus stop. She was warm enough with the two sweaters, two pairs of socks, and newspapers wrapped around her legs. She stared into the distance, hoping to get a sense of how much farther she had to go, but it was impossible to tell. She didn't know the landmarks in the city. Her weaker leg was so tired. She had to push the doubting thoughts from her mind. She wasn't walking as fast as she had been when she started out.

The sun, now directly overhead, was too bright, making her squint. For a time, until her arm started to ache, she held her hand above her eyes to shield them.

Eventually, the homes and evergreens and huge brick government buildings ceased, replaced by expanses of asphalt, motels, grocery stores and gas stations, restaurants and bookstores. She smiled and quickened her pace. She sensed she was getting closer.

As the sun moved past its zenith she reached the highway, the Trans-Canada, Highway One. It wasn't a busy highway and she crossed over the four lanes to the two heading east.

She thought she might cry, standing beneath the expanse of sky. Endless sky. She gave thanks to the Creator for giving her strength to stay vertical, to move her body out of that hospital and back onto the earth. When she looked away from the city, due south, the prairie ran forever. Here and there a small building, a round, grey metal storage unit. Far to the west a couple of grain elevators. She was grateful for the calm. So rare was it that the prairie wind wasn't blowing.

She brought her hand to her forehead and turned to the west. Nothing in sight, but her vision being what it was, that didn't mean there wasn't anything coming. She'd keep moving to stay warm. Eventually, something would come. She needed to get a ride soon. Any time now, Louise was going to arrive at the hospital and find her gone. Elinor chuckled. She wished she could be there to see that. She felt sorry for the nurses. They'd be the ones to get her daughter's fury, tirade of questions, threats of a lawsuit. Her daughter had always had a way with words. Even as a child she'd chatter at Charlie until he was so confused he'd run to Elinor, crawl under her skirt. But she never tried anything with her father. With Joseph she listened, sucked up his stories about bison, owls, and coyotes.

Elinor needed to be out of the city before Louise's discovery. If she was lucky, Louise and Alice would rush to Elinor's house. That would give Elinor time to get farther away, to be on her way to the Manitoba border. Going west to Alberta and British Columbia had never been a consideration. She'd always sensed that Bright Eyes was taken east, where life, in those days, was more civilized — more towns, villages, and farms for a new family and stolen child to get lost in.

She turned and stuck out her thumb for the approaching car. She cursed the long turquoise Chevy as it sped by. A few minutes later, a pickup truck with two dogs in the back didn't stop, either.

She turned from the road to the culvert and the fields beyond.

Flat. Flat as far as any eye could see. Snow sculpted into sweeping curves by wind; yellow stubble, remnants of the harvest, poking through here and there. In spring the stubble would be turned over, and by midsummer the shimmer of golden wheat would run between every road, all the way to the American border.

She was barely moving now. The wind had picked up, and even though the sun was strong, she felt the cold more. She could die out here. Shove that thought from your mind, she told herself. As soon as you find Bright Eyes, give her your message, then you can be with the Creator.

There was a cream-coloured lump by the roadside up ahead. Elinor quickened her pace for a few steps then slowed again. On the other side of the highway, a clump of Canada geese, flying low, wings flapping in long swoops. Remembering that they mated for life, Elinor thought of Joseph and felt warmed. There had to be a reason the Creator had taken him at such a young age, but she'd never been able to figure that out.

The lump on the roadside was a canvas bag the size of a stove, stained with grease and oil, and on it big red letters — DOC — that had no meaning for her. At the end of the bag, which was pulled tight with a cord, the toe of a brown shoe poked through. She kicked at the bag, pushed at it with her hands. Not too hard, not soft, either; bulges and lumps. Possibly the thing was filled with shoes. It didn't matter. She needed to get off her feet. Like a bird settling into its nest, she wiggled her bottom onto the bag until she was reasonably comfortable.

She needed a smoke. A cigarette would wake her up, warm her. She wished she had one of her own, not those store-bought things with the old tobacco that tasted like sawdust. She tried to open the package without taking her mitts off, but it didn't work. She yanked off a mitt with her teeth and slipped a cigarette from the package. Her fingers were freezing. Back turned to the wind, she hovered over the cigarette and the tiny flame, sucking in a long drag until the tip of the cigarette glowed. Then she was coughing and hacking. She hated these store-bought things.

She pushed at the canvas and thought she could feel the outline of a shoe. And another. She traced the letters with her thumb. Who bundled up shoes like this? Why weren't they on people's feet?

"D-O-C, D-O-C." She whispered the letters. Surely it had something to do with government. Governments came up with the stupidest schemes.

She had almost finished her cigarette when the semi pulled onto the side of the road, five or six car lengths ahead of her. The burst of air almost knocked her over and she couldn't breathe from the swath of dirt thrown up. Her ears hurt with the squeal of the brakes. This was her ride; she knew it.

The driver hopped out and strolled to the back of the truck, kicking at the tires, peering under the trailer, tugging on the lock on the back doors. He shuffled toward the front of the truck, scuffing at the road as he moved along. He stopped by the passenger's door. His back toward Elinor, he leaned forward, then stretched back. The yellow stream glinted in the sunlight.

The man stretched his arms over his head, punched the air, bent down, and swatted at the toe of his brown leather western boots. He slouched against the truck and pulled a pack of cigarettes from the chest pocket of his jean jacket. Tall, stocky in legs and body, he wore a red baseball cap and blue jeans.

Elinor moved toward him. She had to believe the Creator would take care of her. In the ditch, or in this man's truck. When she was within ten feet of the man he tossed his cigarette into the snow, turned, and took a step to the front of the truck.

"Hey!" Elinor called out. The man continued. Elinor called louder.

The trucker swung around. He had a dense red beard, a gold chain around his thick neck.

"What do you want?" he asked. He had an accent, English or Irish. Elinor could never tell the two apart.

Now, in the shadow of the man, Elinor saw he was almost twice her size. "I need a ride. To the east. Can't pay you much, but I've got stories to pass the time." She smiled.

The man was shaking his head. "We're not supposed to pick up hitchhikers. They're usually bad news."

"You can check me for weapons if you want," Elinor said, extending her arms. "I'm ninety years plus. I need to get to Ontario, maybe beyond that. I haven't got much time left. I promised my daughter I'd find her before I died."

"Like I said, against the rules to pick up hitchhikers."

"I really need a ride," Elinor said. "What harm can I bring to you? You're twice my size. I'm the mouse; you're the elephant. You could squash me in an instant."

The man took off his hat, ran his fingers through his hair. He kicked at a stone and sent it into a snowbank. "I don't stop much. I'm on a tight schedule. Do you eat a lot?"

"Hardly a thing."

"I'm not much of a talker. I like it quiet."

"I can be quiet. I just need a ride."

"Hope I don't regret this. Get in." He opened the door and went around to his side.

Elinor contemplated the red-and-grey upholstered seat. The step to climb up was three feet off the ground. She lifted her weaker leg but couldn't get it high enough. She almost fell over. The man was stuffing his jacket, lunchbox, a couple of magazines, and a blanket into the cupboard behind him. He shoved paper cups and napkins into a paper bag.

The engine rumbled and the truck vibrated. The smell of diesel and the scent of deodorizer from the paper pine tree that hung from the rear-view mirror were making Elinor sick. The trucker told her to grab the handle near the door. She grabbed it with both hands but still couldn't get herself onto the step. He revved the motor, adjusted the side mirror. Hot air burst onto her face. She started to panic; she had to get inside. She tried again, but her arms were too weak. She was so tired. She thought she might cry.

"Damn it!" she said. "Can you give me a boost?"

He shook his head. "Thought I was taking on an adult, not a kid."

He jumped down from the truck and came around to her. He lifted her up and plunked her on the seat. "You can thank my grandmother for this. She taught me well." He slammed the door.

22

Louise stared at the empty bed, the wrinkled white sheets. She swept back the curtain of the closet looking for, what, she didn't know. Only the faint scent of tobacco remained. She pawed through the drawers in the bedside dresser. A button, a pebble, and a cigarette butt. Everywhere she looked, nothing. She asked the nurse if her mother had left a note. How could no one have noticed her absence?

"When did you last see her?" Louise asked.

"She was here at breakfast." The nurse, half Louise's age, smiled. "She ate everything. The past few days she was eating it all. No complaining. Often, she'd ask for seconds when we came to collect the tray. We would have been discharging her soon. I'm sure she's not far away. Lots of old folks wander off. They get confused. Can't figure how to get back. Or they find a comfortable couch and fall asleep."

Not my mother, Louise thought. Elinor had been hoarding. Saving up for this scheme of hers, whatever it was. At ninety. Had she gone right around the bend this time? Yes, her mother had gotten stronger over the past week, but she wasn't that strong. Was this a protest so she could go back to her own house?

"You're sure she didn't leave a note?" Louise asked. "Maybe with a nurse who's gone off duty? Did she confide in anyone? Was there a favourite nurse?"

"Not that I'm aware of. If you'll excuse the comment, I think your mother hated all the nurses equally. It was only in the past few days that she seemed to be more settled, less argumentative. And she was out walking the halls, going down to the lobby more regularly. We don't lock patients in their rooms. We encourage them to get moving as soon as they can. Now, if you'll excuse me."

Louise nodded. She wanted to kick something.

From the window that overlooked the parking lot, she watched Alice getting out of her truck. Her parka was unzipped. A long red scarf hung to her knees, where it met her black boots. What was Elinor wearing? Louise asked herself. Or was she tucked in at someone's house? An old friend? A new friend? Her mother never seemed to have difficulty picking up people. As cranky as she was with her family members, she exuded warmth and welcome with people in stores, on the street, on the road. If she was holed up at a friend's, Louise had no idea who that might be or where they were. And the worst of it was, they'd lie if Elinor asked them to. Perhaps Lillian knew something.

Alice disappeared from Louise's view; five minutes later she was in the room.

"Dad said you'd be here," Alice said.

"This is probably the last place we should be."

Alice unwound her scarf, tossed it on the bed. She said she shouldn't have brought all the clothes — coat, boots, sweaters, and socks — that Elinor had asked her for. But she kept complaining, telling Alice it was freezing in the hospital. Every time Alice visited, Elinor had the window open, and when Alice tried to close the window, Elinor protested, telling her the air in the room was too dry and stale; the nurses wore too much perfume. So Alice brought her clothes.

"I knew she hated the idea of going into a home. I guess I was naive, thinking we'd find someplace she'd like," Louise said.

She swatted at the pillow on the bed. "It's freezing out there; she's skin and bone. She could be dead in a day."

Alice suggested they go to Elinor's house. Even if she wasn't there, perhaps they'd find a list of her friends, their phone numbers.

"She is so wily," Louise said. "She could convince a dog to give up its bone, a wolf to move away from its kill. Why would she do this? She's after something." She bent down to check under the bed and snatched at a crumpled yellow paper. Seated on the edge of the bed, she flattened the paper on her thigh. *Roper—discharge note. James—enema. Denver—pain meds after lunch.* A nurse's checklist. She scrunched the paper into a ball and threw it into the garbage can.

"Do you recall anything she talked about that might be a clue to where she's gone? She talks to you easier than me," Louise said. She hated to admit that. Probably there were lots of people her mother spoke with easier than her daughter.

"Nothing. She hated it here. She wanted to go home. And she wanted us to be doing a lot more to find Bright Eyes. Go to Ottawa. Talk to the minister of Indian Affairs. Search through church archives. Call the archbishop. Visit every reserve in Saskatchewan." She shrugged and rolled her eyes. "Pretty much drop everything else in our lives."

Louise ran her hand over the sheet, pressing out the wrinkles. "Well, now we know. We were not paying attention. We weren't doing enough by her standards. She has taken matters into her own hands. The problem is, that could kill her."

The hospital cafeteria was deserted, save a pair of doctors in green scrubs against the far wall. The facility was closed for food until lunch, but tea, coffee, and juice were available. Louise poured herself a cup of coffee and took it to a table. She sat with her hands wrapped around the cup but didn't drink. It was her fault, she told herself. She should have guessed her mother would do something like this. She was terrified of hospitals. And she didn't trust Louise to take care of her. They should have had someone at the hospital with her all the time. Charlie would have done that. Louise should have called her brother. She lifted her cup and put it down without drinking. What was she going to do? What did anyone do when a loved one disappeared? Call relatives, call friends, call the police, run notices on radio and television. Of course she would do all that, but she knew, better than most, that if a person wanted to really disappear, they did. She'd done it herself. Now was not the time to think of those matters. She lifted her cup, but her hands were shaking as she took a swallow. She banged her cup onto its saucer.

"Mom. Are you all right?" Alice said, slipping into the chair across from Louise.

"Oh, not really. I think this is all my fault."

Alice sipped her orange juice. Fault was not something her mother easily assumed as far as Alice could remember.

"Why does it take us so long?" Louise said.

"What do you mean?"

"So long to *get it*. I'm past sixty, you're almost thirty. Some days I think we hardly know each other. Why is that? What's your favourite music? What happened to that boyfriend you had a year ago? Do you enjoy teaching? Do you have a best friend? Why does it have to be this way? My mother and I have been sparring for decades. She never told me about Bright Eyes. All this time I've had a sister walking around somewhere, you've had an aunt. And, of course, my mother had a child ripped away from her when she was little more than a child herself. I haven't been a good daughter."

"I don't know …" Alice said.

"Yes, you do. It's you Gran talks to about the old times. You listen to her stories. Everybody needs to be heard."

"So, why haven't you listened to her? There are lots your age who never left; they stayed close."

Louise nodded. "It's true. And the mean part of me says, "'look what became of them.'"

"So you wanted different things. You made a choice."

"I sure did," Louise said. She pressed her lips together, stared past her daughter to the stocky, dark-haired woman who was filling the salt shakers.

"Where do we go from here?" Alice asked.

Nursing staff had started to trickle into the cafeteria. Scents of tomato and onion were rising from the kitchen.

"She's not told you of any secret hiding places?" Louise said.

"No. She loves her little house, the garden, the deer that come by." Alice grinned. "And, of course, she'll spend time in the outhouse. Seems odd to me, but she says it gives her comfort."

Louise slid her hand across the table, gripped Alice's. "You're a good granddaughter."

23

Elinor awoke in the darkness, covered with a blanket that smelled of mothballs and grease. Where was she? Was it Joseph next to her, humming along with the music? She squeezed her fingers together inside her mitts. She was too hot. Her head hurt; the toque was too tight. Her cheek and the side of her nose were cold against the window glass. She cranked her body upright, peered through the windshield, and started when she shifted her gaze to the man behind the wheel. What had she been thinking? He was huge. If he had a mind to, he could snap her in two like a pencil.

She was hungry and she had to pee.

"Have a good nap?" he asked.

"How long did I sleep?"

"Couple of hours." He laughed. "You're great company."

She pulled off her mitts and toque, wiggled her toes in her boots. She wished she could take off a layer of clothing, but she didn't want to expose herself to questions from the man.

In the truck's headlights, snow swirled and slithered over the pavement. In the distance, across the field, she glimpsed a solitary light from a farmhouse. She missed her house.

"Did you say something?" he asked. "Hey, I don't know your name."

She hesitated, uncertain about giving her real name. If she gave him a false name it might give her a few more days before

Louise tracked her down. For most certainly she would find her; of that, Elinor had no doubt.

"Mary … Mary Goodtree," she said. Mary had been her mother's name; Goodtree she made up.

The man extended his right hand. Elinor's hand was the size of a child's in the midst of his. She appreciated the warmth. And she was reminded of Joseph's dry, calloused palms. Perhaps it was a sign. A good sign.

"I'm Edward."

"You weren't born in Canada," she said.

"No. Family's from Ireland. Came to Canada when I was ten."

She wished she could see a bunch of lights telling her there was a town or village coming up soon.

"Where are we?" she asked.

"Coming up to the Manitoba border. I'll be pulling over in a bit for some shut-eye, then an early start in the morning. Where exactly are you wanting to go? And if you'll excuse me asking, what on earth is a woman your age doing hitching a ride? Don't you have family who could help you out?"

"They're all dead. That's why I'm trying to find this last child. I haven't got long."

"What the hell?" Edward's thick fingers gripped the steering wheel hard. He braked and geared down. The truck moaned as if it resented the slowing.

On the road ahead of them, barely visible, flares, a police cruiser, flashing red and white lights.

Elinor stretched out her legs. She drew in a deep breath, told herself to stay calm. She knew her daughter had contacts and was pushy, but surely she'd not called in the police already.

They came to a stop. The snow was falling thick and hard, a dense curtain of fuzzy, swirling flakes of snow. Impenetrable. It was difficult to see beyond the hood of the truck. Edward opened his door and the frigid air surged into the cab. On the radio the announcer spoke of a winter storm coming up from Texas. "Expect two feet of snow by morning. Zero visibility on the roads."

In the long tunnel of light cast by the truck's headlights, Elinor watched Edward, in black vest, red flannel shirt, talking to the RCMP officer, who was barely visible beneath his brown bison coat. Edward was waving his arms, gesturing at his truck. They walked beyond the cruiser and disappeared from her view. Between the snow and the dark, it was impossible to see what they were looking at.

Elinor slumped back on the seat. The radio moved on from weather and road conditions to hockey scores. She rolled her window down. In seconds the sleeve of her coat and her lap were powdered white. Edward, swatting the snow from his vest and hair, was returning to the truck.

"Cold out there," he said, revving the engine.

The policeman waved Edward forward, around the cruiser and the blue car in front of it. Elinor caught a glimpse of a woman huddled in the front seat of the cruiser. The windshield of her car was destroyed. On the road, a rack of antlers and a torso, brown and mangled, the head separated from the body.

A dead deer. It was a sign, Elinor thought. The deer's death instead of her own. She muttered thank you to the deer and the Creator.

Edward turned toward her, asked if she'd said something. Elinor shook her head.

"I've hit my fair share of those," Edward said. "Don't know what the poor thing was doing out on a night like this. You see them mostly in the fall when they're in the midst of the rut." He laughed. "Then they see nothing. They follow their noses after the girls."

Humans were capable of that kind of behaviour, Elinor thought. The not seeing, the blind pursuit of an idea, a passion, a dream. That's what she was doing at the moment. She was following the scent of a hope, a wish. Only the scent she was trying to track was almost odourless, nothing compared to what a female deer gave off when she was ready for sex, ready to begin the next generation.

Edward said he was hoping to get in a couple more hours of driving. The police officer said it was going to get worse. He switched the radio to a station coming out of Minnesota; they played country and western music, songs about riding horses, chasing cattle, hard-drinking women and men.

"Seems odd to me for an Irishman to be listening to country and western," Elinor said.

Edward laughed. "I suppose. You expect me to be listening to sea shanties — stories about boats and fish, nets, high seas. Seems to me both kinds of music are about people living hard, living on the edge, lost loves, love of land and sea.

"Where have you been living?" he asked. "Where were you born?"

She was beginning to tire of the charade and deception she had created. Always a straight-talker, she didn't like having to think and ponder each of his questions. Where was she born? She was glad it was dark and he couldn't see the grin on her face. She was born, she said, many, many years ago on the prairie, when her people were still free to hunt where and when they wanted, to pitch their tipis when and where it suited them, to gather wild berries, pick herbs, dance for days on end.

"You're Indian, then. Picked up a few of your folks over the years. Most of them pretty quiet, but the odd one has been kind of scary. An ear missing. A scar across the chin. Sort of angry. My size is a big help. They get the message that trying to rob me probably won't work. I figure the Irish and Indians have both been pretty messed up by the English. Nasty buggers. Don't know that I've ever met one of them I liked."

She didn't know much about Ireland except that there had been fighting there for a long time. And something about potatoes.

Edward shifted to a lower gear. They rounded a curve and rolled down and down into a river valley, over a snow-covered road. There were no tracks from vehicles that had gone before. Edward sat up straighter, tightened his grip on the steering wheel, geared down further until they seemed to be crawling. Although the wipers moved swiftly, in the brief increment that they were at the bottom of the windshield, snow filled the fan track they had left.

"Not good," Edward said. "Slippery." He said he was going to pull over when he got to the top of the hill. They were about two hours west of Winnipeg.

Elinor felt the truck pull and sway as it crept up the hill, the sound of the engine now urgent and sonorous. She was aware of her body tensing, urging the beast upward. As they reached the crest of the hill, a car sped by on the other side. Edward, shaking his head, watched in his side mirror.

"Silly bastard. Is he drunk? He's going to wipe out at the bottom."

When they were about a quarter-mile beyond the crest of the hill, Edward angled the truck to the side of the road, then leaned back and sighed. "For all the driving I've done, you can never relax when it's coming down like this. That couple of tons behind you has a life of its own. Are you all right?"

"Mostly. But I have to pee."

"You can probably squat under the trailer, but it will be cold, no way around that. I'll help you get out of the truck, then I'm going down the road a bit to see what happened with those folks."

Oh, if her daughter could see her now, Elinor thought, squatting behind the huge tires, the smell of rubber, grease, and gas filling her nostrils. Overhead was a load of beds, tables, chests of drawers, and mattresses, Edward had said. She shuffled her feet a little farther apart and her pee trickled out. Like everything else in her body it moved slowly. In the red glow of the truck's parking lights and the flares Edward had set out, the snow, without wind, fell beautifully and steadily. As ridiculous as it might seem, she preferred this place to that hospital.

Her pee was taking its time leaving her body. She guessed it hated to leave such a warm place. Trying to shift her body so she could get out from under the trailer, pull up her pants, she lost her balance and fell onto her arm. It hurt like hell; she hoped she hadn't broken anything. She tried to move but it was too painful. She'd just rest for a moment. She was so tired. So tired. She curled her legs beneath her, pulled her coat closer, drew her arm over her head.

She loved the sound of the quiet, even though, her hearing being what it was, the sound of quiet had grown softer. Now it was more of a buzzing in her ears. When her hearing was sharper, she'd listen to the crisp whisper of falling snow, each flake announcing its arrival with a tiny crackle or pop, like a fizzy drink but not as vigorous.

Her mind filled with an image of Bright Eyes. She'd come; she was there with her. The pudgy dark skin of her cheeks, arms, and thighs. Black hair soft as a duck's breast. Slight fingers that clamped onto her own like they would never let go. Wet, dark eyes peering into Elinor's, trying to make sense of her new world. So many imaginings Elinor had had over the years. Bright Eyes taking her first steps. Bright Eyes at four, running and chattering.

Bright Eyes at ten, chasing horses, carrying water, learning how to lay beads on deerskin. Bright Eyes as a young woman, tall and strong, coupled with a handsome and intelligent man.

And the snow fell. And fell.

Puffy mounds of silver white. Slender white fingers reaching around the tires, beneath the truck, curving around the perimeter of Elinor's legs, back, and arms. It was so nice to be lying down; she'd sleep for a few minutes. She didn't feel cold. Her thoughts of Bright Eyes kept her warm. She could see her, bathed in a silvery light. So beautiful. Pink-and-green silver, like the scales on a perch's back. Smooth and white and firm like the fish's belly. She needn't leave this place. It was so pleasant.

She blinked hard into the light shining in her eyes. A man's voice calling "Mary, Mary." Why didn't this Mary person answer so she, Elinor, could get back to sleep? She tried to roll away; the pain shot up her arm.

"Go away," she gasped. "Leave me be."

"Trust me, I would," he said, "but you're under my truck and there's a blizzard raging. Come on, then." He crouched down, brushed the snow from her, extended a hand.

Elinor grabbed hold, and with Edward's steadying hand, managed to crank her body into a sitting position. Her heart was racing and the pain in her arm was so intense she thought she might pass out. She cursed the thing. What was she doing here? What had she been thinking? She could hear Louise's voice asking all those questions and more. Somehow, between Edward's tugging and her own feeble movements, she got out from under the truck.

Her teeth were rattling and she couldn't stop them.

There was snow at the roadside — easily two feet of it. All around them snow and more snow. She thought she was going to cry and she didn't want to do that. Maybe she needed to tell Edward the truth and take the first bus back to Regina.

She was grateful for the dry warmth of the truck's cab, the fan blasting, and the cup of sweet, strong tea from Edward's Thermos. He made his tea the way she liked it. Her stomach was growling, which Edward must have heard because he broke off half his sandwich and handed it to her. Usually, she hated cheese. And she wasn't especially fond of dill pickle, either. Edward said they were stuck there until morning. He screwed the top back onto his Thermos and tucked it away in his lunchbox. He lit two candles and set them on the dashboard.

"They'll give a little heat," he said.

He laid a blanket on her lap, pulled another around himself, and yawned, said he needed only a few hours' sleep and as soon as there was some light he'd get moving.

Elinor thanked Edward for the sandwich, the tea, and the blanket.

Edward, eyes closed, didn't respond.

Elinor unfolded her blanket, tucked it beneath her thighs, pulled it over her chest and around her neck. She hoped Edward woke up before they were both frozen.

24

Louise watched the falling whiteness from the living room window: so innocent, so unassuming, so beautiful. Like a baby. It had been snowing for hours and hours. Their driveway had disappeared, as had the sidewalks and sections of the road. Only the shape of their car was discernible now. No colour, no door handles, headlights, or windows. Smaller shrubs and bushes had been transformed into bulges and lumps. Branches on the pine tree and blue spruce hung heavy and low from the accumulation of snow. Schools were closed. Court would probably be cancelled, although that depended on which judge was sitting; Judge Anderson lived within walking distance of the courthouse and he never cancelled.

Snow flowed beneath the illumination of the street lights like a waterfall.

Beautiful as the snow was, it was a deadly beauty.

Cars ended up in snowbanks, branches broke from trees, roofs collapsed. And her mother ... if she fell in it ...

Alice had managed to get to Elinor's house before the worst set in. She said there was nothing to suggest Elinor had gone there and no clues to what had caused her to take off the way she had.

Louise had called the police. They said they would do nothing until her mother had been missing twenty-four hours. It took all of Louise's restraint not to shout at them that her mother might be dead by then, and if that was the case she'd be after the force for shirking its duties. Didn't they make exceptions for ninety-year-olds? With the blizzard, friends and family couldn't drive the countryside and highways, or get out to the reserve to see if she'd gone there. All they could do was wait, and hope.

Lillian had heard nothing from Elinor. She reminded Louise how stubborn her mother could be. Louise didn't need to be reminded.

Louise rubbed her hands together to generate some heat, then placed them over her nose. The house was cold. She went to the hallway, pushed up the thermostat another notch, but the furnace did not come on. She wiggled the dial up and down but there was still no response. She cursed the thing; they'd been talking about replacing it. When she went back to the living room, she saw that the street lights had gone out.

In her study, when she flicked the light switch, darkness prevailed. A shard of light spilled from the window when she pulled up the blind. The top of her desk was strewn with photographs John had left for her. Photographs of Holstein cows and steers, calves with gangly legs, glimmering icicles clinging to eavestroughs, a spider in the middle of its web, golden fields dotted with bales of hay. He wanted her opinion on which three he should submit to the school's photography contest. She gathered the photographs into a pile, examined each in turn, organized them into two piles: the best and the not so good. She was drawn to a photograph of a young boy, six or seven. He wore black pants, a long-sleeved white shirt, suspenders; his hair was cut close, as if someone had placed a bowl on his head and cut around it. A man stood a few feet behind the boy; his attire was the same. They were Hutterites, immigrants from Moravia and the Ukraine. They kept to themselves, bound by their religious beliefs. In Saskatchewan they were flourishing, buying up farmland, which didn't sit well with many local farmers. She was surprised John had gotten this photograph. She didn't think Hutterites permitted photographs. Maybe they needed it for medical or legal reasons. Even though she was drawn to the photograph — the sense of the boy's pride, his future hovering behind him — she put it in the "not so good" pile. She doubted that being the winner in a photo contest was something Hutterites valued. Although she'd be in the minority, she did admire their courage and tenacity, their ability to make a go of things against poor odds. She'd always admired that in people. When she was representing someone through legal aid, if he freely acknowledged to her the error of his ways and indicated a plan, a dream for his future, she'd fight for him. She fought for all her clients, but for those who weren't slackers, she'd fight that extra bit.

She heard a bang from upstairs, then the *swoosh* of the toilet flushing. The furnace came on, ran for a half a minute then went off. She hoped her mother was warm. If something happened to her ... if she was found in the springtime frozen to death under a pile of snow a half-mile from the city.... She'd go after the police, the hospital, the city, for negligence.

She grabbed hold of the banister, headed up the stairs. Her knees ached. The stairs creaked. She'd call the police again in the morning. Her mother wouldn't be a priority. They'd be swamped with car accidents, rescuing people from snowbanks, getting pregnant women to hospital. During the last big snowstorm, a woman had delivered her baby in the backseat of her car, then huddled against the family dog to keep warm until the police found her. Her husband, foolish man, had gone out into the blizzard in search of help but couldn't find his way back.

She pressed her body onto John's back, bent her knees into the notch of his knees. When she rubbed the bottoms of her feet on top of John's, he moaned. In a gravelly voice he said her feet were like blocks of ice and asked what she'd been doing. She laughed, said she'd been out shovelling snow in her slippers. He rolled over, drew her close to him, said he'd go shopping with her so she could buy some new boots. Within minutes he was asleep again; she felt his arms relaxing away from her. The scent of Irish Spring soap, John's favourite, drifted off his body. She'd bought him some citrus-scented soap, but he'd have nothing to do with it.

They'd celebrated their thirty-fifth wedding anniversary a couple of years earlier. It was a small affair, family and a few close friends. John's oldest friend, Gregory, insisted on telling the story about the time the three of them had gone hunting for rabbit in the Moose Jaw hills. He said it was the second time he'd met Louise. He laughed and said he'd had his doubts about how it would work between Louise and John. John wanted to write poetry; Louise wanted to rewrite the Canadian constitution. He didn't think Louise would tolerate a poetic rendition of the constitution, and with the little he knew of poetry, he doubted that John would be satisfied with a bunch of *wherefores, hereins,* and *inasmuches* in his sonnets. Louise was the only one who bagged a rabbit that day. It made Gregory think that at least the two of them wouldn't go hungry; you couldn't eat words.

She rolled away from John. The furnace came on. As the warm air drifted over her, her chest filled up; she thought she might cry. She asked the Creator to keep her mother safe, at least for a few more days, until Louise could bring her home. She hesitated to ask more of the Creator, but she did. She asked for his help finding Bright Eyes.

25

The shaking and rumbling of the truck woke Elinor. She pulled the blanket tighter around herself. A blast of cold air rushed at her as the door opened and Edward climbed back into the truck. He glanced at her, but beyond that it was as if she wasn't there.

Not one for conversation first thing after waking, she didn't mind. Edward propped a mirror on the dash. He smoothed gobs of shaving cream over the areas of his cheeks that were beardless. He stretched the skin taut, drew the blade slowly downward. Three times on the left; three times on the right. The blade scratched over the tough skin and the dark stubble disappeared. He patted his neck and cheeks with an aftershave that smelled like rotten oranges to Elinor. She opened her window a crack; she would have preferred to open the door and wave her arms about to dispel the smell, but she was a guest in this vehicle.

Edward continued to examine his face in the mirror. He grabbed a long hair from his right eyebrow, yanked it out with a quick jerk, and flicked the hair away. He checked the left eyebrow but found nothing in need of pruning. She hadn't spent that much time in front of a mirror in her entire life.

Edward combed his hair, adjusted the collar on his flannel shirt, then returned everything to his kit bag.

"Would you like to have a bit of a wash-up?" Edward said. "I can heat a little water."

Elinor's heart fluttered; such kindness. "Is it that bad?" she asked.

Edward looked at her, moved his head side to side. "Could be worse; could be better. I generally try to keep a bit of civility when I'm on the road." He reached into the storage cabinet behind his head, pulled out a clean towel, a bar of soap, and a small stove. He said he'd be a minute heating the water outside.

Elinor pulled the mirror toward her. "Oh my," she said aloud. It *was* that bad. Clumps of dirt and grass were prominent in her white hair. Her left eye was still half-closed. Her right cheek had a black smudge the length of it. There was a chunk of mustard or margarine at the side of her mouth.

Edward climbed back into the truck, handed her the bowl of water, and asked if it was hot enough.

Elinor dipped her fingers into the water. They tingled with the heat; she left them there for a moment. She dipped the washcloth into the water, then patted it around her face, rubbed at the smudge on her cheek. She pressed the cloth over her eyes and held it there.

"It's wonderful. Wakes you right up," she said.

She smiled at Edward and thanked him. She scrubbed a little soap on the cloth and washed her neck and around her mouth. A scent of pine. He must have a good wife, she thought. She handed the bowl to Edward and he tossed the water out the window. She dried herself. Amazing that such a simple activity could lift her spirits so much.

Edward adjusted the rear-view mirror, slipped the truck into gear, and pulled away from the roadside. They picked up speed gradually, nothing like the way Alice drove her truck. Elinor almost gasped. Alice. Her lovely Alice. She, of everyone, would be worried sick. Elinor wished she could get a message to her, tell her she was all right. Louise, poor thing, was probably raging like a mad cow.

The blizzard of the night before had moved on. The sky was a clear, crisp blue; the sun was still low in the eastern sky. The snowplough had been through and there were heaps of snow on the shoulders of the road. As the truck picked up speed and Edward appeared absorbed with the driving, Elinor's body softened into the warmth of the cab, the thrum of the twelve or sixteen tires rolling over the asphalt. Edward could be her son. She thought of her own sons and wondered if she'd ever see Le Roy again or if he'd managed to kill himself with the drink. So many ruined lives from that stuff. And Charlie — it had been five years or more since they'd been together. She hoped she'd see him before her funeral. After her funeral she'd see Philip again. He'd gone ahead of all of them. Poor boy, only four when he'd died. He'd died alone; must have been so frightening for him. For days she'd wept; the tears poured out of her like a waterfall. The creek had taken him. He'd loved the creek, the ducks, frogs, and fishes that were there. Most years there was barely a trickle of water in the thing. But that spring it had been high and rushing. He must have tripped, banged his head on a rock, swallowed a torrent of water. They found him downstream, tangled up in tree roots. Joseph said he looked peaceful. His pockets were full of stones; there was a fish caught under his shirt. She rocked a little to soothe herself from that remembrance.

A semi approached on the other side of the road. When the two trucks were abreast of each other, Edward honked and waved. Elinor thought she saw Edward's shoulders drop; he stopped leaning so far forward.

"Things are moving again," Edward said. He flicked on the radio, said there was a town a half-hour ahead and they'd get some breakfast.

On the radio, reports of blocked roads after the blizzard, school buses not running, schools and shops closed, meetings cancelled. Then stories about the winners of some book award, the times for the next hockey games, and news of a plane crash in Newfoundland. More protests against the war in Vietnam. Then a police report. They were looking for a missing person. Elinor stiffened and glanced at Edward. *An elderly Indian woman, long white hair, short, walks with a limp. Might be in need of ...*

Edward switched to a station that played country music. Elinor pulled her scarf over her head.

"Are you cold?" Edward asked. "I can turn up the heat."

"No. No. It's fine."

Edward hummed along with the music, then smashed the steering wheel. Elinor jumped.

"You know, if I wasn't driving truck, I'd be out there with those protestors. Not with them. I'd be rounding them up, trying to talk some sense into them. No respect for what those men, soldiers, are trying to do over there."

She thought about asking him what all the soldiers were doing over there, what was the point of it, but decided to leave it. Animals had always seemed so much more sensible about disagreements than humans.

"There we are, just up ahead," Edward said. "Best pancakes in Manitoba."

So, we're in Manitoba, Elinor thought. Good. Eventually, they'd get out of the range of that radio station. And she'd be out of Louise's grasp. She didn't like thinking of her daughter in that way. It wasn't how it was supposed to be. How did it get so mixed up? She, Elinor, had been so confused when Louise ran away. Louise's friends weren't doing that. Why did Louise have to do that? Why didn't she talk to her mother and father, some of the elders? Everyone would have tried to help. She shook her head, and in her mind's eye she swatted herself. It wasn't true. Many on the rez were miserable; they couldn't help themselves, let alone a young girl. Louise was brave, even if she was stubborn and mean sometimes. Elinor hoped she was just a little bit worried about her mother.

The parking lot was filled with transport trucks. Edward wasn't the only one who knew about the pancakes. And such a gentleman, she thought, as he came around to her side of the truck and lifted her down. He said breakfast was on him; his grandmother would have wanted it that way. Elinor was surprised by how hungry she was; most of the time she ate little, except when Alice took her for Chinese food.

Edward said if she wanted to freshen up, the bathrooms were clean at this restaurant, not like some places he stopped.

She rarely looked in a mirror. Why was she doing it now? Despite the wash-up she'd had in the truck, there was still dirt in her hair and the buttons on her sweater weren't done up properly. There was some kind of stain or grease on her skirt. She scrubbed at the spot, but it wasn't interested in leaving. Grinning at herself in the mirror, she hoped she'd find some fresh clothes before she found Bright Eyes.

There was a chair beside the sinks, probably because its upholstery had been slashed. She'd sit there for a moment to gather her thoughts. The police report of the missing woman had scared her. Poor Louise. She must be furious. And worried. She'd always had difficulty sorting out those two feelings. Anger came to her first. Like that mother Elinor had seen in the city, frantic that her child had wandered off, yet cursing and swatting him hard on the backside when she found him. Why not hug the little fellow? Maybe there wasn't enough love there and that was why he had wandered off.

She liked the warmth of this bathroom and the smell of hand soap and wet towels. And pee. What did that say about her, that she found sanctuary in the places where humans left their shit? Shit was part of life and animal shit helped things grow in the garden.

She closed her eyes and saw the expanse of webs the spiders created on her porch in the fall. One morning she'd gone out and there were four perfect webs, each with its resident spider in the centre. Four webs for the four directions, four for the four elements. Air. Water. Fire. Earth.

She was enjoying the image of the webs glimmering in the late afternoon sun, remembering how bad she felt for the spiders the times when the wind got up, tearing at their work, leaving strands of web flapping free, spiders clinging desperately, when she sensed she was no longer alone in the room. The smell had changed; it was sweet. She opened her eyes to a girl of seven or eight standing in front of her. A little older than her great-granddaughter, Catherine's Mariah, the girl wore black boots, and red snow pants with suspenders; her blond hair was arranged in braids. Head cocked to one side, she had an awkward grin. Her top two middle teeth were new. Elinor was about to ask her name when her mother rushed in, glared at Elinor, and took the child to the washroom.

A man's voice was calling for Mary, asking if she was in there. Elinor didn't answer. Then she remembered *she* was Mary. She had forgotten all about Edward. And the pancakes.

After another two hours of driving, they passed Winnipeg; they'd make the Ontario border by late afternoon. Edward had been quiet much of the drive, intent, she assumed, on putting on the miles. That was fine with her, since she wanted to keep her heart and mind on Bright Eyes, continuing to send forth the message that she, her mother, was coming for her. She was trying to decide which town to go to, there were so many to choose from. She asked Edward if he had a map of Ontario.

"Where are you going, then?" he asked, handing her a wrinkled map blackened with fingerprints. "I don't go all the way to the south, you know."

"That shouldn't be a problem," she said. She didn't want to sound like an idiot. She opened the map, which wasn't the help she had hoped it would be since she couldn't read the small letters. All those lines and colours, she wondered how anyone made sense of the thing. For generations her people had travelled great distances using only their eyes, ears, and noses, following rivers, creek beds, remembering clumps of trees, noticing the location of the sun and stars.

She held a section of the map within inches of her eyes. It was still impossible to read and there was no way she was going to get the thing folded back the way Edward had given it to her.

She stuck her finger on the map and said that was the place she was going. Edward said he'd look when they stopped for lunch. She combed her mind for the name of a town in Ontario. She remembered Toronto. She didn't want to go there again.

They were slowing down. She didn't see a town, houses, stores, or cafés. Edward eased the vehicle to the side of the road. He hopped out and disappeared around the back. He passed along her side of the truck, bent over to check something at the front, then climbed back in.

"Heard an odd sound but everything seems all right. Let's have a look at the map, then," he said. "Where was it you were going?"

Ottawa. The nation's capital. She blurted out the name.

"Not going that far east," Edward said. "I'll have to leave you somewhere around Huntsville, Parry Sound."

He folded up the map, grabbed his lunchbox, and sat silently for a moment, his big hands draped over the blue metal box.

Then he turned to her. "Maybe you should tell me what you're really up to, *Mary*." He said her name with extra emphasis, then snapped open his lunchbox and handed her a sandwich.

Elinor stared at the sandwich. What did Edward mean, what was she really up to? Hadn't she been clear? She was trying to find her daughter. Out of the corner of her eye she saw his jaw moving up and down; it was the size of a cow's. And his hands were as big as a cow's hoof. And his neck was as thick as that of the deer that hung about in her garden. For the first time, she was afraid.

"Cat got your tongue?" Edward asked.

"I told you, I'm old. I want to find my daughter before I die."

He bit into an apple, taking half with a single bite.

"I'm happy to help you out, but I don't like it when people lie to me. Too many people have done that to me. Makes you feel like a fool."

It crossed her mind that she couldn't hop out of the truck quickly. She couldn't do anything fast anymore. Except think — she still did that pretty quickly. And she didn't like being lied to, either.

"Why are you asking this now?" she said. "I thought we were getting on. I've been grateful for your help. I don't imagine most truckers would want to have an old woman traipsing along with them."

"You got that one right." He opened his window and threw the apple core across the road.

He left the window half-open. Soon Elinor was shivering. Did he plan to freeze her into submission? He switched on the radio, leaned back into his seat, and closed his eyes. Elinor did up the buttons on her jacket and finished her sandwich. A thick slice of ham with lettuce and mustard; at least she could tell Louise she had been eating well.

A Greyhound bus passed on their side of the road. A few minutes later, going in the opposite direction, moving slowly, a big red farm truck loaded with bales of hay. Next to the driver sat a black dog. The snow swirled on the highway like smoke rising from a fire. She was confused. She'd get Edward to drop her at the next town where a bus stopped. And she'd go home. Maybe she needed to give up on Bright Eyes.

After what seemed forever to Elinor, but was little more than ten minutes, Edward rolled up the window. Elinor was half-frozen.

"Sorry for the cold," he said. "I like to have a little fresh air. Stops me from getting dozy." He put his hand on the stick shift, shoved in the clutch, inched forward a few feet, then stopped the truck. "Okay, *Mary*. I know that's not your real name. You don't, of course, have to tell me the truth, but I'm much less likely to dump you at the side of the road if you're straight-up with me. I know some truckers have a terrible reputation — a woman in every town, fighting, and drugs — but I'm not one of those. So, let's have it, *Elinor* — I'm pretty sure that's you. Why are the Regina police looking for you? And who asked them to do that? You don't strike me as a great threat. Nor do you seem like someone who's lost her marbles and gotten lost."

He reached over and pulled at her hair, hard.

"Ouch," Elinor said, pushing at his hand. "What did you do that for?"

"Just checking to see that it's real, that it's not some kind of costume, disguise."

He grabbed her bag, pawed through it, and tossed it back on the floor.

Damned Louise, she thought. Of course she'd go to the police. "How did you find out?"

"The news on the radio got me thinking, but it was the picture on the television that cinched it."

"When were you watching television?"

"While you were having your little seance in the bathroom this morning. So, what's up, then?"

"Good sandwich," she said, brushing crumbs from her skirt. "I don't know where to start. Do you have children?"

He was watching his side mirror, then pulled back onto the highway. They picked up speed. "Two sons. I hate being away from them, but I make good money driving truck. But this isn't about me and my life."

Some of the tension slipped from her body. It was a good sign he had children. She told him that many years ago she'd had a child taken from her. For a long time she thought she would never see her again, but the closer she got to dying, the more she wanted to see her.

"Did she have a name?" Edward asked. He geared down as they started up a hill, a long, gradual incline.

"I don't know what she's called now. I named her Bright Eyes. She was beautiful. Hadn't been out of my body more than a few hours when she was taken."

The truck, the sound of its engine loud and urgent, crept up the hill. Elinor could feel the backward pull of the load behind them. The landscape was changing; there were more evergreens, rocky protuberances, dark blue lakes. As if they each were holding their breath, awaiting the crest of the hill, their conversation was suspended.

"Who would take a child from its mother?" Edward said as he shifted into a higher gear and the engine quieted. "I'd travel every highway and freeway to track them down."

Elinor sighed against the tears in her heart. There had been so many tears. Tears on her chest and in her tea. Tears in the kitchen sink and in the outhouse. Tears in the grass.

Suddenly, fear eclipsed her sadness. Had he called the police?

Would they be waiting for her at the next town? She fumbled in her bag for her cigarettes.

"So, who called the police?"

She struck the match against the box but it wouldn't light. After three tries Edward offered her the lighter from the truck.

"My daughter, Louise."

"Whoa." Edward hit the brakes. As he did so, he flung his arm in front of Elinor and her cigarette went flying.

"Hang on, hang on. Stay there," Edward said.

A moose, a male with a full rack of antlers, had charged from the bush, across the culvert, and looked like he would continue across the road. They had come almost to a full stop. Edward said the last thing he wanted to hit was a moose; they'd all be dead. The animal paused at the shoulder, then loped across the road and disappeared into the woods.

Edward heaved a big sigh. Elinor rummaged in her skirt and on the floor for her cigarette. They started to move again.

"It's a good thing, don't you think, that your daughter wants to find you?" Edward said. "Means she's worried about you. Maybe you need to call her. Wouldn't you want her to call you if she'd gone missing?"

She had gone missing, Elinor thought. Louise had gone missing for months. It had been horrible. Even all these years later she remembered how awful it had been, how she'd worried and prayed, neglected her chores, almost took up drinking. Maybe Edward was right. She must call Louise, tell her she was safe but not tell her where she was. Or she could pretend to call her.

Now there was a pain in her chest. She was feeling light-headed, having trouble breathing. She cranked open her window a crack.

"Hot?" Edward asked.

The pain was worse. She couldn't get her breath; she thought she might throw up, pass out, or both.

She closed her eyes and tried to calm herself. No, she didn't want to die here. Not here.

Elinor blinked at the bright lights. It was almost dark. The truck was stopped. Edward was gone and she was lying across the entire seat. She grabbed the steering wheel and gave it a squeeze, first with one hand and then the other. She heard the low throb of truck engines that had been left running and the louder rumble of others as they started to move.

She sat up although her body longed to remain horizontal.

They were parked at the edge of a big parking lot, more semis than she had ever seen in one place. Had they been mating like gophers? Across the lot she saw gas pumps and a sprawling restaurant with a bright red neon sign: SUZY'S PLACE. People were coming and going. She didn't see Edward. She'd opened the door and was calculating how to get herself down from the height when he appeared.

"Where do you think you're going?" he said. "I've had enough. I thought you were dying back there. I'm so far behind schedule for this run I'm losing money. I've called the police, another expense out of my pocket, and in a few minutes I'll call them again, after they've talked to your daughter and she figures out what to do with this nutcase mother of hers."

"Can you please help me down? I need to use the washroom."

"I don't know if I can trust you. Are you going to take off? Well, actually, it's no concern of mine if you take off. I'll be free of you." He slipped his huge hands under her arms and swung her to the ground.

Elinor, hunched over, her knees stiff and sore, began inching herself toward the restaurant. Edward came alongside of her and slipped his arm under hers. He told her to thank his grandmother; that was the only reason he was sticking around. He'd never be able to face her if he'd abandoned someone's grandmother at a truck stop.

Elinor wanted to tell him she'd give him all the money she had and she'd tell Louise to pay for any expenses beyond that, but it was taking all her energy and breath just to get across the parking lot.

Dinnertime, the restaurant was crowded. Truckers, families with young children, teenagers, and a couple of tables with priests — stiff white collars, black shirts and pants, blue and maroon sweaters. Damned priests. What were they doing there? Smiling, laughing, gobbling up pie. She wanted to tell all the parents to keep an eye on their children.

From the jukebox in the corner, strains of that Elvis guy singing "Love Me Tender." The smell of coffee, tomato sauce, and fried foods — onions, french fries, hamburgers. She wasn't hungry.

She didn't look at the menu and told Edward to order for both of them, except that she wanted a pot of strong tea, and to keep in mind that she wasn't very hungry. Edward told the waitress to bring two orders of ribs, mashed potatoes, and peas.

"I'm sorry for getting so mad at you," Edward told Elinor when she returned from the washroom. "You scared me there in the truck when you passed out. Have you got heart problems? Why isn't your family helping you?"

What was there that she didn't have problems with? Elinor thought. "I don't know what problems I have," she said. "My doctors and daughter tell me but I don't listen to them. There's nothing to be done. I'm old. And I've only ever had one problem: my first child being taken from me. I had so hoped to see her before they put me in the ground, but I don't think it's going to happen. For sure I'll be going into the ground."

The waitress slid two enormous plates of food onto the table.

Elinor's arm hurt; it was difficult to cut the ribs, so Edward did it for her. They were delicious but she had little appetite for them. The mashed potatoes were too dry and she found them hard to swallow.

Edward pointed his knife at her, said he could eat and listen at the same time and he wanted to hear her story. This time he wanted the truth. He jabbed his knife at her again.

Elinor waved at the toddler at the table next to them, a dark-haired boy with a forkful of spaghetti at his mouth and sauce all over his face. Her heart ached. Babies and young children were so precious. She didn't know how to tell Edward what had been done to her. She'd never told Joseph, her own husband. But she was going to die soon. What good had keeping silent all these years done for her?

In as few words as possible, she told him what had happened.

"Why wait so long to find her?" Edward asked.

Elinor shook her head, rubbed her palms in circles over the table. "I've asked myself the same question. I wish I knew. Scared? Stupid? Maybe I was afraid she wouldn't want to see me."

She'd not tell Edward this, but deep inside she'd believed it was all her fault; she should have been strong enough to resist the man. Having the child taken from her was her punishment. One of the nuns told her that. Sex before marriage was a sin, they said in that church. She'd cried so hard she thought she was never going to stop. After doing such a horrid thing (according to the church), she didn't deserve to ever see her child. Now she knew better, but it had taken so many years.

"You don't strike me as stupid. And a fearful woman doesn't head off across the country with a stranger."

"I've gone from scared and stupid to desperate."

The telephone booth was outside. It was dark and snowing again. A gentle, wet snowfall that looked like it might continue for hours. Many of the trucks had gone from the parking lot.

Edward dialled Louise's number.

26

"**M**om? Are you all right? Where are you? Can you speak
up? I can hardly hear you."

Louise heard trucks revving up, her mother whispering,
then a man, Edward, came on the phone and said they were just
over the Manitoba border into Ontario. He was heading east,
had a run to finish. As soon as he could find a motel for Elinor,
he'd call Louise to tell her where she was staying.

"Thank you. Thank you very much for looking after my
mother," Louise said. She hesitated. "How is she? Does she need
a doctor?"

"She may," Edward said. "But first I think she needs her family. I have to tell you, if she was a child I'd be calling Children's
Services. How could you let someone so frail end up on the
highway?"

Louise knew she needed to let that one go. She asked how
long before she'd hear from Edward. He said an hour or two; he
didn't think there was a decent motel any closer. Blinking away
tears, Louise returned the phone to its cradle. Of course it was a
relief to hear from her mother, but her voice was barely audible.
She sounded so weak. That she had gotten as far as Ontario was
a bit of a shock; she was one tough bird. Even so, Louise prayed
they'd get her back home before something more serious set
in. Or before she took off again. Something had propelled her

to do what she had done. And probably she wasn't happy with the outcome.

John, in his favourite cardigan, the maroon one with the two missing buttons and a hole at the left wrist, sat on the couch, a thick textbook on his lap, student papers strewn about him. Whenever Alice looked at him, he had nodded off. Alice, shoes off, feet up on the footstool, was slouched in the wing chair with a book on her lap. She twirled a strand of hair, tighter then looser, and bit at the corner of her mouth.

Louise, in navy velour pants, white turtleneck, and black vest, paced in front of the fireplace, then around the room. She glared at her husband and her daughter and then chastised herself. She jabbed at the embers in the fire, shoved in another log, stood with her back to the fire. Why hadn't she gotten more information from this Edward fellow? At least the name of the trucking company he worked for.

"How can you two just sit there? How can you concentrate on what you're reading? It's been four hours since I talked to her. He said he'd have her in a hotel in an hour or two. Maybe we should be looking into flights. Or two of us should just start driving. We're going to have to go east, anyway."

"Are you sure they're in Ontario?" Alice asked. "Maybe they're in Alberta. Or maybe this guy doesn't really have Gran at all."

"No, I talked to her. I know it's her."

"Are you sure? Did you ask the person something only Gran would know?"

"No, I did not. I think I know the sound of my mother's voice."

Alice rolled her eyes.

"I'm not always the lawyer," Louise said.

"Do you think this guy might want a ransom?" Alice asked.

"I have no idea."

John slammed his book shut and dropped it on the coffee table. He slipped off his glasses, stared at them for a moment, closed the shanks, and placed them on top of his book. He said it was late; they should all go to bed.

Louise said she was staying up; Alice said she wasn't tired.

John went to Louise, rubbed the top of her back and suggested she try to relax. Perhaps they had a flat tire, he said, or the motels were full.

"Or Mom's in some emergency room hanging on by a thread."

"Maybe, maybe not," he said. He kissed Louise on the cheek and shuffled to the stairs.

Alice closed her book, stood at the fire for a moment, then went to the window. She didn't want to think it, but prayed her gran would still be alive when they got to her. It was snowing again, large, fluffy flakes dancing in the street lights. She longed to call Wanda, but she couldn't risk calling from her parents' house. She didn't know when she'd see her again. She'd have to go with her mother to Ontario, or wherever her gran was. What hope was there for her and Wanda? To always be hiding, skulking about, going to illegal clubs? She glanced at her mother, who was running a finger along the edge of the mantel.

Louise examined the smear of grey dust her finger had collected. She rubbed it between her fingertips and scanned the jumble of photographs and souvenirs on the mantel. She ran the palm of her hand over the photograph of her granddaughter, Mariah. Her only grandchild. Mariah, in pink pants and T-shirt, was at the piano, grinning, legs dangling over the piano bench. Louise's heart stirred. Such an imp. So bright. Too bad she lived so far away. In Ottawa. Had Elinor been trying to get to Ottawa?

Tucked behind Mariah was a photograph from Alice's graduation from teachers' college. It had been a good day, everyone in fine form. Alice, so proud in her black cap and black gown with the purple-and-red trim, Andrew and Catherine standing on either side of her. Hands clasped, they were consumed by laughter. Just at the moment that Louise snapped the picture, John had said something (she couldn't remember what it was), and the three of them had erupted. If it had been up to her, they'd have had only one child, but John was insistent on more. He was the third of five children and he'd loved the constant chatter, play, and busyness. Only children were spoiled and selfish, he said. He'd kept his promise that he'd do his share of changing diapers, wiping runny noses, helping with homework, packing lunches, shopping for shoes.

Louise grasped the seashell Alice had brought from Mexico. Pink, purple, and taupe, the smooth curve of the hard shell fit perfectly into her palm. She rubbed it between her hands and it clattered against her ring. When she held it to her ear, an echo and gargling sound came back. At the base of the cavity was a pinch of fine sand. She yawned and sighed.

Alice turned from the window. "Tired?"

"I guess. This waiting and not knowing drives me crazy. It's worse than waiting for a judge or jury to render a verdict."

Alice dropped back into her chair, picked up her book but didn't open it. "What's it like when you lose a case?" she asked.

Louise gathered John's papers into a tidy pile, tossed a sheet of crumpled paper into the fire, then plunked down into the navy wing chair opposite Alice.

"It varies," she said. "It's always hard, but sometimes it's worse than others."

The law, she said, could be an ass. The prosecution finds a bit of compelling evidence that sways the jury. A judge decides to make an example of your client. Or he instructs the jury to return a specific verdict when they might actually have found the opposite. She spoke of a case, not one of her own, in which the prosecutor went with a charge of murder, when it should have been manslaughter or less. It was clearly self-defence, but the prosecution argued that the kid had gone too far, didn't need to kill his attacker. He was found guilty, and because of the murder charge he got a much longer jail term than if he had been found guilty under a manslaughter charge.

"From what I understood," Louise said, "the attacker was a madman. The kid shot him in the leg but he kept coming at him." She shook her head, lined up John's pencils, made the erasers at the end of the pencils even with each other. "The law is applied, but justice is not always obtained." She stared at the pencils, then gathered them in a bunch and placed them on top of John's papers.

"What about you? When you have to fail a student? I know your father hates that."

"Me, too," Alice said, "especially if the kid, and the parents, too, have worked really hard." Often, she said, it was worse for the parents than for the kid. Most kids, she said, knew when they weren't getting it like the rest of the class. They'd tell you how relieved they were not to be going on to the next grade.

"A few times, even against the principal's advice, I've shoved a kid ahead, thinking if she worked a little harder, she'd be all right. One girl I still remember. It was a disaster. She failed miserably and I felt so responsible, so guilty. I hate being wrong."

Louise smiled. "Yes, I know. I was so glad when you turned eighteen."

"What do you mean?" Alice said.

"I could kick you out of the house then. You were of legal age."

"Was it that bad?" Alice asked.

"It was that bad. It's a good thing you had your father. I might have killed you otherwise."

"Come on, Mom. I don't think I was doing anything worse than what my friends were doing."

"That was the problem — the friends. You seemed to be drawn to the ones who liked to race up and down Albert Street at midnight, run half-naked over the grounds of the legislative buildings, dump purple dye into the fountains. You and your so-called friends almost burned down the tennis club. What were you thinking?"

"We were drunk. I never killed anybody."

"No, but you almost slaughtered any reputation I might have acquired in the legal community. Not just a little embarrassing to see the article, and photograph, in the newspaper. My daughter, in nun's garb, and her friends stopping traffic on the Albert Street Bridge, refusing to let people pass until they contributed to your fund for … what was it for? Some church you didn't belong to? Stray cats? Orphans in Africa?"

Alice laughed. "I forgot about that." She stretched out her legs, jiggled them up and down, then stood at the fire with her back to her mother. "I guess I came by my outrageous behaviour honestly."

"What's that supposed to mean?"

"You ran away from home when you were, what, fifteen? Sixteen?"

"That was different. Different times. You have no idea."

"Tell me about it."

"It was so long ago."

"You don't like talking about it. I have friends whose parents never stop talking about the good old days. Not you."

Louise leaned over to rub at a spot on the toe of her shoe. When she straightened up, the yellow light of the lamp caught the side of her face, and Alice saw the lines at the corners of her mother's mouth.

"What happened when you left the rez?"

"It's not very pretty. You don't want to know."

"I wish you wouldn't do that, Mom. Presume what I do and don't want to know."

"Fair enough. It's not a good time to talk about it."

"It's never a good time with you. Why is that? If we weren't waiting for a phone call about Gran, you know I'd be out of here." *And in Wanda's bed*, she thought. "I bet you'd tell Catherine or Andrew if they asked."

"Not so. But let's not have a thing about it now. They've never asked. You have. And I promise we'll find a time."

"It's not like we learned anything about Indian history and lives in school. Gran is always happy to talk about the past."

"That's where we differ. I look to the future," Louise said.

"Gran says nobody ever goes forward without the ancestors, without their knowledge."

Louise sighed. "Maybe so."

"Are you going to call Le Roy and Charlie?" Alice asked.

"I don't know. We rarely speak."

"What if they've seen Gran on television?"

"They'd call. Charlie would, at least. Le Roy's another story."

"You don't like him much," Alice said.

"When we were young he was funny, silly. He had a big heart. We found this injured hawk once, and he nursed that thing, caught gophers, frogs, and mice for it to eat, until its wing had healed and it was able to fly again. It's not so much not liking him as not liking what he does."

"Which is?"

"The drinking. Non-stop. Mom doesn't talk to him anymore, either."

"Sad," Alice said.

"Dad's death, the way he died, was hard on all of us. But for Le Roy, it was as if he'd lost his will to live, to keep going. Slow suicide, I call it."

Louise glanced at the clock on the mantel. "It's past midnight. Why don't they call?"

"Go to bed, Mom. I'll stay up."

Louise crept into the bedroom. John had flung off the covers; his arms were crossed over his chest. Had his hair gotten greyer? Was he thinner? In the past few years he seemed to have less patience for the students who got into fights, the teachers who came to work without lessons prepared or tests graded. She took off her clothes and slipped into her nightgown.

"Coming to bed?" John mumbled, rubbing his eyes. "Did he call?"

"Yes. And no, he hasn't called."

John yawned. "He'll call. I'm sure he'll call. Get some rest."

She drifted into sleep and dreamt of a car accident — her own. The driver she rear-ended coming toward her, furious at her for ramming his car, his beautiful car that he'd bought the day before. She wasn't paying attention when she ran into him. She's trying to explain herself, her preoccupation with finding her dog. He doesn't believe her. He's got a knife, says he'll make sure she never sees her dog again after what she did to his car. She starts to run. She runs and runs and every time she looks back, the guy is behind her and getting closer. The last time she looks back, she recognizes the man. It's Ian Scott.

Alice tugged a blanket around herself and snuggled into the big armchair. She yawned and wondered if her mother would keep her promise. Had it been that hard a time? Had something horrible happened to her that was too painful to talk about?

She thought she might drift off, get a few minutes of sleep, but her thoughts went to Wanda. Wanda was a night owl and was probably still awake. Alice couldn't risk it. She couldn't risk her parents hearing her talk to Wanda. But more important, she couldn't risk tying up the phone lines if Edward was trying to get through. She curled tighter into herself, squeezed her thighs together, imagined them being enveloped by Wanda's legs, Wanda's tongue dipping into her ear, licking her neck. She was moaning with more imaginings when the phone rang.

Louise followed Alice into the hallway. She tried to focus on what Alice was saying, but she kept seeing Ian Scott. She was shivering with fear.

"Did you get what I said?" Alice asked. "Edward called. Are you all right?"

"I'm fine, fine. A bad dream. Thank God he called."

There was a whiteout, Alice said, shortly after Edward got on the road. They couldn't go anywhere for at least an hour. It had been more difficult to find a decent motel than he'd thought it would be. Elinor was safe and asleep at the Lone Pine Motel.

27

O n the third day, Louise and Alice arrived at the motel in the last hour of light. The trip had been exhausting, especially the winding roads through northern Ontario. And because neither had wanted to drive at night, it took longer than either would have liked.

The Lone Pine Motel had a single, pitiful, to Louise's way of thinking, pine tree in the middle of the parking lot. There were four small cabins and eight motel units, all in varying stages of decline, all a faded green with peeling white trim. One of the parking spaces was taken up by a pile of snow higher than the building. Behind the motel, a wall of scraggly pine trees and an outcropping of grey and maroon rock that towered over the small building. The rock was carved with rivulets of ice.

Elinor's room, 214, was the second door to the left of the office.

Louise's heart was racing and she realized she was scared. Scared of what state she might find her mother in. Had she suffered another stroke? Had she been harmed, injured during the time with Edward? Even though Edward said Elinor was all right, she might be deathly ill. He didn't know her, and Elinor was skilled at denying, even lying, about physical ailments.

Louise had phoned Elinor a few times when they were on the road. Most times Elinor didn't pick up. The one time she did she said she was exhausted and had little to say.

Alice rapped on the door, waited little more than a few seconds before turning the knob when Elinor didn't answer.

"Typical," Alice said when the door, unlocked, came open.

The small room was painted a dull pink. Above the unmade bed hung a faded painting of a country scene with an English cottage, thatched roof, and cows in a field. Next to the window, which looked like it hadn't been washed since the motel was built, were a table and chair. Elinor's coat, red stockings, and purple scarf were piled in a jumble on the back of the chair. A white bowl and mug, spoon and glass, tea bags and sugar, a packet of cigarettes, and a couple of stones were strewn across the table.

The toilet flushed; Alice and Louise grinned at each other. The toilet flushed again, then the sound of running water.

Alice tapped on the bathroom door. "Gran. It's Alice."

No answer. Alice cracked the door.

Elinor faced the bathtub as water rushed into it. Half-dressed, shoulders curled, knees bent, she wore a white T-shirt, baggy white pantaloons, and thick blue socks that reached her knees. On her left arm a bandage that ran from her elbow to her wrist. Her creamy hair hung to her non-existent bum. She was skin and bone. Alice blinked away tears.

In the interval between Alice placing her hand on her gran's shoulder and Elinor turning toward her granddaughter, Louise glimpsed the thin frailness and stubborn courage that was her mother. What was she going to do with her? They needed to find Bright Eyes.

28

Elinor twittered at her daughter's blue and green budgies, then poked a finger through the rungs of the cage. When none of the birds showed interest, she opened the door and slipped her hand in. She rested a finger at the breast of one of the turquoise birds. Her own heart, she thought, wasn't beating much stronger than that of the bird. Eventually, the budgie curled its cool claws around Elinor's finger and she withdrew her hand.

"You poor thing," she said. Then she laughed, a dry, weak sound. "I'm not any different than you, am I? We're both caged. My cage is a little bigger than yours, but it's just about as hard to get out of. I have to wait for my granddaughter, daughter, or son-in-law before I can go anywhere, do anything. Let's you and I go for a walk, shall we?"

She shuffled from the kitchen into the hallway and then the dining room. She extended her arm and asked the bird what he thought of this place. "This is where we eat. Quite a bit grander than the plastic dish you sup from," she said. She waved her arm, trying to get the bird to fly, but it only gripped harder onto her finger. She laughed. "What? Have you forgotten how to move those wings of yours?" She dragged a chair away from the table and sat down.

"What's your name? Buddy? Petey? Birdy?" She flicked her arm quickly. "Come on. You can do it. Give us a show." The bird flapped its wings but didn't take flight. "That's it. Do a little warm-up. If this old woman can get herself out of the hospital and halfway across the country, you can have a little spin around the dining room. I won't tell Louise. It will be our secret." She flapped her arm again, then tried to nudge the bird from her finger with her other hand. "Come on, away you go. I know it's not the jungles of Brazil, but there are a couple of plants by the window and some pretty pictures on the wall. Let your imagination go a bit."

Some of the pictures were lovely, but not all of them. She was surprised to see that Louise had hung a few of her paintings, the ones of the valley. She didn't care for the modern things, with bright colours, lines, and designs. She didn't see any creatures in them. What kind of person made pictures without birds, fishes, antelope?

She flung her arm again and this time the bird took flight.

"Yes. Isn't that lovely?"

The bird circled the room, landed on the frame of a large modern piece of art, shit, then took flight again. Elinor's eyesight being what it was, she didn't notice the deposit the bird had left. It flew to the sideboard, a dark walnut piece, and toddled from one end to the other.

At the window, watching the neighbourhood children in their scarves and mitts, red and blue snow suits, throwing snowballs, leaping into piles of snow, Elinor wondered if Bright Eyes had ever done those things. There was so much she didn't know about her daughter. Did she like to play bingo, eat fried fish, watch the seasons come and go? Did she have children?

Elinor forgot about the bird.

She wandered into the living room and plunked down onto the couch. Just this one room was almost half the size of her little cottage, which she missed desperately. Now the lake would be covered in ice, a long expanse of white, quiet and still. When she was younger and better able, she'd walk along the shoreline looking for deer, muskrat, and duck tracks. She loved the springtime, the tinkle of the ice breaking up, the crackle of red-winged blackbirds clinging to bulrushes, soft puffs of fluff on willow bushes. As soon as most of the snow was gone, the hillsides were covered in purple crocus, the fuzzy blooms crouching low to the ground to escape the prairie winds.

The couch was too soft. She'd ask Alice to bring her rocker in. She liked to rock, not sink down into cushions; too hard to get up. She inched her body to the edge of the couch and pushed herself up. The tiredness was coming again. She'd take a nap soon. Louise thought that was all she did but Elinor made herself roam about the house to keep the blood flowing through her veins until Bright Eyes came. She knew she was coming; she must hang on until then.

How did she manage to work in this place? Elinor wondered, standing at the doorway of her daughter's study. The desk was strewn with papers. There were stacks of books around the edges of the desk. Larger than Elinor's living room, the study contained what to Elinor was an enormous desk, a brown-leather high-backed chair, and two floor-to-ceiling bookshelves crammed with books and magazines. The window overlooked the garden. Elinor thought it was one of the nicest views in the house.

She remembered the summer John had made the pond. How hard he had worked, digging a hole in the heavy clay soil, filling it with a layer of cement, then securing stones around the perimeter, piling others up for the waterfall. He was so proud of the goldfish. He loved feeding them, seeing them dart to the top, snap the pellets off the surface of the water. He was delighted that the fish were growing in length, getting plump. One morning he'd noticed that one of the fish was missing. Perhaps it had died and sunk to the bottom of the pond, although the day before all four had seemed healthy. When he fed them that evening he saw only two fish. The following morning there was only one. Then he saw the scat by the pond. He stayed up late that night waiting, until he couldn't stay awake any longer. The next morning there were no fish. More scat. Raccoon scat.

The pond was a lovely place to sit near in the summer, the sound of water trickling over the stones. The chicken wire John stretched over the water seemed to deter the raccoons.

Elinor shuffled to the desk. Piles of files. One pile easily two feet high. She'd never seen such a huge briefcase as her daughter dragged around. No wonder she had problems with her back and neck.

Fingers grasping the perimeter of the desk, Elinor moved to the chair and sat down; her feet didn't touch the floor. The back of the chair was straighter than she liked. It had wheels; she tried to roll it closer to the desk but it was too heavy for her to move. She spotted the purple glass at the edge of the blotter and wiggled to the edge of the chair. The size and shape of an egg, the chunk of glass fit into her hand. Smooth and cool, she was reminded of the stones she had found in stream and creek beds, where years of flowing water left them equally smooth. She returned the glass egg to its spot, grabbed the gavel, and pounded it down on its square of wood. She chuckled at what a satisfying sound it made.

The day Joseph came back from the city, from that woman's house where Louise was staying, and told Elinor their daughter was going to law school, Elinor almost fell off her chair. And she did drop her mug of tea. Then she laughed and pointed her finger at him, said she'd never thought him to be such a fool. Why would Louise want to do that? How could she manage to do that? People who did that had money. And their skins were white. Louise had neither of those.

When Joseph insisted their daughter was smarter and more resourceful than either of them knew, Elinor decided to calm herself. Even so, she wasn't convinced anything would come of it. A small number of their people were managing to do well — a very small number. Some had started to have success with their farms, growing big crops of potatoes and onions, grains, raising healthy cattle. A few had finished school and were working as carpenters, cooks, even some teachers. But most were struggling, barely getting by, in her estimation. Sickness, hunger, too much drinking, shacks for homes, children dying, leaving their families way too early.

The day Louise left — disappeared — Elinor had been happy. She'd been making birchbark pictures, something her mother had shown her how to do. Strips of bark, young and thin, moist and malleable, were cut from birch trees. The strips were folded into quarters or eighths, then a design was marked on them. Using her eye tooth, she bit along the design without puncturing the bark. Sometimes she made flowers and leaves, dragonflies, other times just designs. It was always exciting to see what had been created when she unfolded the bark, the same figure or design mirroring itself four or six times. Little dark dots where she'd bitten transformed into a flower, a dragonfly.

At first Elinor wasn't worried when Louise wasn't there for supper. She thought she'd wandered into the woods with the other girls. Even when Louise stayed away the first night, Elinor thought little of it; Louise was getting older and she was well able to take care of herself. But by the third day Elinor was frantic. No one on the reserve had seen Louise. All of her friends were with their families.

Philip had been dead about three years when Louise left. Yet for Elinor, it seemed as if it was just the day before that he had been taken from them. He came to her in her dreams.

Sometimes she'd see him in the clouds. The war in Europe had ended a year or two before. Cousins and friends of hers had gone to France. They wrote letters about the horrid mud, rain, and rats, guys dead all around them. The letters stopped and when the war ended, some didn't come home. Others came back without arms or legs, or with half their face shot off.

Elinor didn't know if she could bear the loss of another child. A week went by. Maybe the coyotes had gotten her. After another week and no word from or about her daughter, Louise's friend Blanche finally told Elinor what Louise had been planning. It was small comfort to Elinor; her daughter might as well be dead. On her own off the reserve. What would she eat? Where would she sleep? Who would watch out for her? Certainly not white people. They only knew how to take from Indians, never to give back.

Joseph went to the city, over and over, to search for Louise. After three months he found her. So many things Elinor had forgotten, but she remembered Joseph's look when he walked through the door the day he found her. If she had made a painting of his face, it would be like one of those modern paintings with colours thrown about, weird shapes and designs, a painting that made no sense to her. Most of the time she could read Joseph; she knew the colour of his happiness, the patina of his anger, the brush of satisfaction in his eyes and on his mouth when he'd managed to catch a couple of rabbits. That day she fussed around, asking him if he was sick, had he been drinking, did he want tea. All he said was she should sit down, get herself a drink, she might need it. As soon as he started to speak, she knew his heart was broken, and by the end of the telling, hers was also. Yes, he had found their daughter. At the moment she was safe. And she was not coming home. Not for a visit, not to get food. Not ever.

* * *

When Elinor returned to the kitchen she noticed the open door of the birdcage and closed it. "Silly birds. Door wide open and you don't go out for a fly. What's the matter with you?"

A flutter came in her mind and she counted the birds. She was pretty sure there should be five but she counted only four. Then she remembered. Fear clenched her chest like a hawk's claws held tight to a gopher. Louise would chop off her hands. Her mind raced to the dining room but her body couldn't keep up. She tripped. Sprawled on the floor, she cursed her feet for refusing to follow her wishes. The birds chirped and she told them to shut up. She stared at the ceiling, watching the shadows shift and jiggle.

As a young girl she'd lie on her blanket watching the smoke from the fire weave its way to the opening at the top of the tipi. Every once in a while a drop of fat would slip from the rabbit's or duck's body and sizzle in the fire.

The shadows on the ceiling darkened and Elinor remembered the bird.

Where was that damned bird?

She rolled onto her side, urged her body onto her hands and knees. It was a miracle she hadn't broken something. She prayed this wasn't a day that Louise came home early from work. There would be no explaining herself. Louise would be rushing her off to a doctor. Her heart was running so fast she thought it might burst through her chest. She'd stay in this spot for a moment to get her breath. She didn't want to pass out.

This was the world view enjoyed by dogs and cats, she thought — table and chair legs, crusts of bread, a green pea under the counter, a splatter of gravy or ketchup on the floor. She lifted her head. She could see the edge of the kitchen counter, the white enamel of the oven door, the doors of the lower cupboards, the garbage can. A dog's experience was made richer by all the scents its nose gathered. She sniffed a couple of times but didn't bring in anything interesting. She sucked in a breath, grabbed hold of a table leg, and pulled herself up. Head spinning and light, she gripped the edge of the table and remained there for a moment.

Somehow she got from the kitchen to the dining room.

The absence of sunlight in the room told her it was mid afternoon. John often came home early. If she wasn't napping, they'd have a cigarette together on the back porch. He'd talk about his students. The things they got up to: The one who claimed he lost his homework in a mailbox. Another whose mother called every day to say her daughter's homework was too hard. John figured the mother was doing the homework. The student who tossed another student's lunch onto the roof of the school.

Elinor scanned the dining room. Where was the damned bird? She called and whistled but saw and heard nothing. Did it get outside? She was pretty sure she hadn't opened any doors. She shuffled across the room. A few feet from the window she felt a lump beneath her foot. She looked down and cursed.

"Must have flown into the window," she whispered to herself as she scooped up the little creature. *Don't let it be dead.* She cupped the bird to her chest and stroked the tiny head. Maybe the beating of her own heart would spur the bird's to action.

"Come on, then," she said, "you're tougher than that. Just a little bonk. I tripped a few minutes ago but got myself back up." She held the bird away from her chest. Was there some movement in the bird's throat or chest? Some quivering inside? She brought the bird to her mouth and breathed on it. Still nothing. She might as well die. Louise would never forgive her. Maybe the bird needed to be with the others. Maybe they'd know what to do. Yes. Creatures always looked after their own. Well, mostly. Sometimes they abandoned them. She placed the bird in the bottom of the cage, prayed to the Creator to help it heal.

29

Louise flipped through the pile of messages Anita, her assistant, had left on her desk while she was in court. A request for a donation from the Canadian Cancer Society, a notice of a meeting at the animal shelter, a reminder about the monthly dinner of the Law Society, a reminder that her dry cleaning was ready for pickup. Several calls from clients and colleagues. A message with a long-distance, out-of-province number. She didn't recognize the name. The message said URGENT PERSONAL MATTER, PLEASE CALL. Usually her assistant screened out these kinds of calls. This person had been persistent.

Maybe it was Louise's fatigue that caused her to let her guard down. Since Elinor had come to live with her, Louise hadn't been sleeping well. She spent far more time than she'd like worrying about Elinor. Worrying that she'd fall down the stairs, worrying that she'd fall asleep with a cigarette still burning, worrying that her mother would burn the house down. One day Louise came home from work to find her mother with the oven on and the oven door wide open. When Louise suggested Elinor turn up the furnace, Elinor said there was no need to heat the whole house, and she liked seeing the red of the oven coils. Louise prayed her mother didn't toss paper or scraps of wood into the oven to see the element glow even redder.

Louise dialled the number. Later her mother would say it was meant to be. The signs were all there: her assistant out of the office, Louise distracted, restless, more likely to act on impulse. If Anita had returned the call, she might have dismissed the person as a crank.

After two rings a woman answered.

"It's Louise Preston. You left a message?"

"Yes. Yes I did. Thank you. Thank you for calling. How are you today?"

"Fine."

Bad idea to have called, Louise thought.

"I wondered if you would …. I'm … I'm not quite sure how to say this."

Louise crumpled the message and threw it at the wastebasket.

"Is Elinor Greystone your mother?"

Louise hesitated. "Why do you ask?"

"I'm sorry to intrude. Is she your mother? Did you find her?"

"I'm not in the habit of giving out personal information over the telephone." Louise wove her fingers through the coils of the telephone cord.

"Of course, and I wouldn't, either. It's just that I've been searching for my mother for months. Well, years really. And when I saw that picture of that woman on the television a few months ago, I thought there was a strong resemblance. I should have called sooner, but for a couple of weeks I thought it wasn't so. Then I was quite sick and not able to do anything."

The woman took in a deep breath. "My name is Victoria Witherspoon. I was adopted at birth, never met my mother, but my parents told me she was Indian and I was born in Saskatchewan. There was no birth certificate."

In the past few weeks Louise and Alice, on weekends and after work when they could manage it, had increased their search efforts. Alice had visited reserves near the location of the residential school. She'd talked with chiefs and elders, even a couple of students who'd been at the school when Elinor was there. One woman remembered Elinor, even that there had been a child. No one had any idea what happened to the child. Louise had made repeated calls to Indian Affairs; they had not been co-operative. Whatever records they had, they weren't letting go of. She contacted Vital Statistics; no birth had been registered. John, bless his heart, knew a couple of priests. He called them, asked for their help in accessing church records. He was still trying. Louise yearned to find the name of the nun who had taken the child, and the names of the priests. Probably all dead. Did they need to start visiting cemeteries in the area?

Louise pushed back her chair and moved to the corner of her desk, as far as the phone cord would allow.

"Is Elinor your mother? Did you find her?" Victoria asked again.

"Yes. And yes."

"Surely this is awkward for you. Perhaps a letter? I could tell you more about myself. I have so many questions. Would that be all right? If I sent a letter?"

Louise pawed through the leaves of the ivy plant that trailed over her desk, pinching off yellowed and brown leaves. She poked her finger into the soil, still moist. "Pardon?"

"Could I send you a letter?"

Louise guided her body back into her chair. Bright Eyes? Her mother's child? Probably some gold digger. Maybe she should tell her that up front, save her the cost of the postage. Her mother had no money. "Sure ... I'll look out for it."

"In a few days I'll get it over to you. Maybe a bit longer; my energy is limited these days."

"Do you mind if I ask where you live?"

"In southern Ontario, a small town called Kincardine. Do you know it? It's on Lake Huron. Quite a lovely area."

"I'm not familiar with it."

"Well then, I won't keep you," Victoria said.

"Hang on. I want to get your name down. And your phone number, can you give it to me again?"

"Of course." Victoria recited her number.

"What's your birthdate?"

"Well, like I said, I don't have my original certificate. I do have a birth certificate. I guess my father, being a physician, he managed to get one."

"And what's the date on it?"

"It says April 27, 1893."

"Thank you. And ... and for place of birth, what does it say?"

"Yes, well, that's the funny part that I will tell you more about in my letter. Ontario. It gives Ontario as my place of birth, but that's not what my father told me."

Louise emptied her briefcase. She stared at the stack of files. She picked up one, fanned through the pages, and dropped it to one side. The likelihood that this woman was Elinor's daughter was such a long shot. Hundred to one, thousand to one odds. She had a sudden flash of worry. *Where was the paper with the woman's information?* She slammed files around on her desk before noticing the paper on her chair: April 27, 1893. Her mother would have been fifteen or sixteen years old.

She folded the paper in half and looked up to the photograph of her father.

"Now what, Daddy? Should I tell her? Get her all excited. And if it doesn't come to anything? If I never hear from this Victoria woman again?"

She tucked the slip of paper into a drawer in her desk that she kept for confidential files. She was not going to tell Elinor, or Alice, about the call. Not yet.

Like a lawyer building a case, she needed more evidence.

30

They met in the north end of the city, a part of town that Alice rarely had cause to go to, it being the poorer, more industrial area. Most of the people who'd come for the meeting — rarely were there more than twelve or fifteen — were at the snack table at the back of the room, chatting, joking, fixing coffee or tea, grabbing cookies, an apple or orange. The numbers hadn't diminished since Alice's first meeting, but they'd not grown, either. It was a fluke that Alice had found out about the meetings. Wanda had hired a Native man to repair her fence. When he'd finished the work she'd invited him in for tea. She asked him what he thought about the plans for the amusement park on Indian burial lands. At first he didn't want to talk about it, but when Wanda said she thought it was appalling, he agreed and told her there were plans to protest. Wanda later told Alice she must go to these meetings. Although fearful, Alice knew Wanda was right.

One of the elders, a stocky man with a pocked face wearing a blue bomber jacket bearing the insignia of a local electrical firm, rose to give the prayer. He spoke first in Cree, then in English. He thanked the Creator for his support at this difficult time, for bringing everyone safely to the meeting, for the food and everyone's good health.

Thomas, a tall, muscled man with a braid down his back who was dressed in faded blue jeans and a blue Toronto Maple

Leafs T-shirt, spoke next. One of the organizers, Thomas, had a voice that was deep and resonant. Alice thought he'd be good on the school playground during recess when you wanted to get the kids' attention. Thomas said their letters and petitions and telephone calls to municipal and provincial officials had gone unnoticed. "No more attention given to them than a waterfall gives to a grain of sand," he said. The groundbreaking was going to happen within the next couple of weeks. It seemed their cause was of less importance than a gopher in a wheat field. (The province had recently approved funding to assist farmers with containing an outbreak of gopher activity on farmland.)

After Thomas's update, a skinny man with braids and a scar that ran the length of his left cheek spoke. He said they'd all heard the stories from their ancestors. "We're agreeable and helpful, and the next thing we know we're living in a corral, with barely enough land to support three horses. I don't think we've got any choice. We are not amused. We don't care to be amused. We don't think our ancestors will be amused. And we've been riding real horses for a couple of hundred years. I, for one, am not getting on a pink-and-green horse that has a pole stuck through its belly and never shits."

Some chuckled and nodded. Others refilled their coffee, lit cigarettes. There was a communal exhalation of smoke.

A young woman, her hair in braids, her hands covered in scabs, who seemed to need a drag off her cigarette after every fifth word, said they needed to stop holding on to their anger. Indian agents had been selling parcels of land to the local farmers in her grandparents' time, before she was born. "What kind of progress is it that shows no respect for the dead, or the living, for that matter?" she asked. "I say we go there, join hands, lie down, and put a stop to progress."

Although she had been to five or six meetings and was growing fond of many of the people, especially Thomas and his mother,

Elizabeth, Alice had not spoken to the larger group. It was time.

"Last week my VP, whom I thought understood, pulled me aside. He was polite, chose his words carefully. He told me there had been complaints from some parents, wouldn't tell me which parents. Maybe I should cut back on the Indian 'handicrafts,' as he called them — stories about animals, visits from elders." She shoved her hands into her pockets, made them into fists. "I was a fool to think he cared, that he understood. He understands as far as it meets his needs. I thought he wanted me at Northview so that the Indian students got a better deal. Now I'm thinking he saw me as a policewoman. Maybe I'd keep them in check. He could put in his annual report that he had an Indian staff member and there were fewer stabbings, drunken parents at the school. Maybe a couple of the Indian kids actually got some passing marks, learned how to do their multiplication tables." She threw up her hands. "I'm sorry. I've gotten way off track. I think we need to act. Maybe set up a few bingo tables in one of their cemeteries."

The group nodded and cheered, banged on the tabletops. Others spoke, echoing Alice's comments. When the meeting ended, the woman who was the chain smoker, Raylene, slapped Alice on the back and said she wished she'd had Alice for a teacher. She said she couldn't take the name-calling, the bullying, and that the teachers were as bad as the students. She'd dropped out of school in grade seven.

After the meeting, lingering with Thomas and Elizabeth in the parking lot, swirls of smoke from Thomas's cigarette filling the space between them, Alice was restless, excited. With Thomas, Elizabeth, and the others, she had a sense of connection, kinship, a shared vision, a sense of community and history.

Elizabeth said she'd make a batch of doughnuts for the protest. Thomas laughed and said if the going got tough, they'd make a peace offering of doughnuts to the police.

"Or we could use them as ammunition," he said.

"A waste of good food," said Elizabeth.

"I can see the headline already," Thomas said, "Indians charged with pastry assault on RCMP. Their punishment: provide a thorough scrubbing of all police uniforms until they are free of Indian crumbs."

"Thomas!" his mother said, giggling and swatting at him.

"I like the image of a doughnut with white icing and sprinkles dangling from the end of a gun," Alice said.

"Do you two have any idea how much work doughnuts take?" Elizabeth asked.

Thomas put an arm around his mother. "I'll help you. We'll make chocolate ones with red icing for us and white ones with especially big holes for the white cops. They can put two donuts together to make a pair of binoculars. Help them to see things more clearly."

"You are nuts," his mother said.

"But you love me anyway," Thomas said, a grin on his face.

"Don't push it."

They were readying to part when Elizabeth asked about Elinor. How was her health? Did they need help with her? Would she like a visitor?

"She's frail … but she's all right." Alice hesitated, surprised by her own tears. "I think her time is coming." Her mother had been adamant that they not tell others why Elinor had taken off, the fact that there had been a child.

Elizabeth squeezed Alice's hand, then drew her into a hug, patted her back. "Sometimes it's a blessing," Elizabeth said.

Alice strolled to her truck. Thomas honked and waved and shouted, "Doughnuts!" as he sputtered by in his green Volkswagen Beetle. When Alice had first seen Thomas's contortions trying to cram his six-and-a-half-foot, two-hundred-pound body into the car, she'd asked why he'd chosen that vehicle. He said it served as a daily reminder of a body, a person trying to get somewhere and into something where he doesn't fit. "Kind of like Indians in white society," he said. "You never really get comfortable. That's why you have to keep your own culture."

There was chaos on the prairie when the fires came.

A time of drought; hardly a day went by without a fire. The herd hung in one place, thirsting but too hot to seek out water. The grass was so dry it crackled with a breeze and crunched beneath one's hooves.

Fires on the prairie move like the wind. They can leap higher than a rubbing stone.

The fire I remember best came up fast and moved with the speed of a hawk plunging to earth.

I outran that fire. Others did not. Not the young. Nor the very old.

Screeches of panic.

Hair and flesh on fire. The air filled with smoke and the bitter scent of flesh.

Skin blackened and charred.

I wanted to run as far as the great waters.

Many of the bison who were burned but survived had their eyes swollen shut. The poor creatures bumped into one another, tripped over those who had died, and stumbled into the coulees. Eventually, they fell to the ground, weakened from starvation.

Soon the vultures, owls, and wolves came.

The fire in this museum was worse than the fires on the prairie.

You hope that the curator, janitor, a fireman gets to you before it's too late.

For some, it was a second death.

The museum got hotter and hotter. Walls collapsed. The glass burst, scattering fragments like raindrops.

I wanted to turn away. I didn't want to watch the gallery opposite mine.

The fire flew across the floor and shot up the legs of the antelope. I saw the terror in the creature's eyes. For a second I saw the wires and bits of wood. Then, only triumphant flames.

I feel cold thinking of that time.

The odour of smoke in my coat stayed for weeks.

The worst was the curator. Shouting and shouting. Save the bison. Save the bison. Never mind about the others.

Save the damned bison.

The old Indian woman came again. She looks so tired; she doesn't talk to me much even though I have tried to speak to her. She speaks often to someone else while she draws — Bright Eyes, I think the name is.

31

Shivering from the March winds and the dash across the park to her office, Louise wriggled into a thick sweater, shoved off her shoes, and sought out the worn brown moccasins beneath her desk. She leaned back in her chair as a wide yawn escaped her mouth. She'd had the same dream, the one with Ian Scott, again last night. It was the third time in the past two weeks. She dreaded sleep; she stayed late in her study, hoping that reaching a place of exhaustion would let her get through the night. In last night's dream, Scott's eyes were squinting and dark, filled with anger. He didn't grab or chase after her as he had in other dreams, but no matter how far she ran from him or where she went, he was always waiting. And watching.

She couldn't talk to John. She couldn't talk to anyone. To do that would incriminate herself. She must speak to Mary.

She pulled the day's mail toward her and flipped through the newspapers, brown manila and white legal envelopes. Her secretary had sorted the letters into professional and personal. Louise rarely got personal mail at her office. She stared at the large, awkward script on the plump pale pink envelope with its Ontario return address. Since their phone call seven or eight days earlier, Louise had thought often of Victoria, wondering when, or if, she'd send a letter. Wondering if there was anything she could do if no letter came.

Louise sliced the letter opener through the fold of the envelope and slipped out the contents — several pages of unlined paper. On many pages, the writing drifted downward. In places the script was shaky. But despite these penmanship characteristics, what was written was legible.

March 24, 1969
Kincardine, Ontario

Dear Mrs. Louise Preston:
I have had a good life. I was blessed with wonderful adoptive parents. Nevertheless, in the last few years the desire to know my real parents has grown intense. Hardly a day goes by when I don't wonder who my mother was. I confess I don't understand this. Maybe it comes with age, since I hardly gave it a thought when I was younger. My parents were always truthful with me that they were not my birth parents. As soon as I was of an age where I could think of such things, it was pretty obvious that I didn't look like either of them. They were both fair, and there was me, with my black hair and dark skin.
My father was a physician. In Saskatchewan he had been the doctor for the Indian residential school in the valley. I never knew its name. Not until I was in my twenties did Father tell me that the priest at the school had asked for his help. One of the students had had a child. The priest asked Father if someone in his practice might take her. That was me! How simply things were done in those days.

Father told me he and Mother had wanted a child of their own but Mother hadn't been able to carry a pregnancy and had had several miscarriages. They were planning to move to Ontario, where they understood life was a little more civilized. Father couldn't remember if he had already told the priest of those plans when the priest made the request.

Father said he took me on the condition that the priest gave him the names of the mother and father of the child. He didn't know if I would want to contact these people, but he wanted it to be an option. I remember the day he told me; I was nineteen, twenty. He was so upset, rushing around the house, looking for some book. It was the book into which he'd tucked the piece of paper with my parents' names. He never did find the book or that piece of paper. We had moved several times over the years. Right then I didn't much care. I couldn't imagine contacting my birth mother. The people I had lived with all my life were my parents; they were the only parents I knew. We didn't talk about it again.

After I had my son, it passed through my mind to know who my birth parents were. But I was busy with raising Andrew, my husband was with the bank, and soon after Andrew was born, my husband was transferred to Manitoba. What an adjustment that was! It took me a long time to get used to the constant blowing of the wind.

Even without the piece of paper, Father did remember I was the offspring of a student at the residential school. He knew the year but not the date of my birth. It was 1893 or '94, the year they had moved to Ontario. My mother had a bad heart; she died early, at fifty-eight years of age. I had just turned thirty-one. We were very close. I thought a lot then about finding my birth mother. Still, I did nothing about it. Probably I was afraid. That it would be too painful if she didn't want to see me, or if she, too, was dead. More years passed. My husband was transferred to Ontario, to the very town I live in now.

Two years ago I had a serious heart attack, almost died. And when I was clinging to life, the strangest thing happened. I saw a woman in the corner of the hospital room early one morning before the nurses made their rounds. She wasn't really a woman, more like a child, a teenager. She was beautiful. Dark hair and skin, twinkling eyes. And she had the most wonderful smile. She stood there smiling at me. And another strange thing — I smelled smoke, sweet smoke, like grass or incense.

I wondered if that woman was my mother. I took it as a sign and thought I must find her, all the while knowing that she might be dead or have changed her name. It seemed hopeless. I knew so little about her. Only that she was Indian and had gone to some Indian school in southern Saskatchewan. By then my father had died, so there was no one I knew who had any information.

My son helped me contact the churches that had run schools in that part of the country. They would not give up any information. I had an idea of travelling through the reserves, looking for my mother, but perhaps you're aware of the tension in this country between the Indians and the whites. So I gave up on the whole thing and put it out of my mind.

Last winter when your mother's picture came on the television, I was stunned. I thought it might be my mother. I don't know why except I had a strong sense, kind of the way it was in the hospital. I'd smell sweetgrass and smoke where you'd not expect it — in the car, the grocery store, at the library. I felt drawn to your mother. I couldn't get her picture out of my mind. One day I'd tell myself to call about it. The next day I'd think it was craziness, impossible that we might be related.

I was so worried. They don't tell you if the missing person has been found. I called the police, but of course they wanted information; they weren't looking to give out information. Then I thought she wouldn't want to see me, anyway. All this time had gone by and she hadn't tried to contact me, although I don't know how she would. My son encouraged me to call or write. I was so nervous. I had never known, nor did my father, the circumstances of my adoption. Maybe my mother didn't want to see me. Maybe she wanted to be rid of me.

Please write to me at the address I've given. Perhaps we are sisters and could meet at least once before I die.

Yours truly,
Victoria Witherspoon

Louise laid out the pages one by one on her desk. She stared at the jumble of letters sprawling across the pages. She picked up the first page, reread it, then brought it to her nose. A scent of perfume or soap, lavender or peppermint, she wasn't sure. She didn't use perfume herself. She envisioned all the fingerprints that Victoria had left on the pages. And now her own, comingling with those of Victoria. She reread the entire letter before dropping it on her desk. It was too impossible. Affidavits, wills, and summations she knew how to write. A letter to a strange woman claiming to be her mother's lost child. What did one say? Maybe she should forget letters, fly to Ontario, meet the woman, draw her own conclusions. But haste had never been a lawyer's friend. The facts must be gathered, each piece of information, detail, carefully weighed and considered. A case had to be built up with a solid foundation. That was why she had decided to keep this to herself for a while longer. Alice and Elinor would rush ahead without due consideration. She knew the path she was choosing was not without risk, and she'd done enough risking in the first twenty years of her life to last a lifetime. Nevertheless, she pulled out a clean sheet of paper from her desk. She wrote slowly. Her handwriting was small and tight, not easily read. But she would not ask her secretary to type this letter.

April 1, 1969
Regina, Saskatchewan

Dear Victoria Witherspoon:
Only in the past year has my mother spoken about
the child she bore in residential school. The child,
whom she'd named Bright Eyes, was taken from
her, without her consent, shortly after her birth.
She asked me and my daughter to help her find

this child, but we had little sense of where to look. Anyone who knew of her had died years ago.

I cannot, of course, confirm for you that you are my mother's child — and my half-sister. Although I can tell you that no one else has come forward claiming to be her child.

Perhaps you could send a photograph of yourself. That might be helpful.

Sincerely,
Louise Preston

Louise started a trial the day after she mailed her letter to Victoria. Her days, and some of her nights, were spent gathering her facts, reviewing documents, and preparing for the next day's arguments. She forgot about Victoria and was admittedly surprised to see the familiar pink envelope amidst the day's mail two weeks later. She squeezed the envelope, ran her fingers around the perimeter; it was bulkier than the other had been. Then she remembered: photographs. She had asked for photographs. With that thought came queasiness in her stomach.

She propped the envelope against her desk lamp and popped out of her office to the kitchenette area, where she plugged in the kettle. She needed a cup of tea. She went back to her office, glanced at the envelope, and went to the window. Mid afternoon, the descending but still-bright prairie sun bouncing off the windows of the office building across the street. In the past few weeks the sun had been getting higher in the sky. On the street, two women, their only winter attire boots and turtleneck sweaters, stomped their feet and clapped their hands as they waited for the traffic light to change. As soon as the light changed they rushed across the street, continuing to run until they reached the next corner and turned and Louise couldn't see them anymore. Louise recalled her shouting matches with Alice, trying to get her to dress for the cold weather. Maybe it was an obsession of hers from the days when she'd had few heavy clothes and spent long nights shivering and stiff in the Scotts' unheated shed.

Ardith, her secretary, rapped on the door, said Louise's kettle had boiled. Louise never asked Ardith to make her tea. Ardith had been clear about that. Secretaries did secretarial work and nothing else. Louise knew about this because Ardith had told her that many of Louise's male colleagues got their secretaries to pick up their dry cleaning, buy their wives' birthday presents, and wash up everyone's dishes in the office.

Louise made her tea and took it to her office. She had a couple of sips — black orange pekoe with milk, no sugar — then put down the cup. She sliced the letter opener across the top flap of the envelope and wiggled out the thick wad of paper. Four sheets were folded over two black-and-white photographs. One picture was of a child, the other of an adult. Louise turned on her desk lamp and drew it closer to the photographs. The child was skinny-armed with an impish grin, probably about four years old. She wore a light dress, white socks, and black shoes. She was clutching a chicken. She bore a strong resemblance to Alice at a similar age. Since there were no photographs of Elinor as a young child, that comparison couldn't be drawn.

The picture of Victoria as an adult was taken in the midst of what looked like a backyard vegetable garden. She was holding a bunch of roses and a pair of shears. She wore a light blouse, a sweater vest, and a dark skirt that hung below her knees. Her grey-white hair was loosely pulled back. She was standing especially straight and smiling. It was a calm, self-assured smile, not a smile of giddiness or a smile that arose from great laughter. There wasn't much resemblance to Elinor. Maybe she took her looks from her father. Louise would never see a photograph of that man.

Louise thought of her own children. Andrew had been the spitting image of John, each with chin dimples, a large shock of hair, and pouty lips; their baby pictures were interchangeable. Catherine had looked very much like Louise, although baby pictures could not be compared since there were none of Louise. They teased Alice that she was the mutt; didn't look like Louise or John. Always her own person, Louise would say, right up to present day.

There were prickles on the back of Louise's neck as she looked at the photos. She wasn't a religious person; she didn't believe in miracles. She didn't think that people were basically good, that governments looked after their citizens, that the meek would inherit the Earth. She certainly didn't believe that justice always won out. Some days she wondered what she did believe in, what she had faith in, what she drew her strength from. Some of the choices she'd made in life implied she believed in herself or that people could be trusted. That seemed implicit in her decision to run away from her family and the reserve. But that had been a decision made out of desperation. Was there also an element of hope and trust that she'd find a better world? She couldn't say. She happened to get lucky. She happened to be in the café with the Scotts on a day Mary was working. And she happened to be in the library on a few days when Evelyn McKellar was there. What if she hadn't found them? Maybe she had absorbed more of her parents' teachings than she realized or wanted to admit to. The notion that the Creator was watching over her, that he would provide for her.

As she was attempting to return the photos to the envelope, she discovered another paper, folded into fours. The letter was brief, and as she read it she shook her head in disbelief. This woman, who was easily seventy years old, was prepared to traipse across the country, spend her own money, no prize or cash award being offered, on the hunch that Elinor might be her mother.

Was it possible that this woman was Elinor's stolen child? What possible incentive could there be? Just because Louise couldn't think of anything at the moment didn't mean that there wasn't an ulterior motive. Thirty-plus years of practising law had shown her the infinite ways in which humans could be devious and calculating. Louise cautioned herself. She must not let her emotions dictate what she must do. Build the case, gather the evidence.

Even so, she'd telephone Victoria.

She'd take the photographs to Elinor and Alice.

32

Elinor, hunched over, eyes inches from the paper, pencil barely moving, made minute strokes around the bison's eyes. The small drawing on the wrinkled four-by-six sheet of paper was what she had been working on for weeks. It was the one thing she seemed to have energy for these days.

Mid-morning, the two of them were in the kitchen, Elinor at the table, Louise, in a white apron, pulling bowls and containers from the fridge. The budgies, seemingly happy for the company, chattered and burbled and clamoured up and down the rungs of their cage with the aid of their beaks.

Louise muttered and groaned about the state of the contents of the bowls she'd taken from the fridge. Invaded by brown or green mould, the original food in the containers was barely recognizable.

Elinor held out her drawing to Louise, asked her how it looked. Louise wiped her hands on her apron, came over to the table.

"Perfect. It looks perfect, Mom." The bison head, drawn straight on, was a strong likeness. Small eyes, massive furry head, flat black snout.

Elinor grunted and leaned back in her chair.

Louise glanced at the clock.

"Do you have to be somewhere?" Elinor asked.

"No, why?"

"You keep looking at the clock."

"Shall I find a frame for your drawing?" Louise asked.

"That would be nice." Elinor rubbed her hands over her cheeks, cheeks that were sunken in and hung like a hound dog's "Was it really that bad when you left?" Elinor asked. She sighed. "I have wanted to ask you that for so long. All these years trying to find a reason why a daughter would leave her mother like that. And her people." She held the drawing of the bison at arm's length, squinted, then brought it closer. "It wasn't natural, you know."

"I know," Louise said. "I planned to come back. I even started out one night."

"Where did you live? With some woman, what was her name?"

"Evelyn McKellar."

Evelyn volunteered at the library. She valued books and learning as much as Louise had come to. Louise lied to her, said she'd run away from an orphanage. One day Evelyn asked Louise to leave the tiny room she shared with Mary above the café and come live with her. Evelyn McKellar sent Louise to school, she made her read the Bible every day, and corrected her English, both spoken and written. Evelyn was strict. She'd clip clothespins on Louise's ears to get her to listen better, to remind her to press every wrinkle on every sheet when she ironed.

"You'd rather live with her than your own family?"

"I was a kid. What did I know?"

"You said you started to come back. What happened?"

Louise hesitated. "Mary stopped me, told me it was a bad idea, said nothing on the rez would be any different or better."

Elinor rubbed her hands in circles over the table. "Well, she got that part right. But you still should have come. Even to visit. Have you ever thought what it's like for a mother to have a child disappear? You were the second one gone from me. Well, there were more than that, but I knew where they were, that they had died. After you disappeared, I wondered what I had done wrong to deserve such things."

Louise sat across from Elinor, placed her own hands on top of her mother's. "I was stupid. I was wrong." She wouldn't tell her mother that if she had to do it all over again, she would still leave.

Elinor grunted.

Louise studied her mother's hands. So small, so gnarled. In places, the skin was almost translucent. There was a sizeable bruise over her left thumb. "What did you do there?"

Elinor brought her hand closer to her eyes. "No idea. Caught it in a cupboard door, banged it against the wall in my sleep." She poked at the bruise. "Doesn't hurt."

She ran her palms in circles on the table again, closed her eyes, and hummed a tune Louise did not recognize.

"I should see Lillian one more time," Elinor said. "Have you talked to her?"

"We talked after you got home."

"Is she still with that Leonard fellow?"

"Of course, Mom. He's her husband."

"I never liked him. Don't know what she sees in him. He's not like John."

"I always thought he was kind enough," Louise said.

"Maybe so. But he never gave her children. And that's not right."

"Sometimes it's not meant to be," Louise said.

"I think he was punishing her."

"Punishing her for what?"

Louise heard a squeak, the sound the front door made when it opened and closed. Finally, she was here; Louise had asked her to come.

Alice went directly to Elinor, hugged her, told her she looked terrific. She said the temperature was getting warmer; soon they could go to the valley, have a picnic.

Elinor said that would be nice. She asked how the children were, the children in Alice's class. She told her teaching children was an honourable thing to do. More people should do it. Children were the future. She closed her eyes again, started to rock. Alice turned to Louise, mouthed the words "Is she okay?" Louise nodded yes.

"I have news," Louise said.

Elinor shook her head from side to side, then up and down. She seemed oblivious to her daughter's words.

Straining against the dryness in her throat, Louise pushed out the words. "It's about Bright Eyes."

"You found her?" Alice blurted out.

"Maybe."

"Who? How?" Alice asked.

Elinor smiled.

"She's on her way," Louise said.

"From where?" Alice threw her arms around Elinor, who had started to rock. Then Elinor's body stiffened and crumbled into itself. She tried to speak but there was only choking and coughing.

When Alice mentioned an ambulance, Elinor rallied, told them she was fine. With Louise on one side and Alice on the other, they guided her to the couch in the living room. They propped pillows behind her and tucked a blanket around her thin body. Elinor closed her eyes, said she needed to rest before she heard more.

Elinor needed this time alone, behind her eyelids, to gather her strength, to take in this so-called news of her daughter's that had entered her body like a bolt of lightning. It was almost too much to bear. Even though her thoughts were never far from Bright Eyes, even though she had worked for weeks on the bison head, talked endlessly during the day to the budgies about Bright Eyes, she knew they were all efforts on her part to keep the child alive in her mind. Because in most parts of her body — arms, legs, belly, neck, and toes — she had given up on Bright Eyes being found.

And there was more. She was afraid of what Bright Eyes might say. Why so many years had gone by and Elinor had made no effort to look for her? What kind of mother was she? How could she answer these questions?

She let her eyelids flicker to show Louise and Alice she was still alive, to get a glimpse of what they were up to. When she didn't see either of them, she opened her eyes fully and discovered Alice's face within inches of her own.

"What happened?" Alice asked.

"A little too much excitement for the old ticker," Elinor said.

Louise told them what little she knew of Victoria through the letters. She handed the photographs of Victoria to her mother. If it was possible to caress and embrace a photograph, that was what Elinor did as she gazed at Victoria.

Alice devoured the letters.

Elinor was transformed by the news. Her eyes were open wider, her back straighter. She was more talkative and feisty. She said she had things to do. They must go to the valley, clean up her house, plant her garden, frame her drawing of the bison, go through her paintings to see if there were others Victoria might like to have. She wanted Victoria to feel welcome. And to meet Lillian and Mariah, Le Roy, Charlie — the entire family.

"When does she come?" Elinor asked.

"Very soon. A week or so," Louise said. "It's a long drive. And she's getting on."

"Why doesn't she come in a plane?" Elinor asked. "Tell her to take a plane."

"It's all right," Louise said. "I think she wants it this way. It is her choice."

"I need to get out to my house," Elinor said, "tidy things up. She needs to come out there, where I'm comfortable, where I have all the memories."

"Let's wait until she gets here," Alice said.

"I hope she's got a fast driver," Elinor said.

The door to Elinor's bedroom was ajar, the lamp on. Louise listened for a sound — a cough, a moan, the creak of the rocker. Hearing nothing, she pushed open the door. The blankets were thrown back, the pillows at the foot of the bed. Elinor's heavy blue sweater and flowered head scarf were flung over the chair. In the half-light Louise marvelled at what the guest room had become: her mother's valley home squeezed into one room. The space smelled of sweet-grass, tobacco, and the Chinese ointment her mother rubbed on her joints. Her rocker, shawl, and slippers faced the window that over-looked the back garden. On the little pine table, a box of matches, a pair of socks, pencils, a pad of paper, a small pile of stones, and the photograph of Bright Eyes as an infant, now framed.

The chest of drawers was so stuffed that none of the draw-ers closed. The Dickens book was on the corner of the dresser. But where was her mother? It was late. Most nights Elinor was asleep by eight o'clock. Last night, the night Louise had told her of Victoria, Elinor had been up past ten o'clock worrying about what Victoria would want to know about her, how long she would stay, whether there would be enough time to tell her everything Elinor thought she should know.

Louise didn't find her mother in the kitchen with the birds or asleep on the couch. "Not again," Louise muttered. Surely she wasn't trying to get to her house on her own.

Living with her mother the past few months hadn't been all bad. Perhaps they had both changed: her mother a little less abrasive, opinionated; Louise, more ready and able to listen to what her mother had to say. She was surprised when she realized that she had started to look forward to finding her mother in the kitchen or beside the pond in the back garden when she got home from work. And on the days Louise arrived home exhausted and frustrated from a difficult trial, her mother seemed to sense that. She'd put on the kettle, tell Louise to sit down, take her shoes off. She'd present her with a dandelion, a sweet pea in a glass of water. She'd make an herbed tea that tasted like boiled cabbage, and she'd chat, ramble, meander through her life, her experiences from sixty or seventy years ago, or her opinions of what had been going on in the world in the last five years.

Last week Elinor talked about how it pained her when she'd hear about an Indian person living on the street, nothing to eat, nowhere to bathe. She'd ask herself, *How can that be?* When she was young there was food enough for everyone. Because everyone shared what they had and they looked out for each other. She chuckled, remembering all the foods they ate in those days: Rhubarb, wild turnip, and onion. So many berries. Strawberry and raspberry in early summer; chokecherry, pin cherry, and saskatoon berry later on. There were fish, ducks, partridges, and prairie chickens. And there was a time when they ate lots of gophers. They'd cut off the tails, because they got money from the government for them, then they'd hold the little fellow over the fire, singe off his hair, gut him, and fry him up. They were tasty, she said.

Elinor told of the time at the school when a boy fell from a ladder, broke his ankle. The nuns insisted it was only a sprain, no need to get a doctor. The boy spent two weeks in the infirmary. They made him get up after that time. He couldn't stand on that leg; he fell over and broke it some more. Finally, they called the doctor, who said the ankle was broken, in need of a cast. Elinor said in the time she had been at that school, four children had died. One had been sent home because he wasn't learning fast enough. Elinor laughed, said she wished she had thought of that.

Louise found her mother outside, squatting in the middle of the front lawn beside a small, smoky fire. Her arms were curved upward; she was singing in Cree. A clear, warm night, the stars of the Big Dipper overhead. Louise was grateful it was the middle of the night or her neighbours would be calling the fire department. When Elinor tried to stand up, she almost fell over, and Louise ran to her.

"I knew you were there," Elinor said.

"What are you doing?" Louise asked, her arm around Elinor's waist.

Elinor said she was sending a message to Bright Eyes through the stars, in the smoke. "Telling her to take care, asking the Creator to keep her safe."

She said it was a beautiful night but all the street lights made it impossible to see the stars. "What's the point of them?" she asked. "Damned waste. Everybody's asleep, nobody out here cutting their grass, walking their dog, making dinner, so why does the city bother with them?"

Louise supposed her mother had a point. They inched their way across the grass.

"I think she's coming tomorrow," Elinor said. "Not a day too soon."

Elinor told Louise that the last few mornings when she awoke, her head was fuzzy like dandelion puff, her legs were stiff as fence posts, and she couldn't move. She wasn't sure if she was still at Louise's or had passed over. But it wasn't bad; she felt comfortable and warm. Joseph was there smiling at her. Philip was running and laughing, his fat fingers bulging with stones, a clump of sticks. She'd even seen her parents, who had been gone such a long time.

They settled into the white wicker chairs on the porch and soon Elinor was asleep.

Louise had never sat out on her porch at two in the morning. It was pleasant.

Clouds had moved in, occluding some of the stars.

Maybe Victoria was looking up at the same sky.

33

They pulled off the highway into the small half-circle of elm and maple trees, a strange oasis amidst the flat landscape of miles and acres of wild grasses, fields of wheat that ran to the horizon. The solitary picnic table was patrolled by a pair of black birds, necks jutting forward with each step. Squawking their discontent at the new arrivals, they flew off, but not far. A breeze that came and went lessened the blazing heat that had been with them since early in the day.

Victoria, in a white blouse and pale yellow cotton skirt with a motif of pink flowers, was glad for the stop. She found the prairie heat tiring, although, given its dryness and ever-present wind, not as fatiguing as the lingering, humid summers of southern Ontario. She rolled down her window, bringing in the scent of soil and grass, the constant buzz of crickets, the intermittent click of grasshoppers. She took a white handkerchief from a pocket of her skirt, patted the moisture from her forehead, cheeks, and neck.

Gloria, her twenty-four-year-old driver and companion, had been a gem and completely undaunted by Victoria's needs. Some days it seemed they travelled little more than a hundred miles. One day they didn't get farther than the distance between the hotel room and the local hospital. Victoria had had trouble breathing in the night; she couldn't catch her breath. They stayed on an extra day in that place for her to rest.

Either Gloria was a good liar or this wasn't her first trip travelling cross-country with a seventy-five-year-old woman. She said she'd had a great time of it, learning the history of mining in the area while Victoria slept and rested. That's where they'd been stuck: Sudbury. The heart of Canada's nickel-mining industry. Gloria had lunch on the main street in a Chinese restaurant and brought back sweet-and-sour spareribs and stir-fried rice that Victoria had eaten very little of. As long as she could remember, she'd always had a queasy stomach. Bland foods without sauces and spice suited her best.

Gloria dragged the cooler and basket of food and dishes from the car to the picnic table. A short, slight woman with a wiry muscularity to her body, she wore blue cotton shorts and a sleeveless yellow blouse. Her blond hair was pulled back into a ponytail. She'd said little about her deceased twin, but there were patches of time when she was so distant Victoria worried about her. Gloria unfolded the tablecloth, shook it over the table, ran her hands over the cloth to push away the wrinkles. On her way to the water pump, Gloria called to Victoria, still at the car, and asked if she needed help. Victoria waved and said she was all right.

Gloria grasped the end of the long wooden handle of the pump. When the handle barely moved she shifted her position, squatted, and pulled down harder. The pump squeaked, the handle came back up; she hung on and drew it down again. No water. She stood up, pulled down again. Still no water.

She needs to get it going faster, Victoria thought, *that's what draws the water up*. She'd not say anything and wait to see what Gloria was able to figure out. If Gloria was taller she'd get more leverage with the handle. Now she was getting the hang of it, pumping more swiftly, and finally, a trickle of water. With the next downward push a gush came, spilling beyond the pot beneath it, scurrying over the dry soil.

Victoria pushed open the car door, grabbed her cane, and started toward the picnic table.

The green rusted Coleman stove that Victoria had owned forever rattled and shook as Gloria pushed the plunger in and out of the fuel tank, building up the pressure to light the stove, to heat water for Victoria's tea.

Victoria thought she had gotten the better part of the deal, but Gloria seemed happy to be away from the sadness of the past three months — the sudden death of her twin sister in a boating accident. Gloria said she was getting a paid vacation across the country — country she had never seen.

Victoria wondered if Gloria's enthusiasm was left over from all the flag-waving and celebrations of two years ago: 1967, Canada's one hundredth birthday. Victoria regretted she'd not gone to Montreal, taken in Expo, but it was during a time when she'd been unwell. She went there in every other way possible — television, radio, newspapers. A neighbour had gone and Victoria devoured her stories, pored over her photographs of the pavilions from France and Japan, Spain, England, and Morocco, with their sweeping buttresses, shiny silver and gold materials. Buildings with fountains and canals, spires and pagodas. Buildings in the round, like a giant globe.

Halfway to the picnic table, Victoria stopped and looked back to the car and the highway. On a grid road parallel to the highway, some distance away, a truck travelling fast left a plume of dust, a tawny wake six or eight truck-lengths long.

A croaky, singular note from a bird pierced the prairie silence. She located the songster on the fencing across the road. She walked a few feet toward the bird, hoping to get a closer look. Yellow breast, neck extended, the deep note burbled from its throat again.

She'd been thinking of sharing her mother's diary with Elinor.

Perhaps her early jottings, the entries about Victoria as a baby and young girl, would interest Elinor.

It was strange, Victoria thought, to know herself through her mother's notes. As a baby, her mother wrote, Victoria had fed voraciously, as if there might not be another meal. She'd been fascinated by spiders and ants, worms in the garden. She'd watch them for hours, putting stones and twigs in their paths, watching how they overcame the challenges. She'd walked far sooner than other children and was soon climbing onto chairs and tables, jumping from fences. Her mother had written that Victoria loved to be outdoors and cried fiercely whenever she had to come in. A teacher, Victoria's adoptive mother soon had Victoria reading books. Victoria's favourite book, according to her mother's notes, had been *The Jungle Book* by Rudyard Kipling. Victoria adored the monkeys; she'd laugh and hop about like them.

The yellow-breasted bird flew off and Victoria continued to the picnic table. A soft breeze swept over her face; the tablecloth puffed and sighed with the bursts of air. The water in the pot had begun to mumble. Victoria sat down and unwrapped one of the sandwiches: ham with mustard. She had never cared for mustard. She rewrapped the sandwich and opened another. Chicken. She liked chicken and immediately took a bite.

The lid on the pot began to rattle. Where was Gloria? Victoria preferred that Gloria deal with the hot water because Victoria's hands were unsteady. Another minute and the water was sloshing out of the pot, sizzling onto the blue flame. Victoria called Gloria. No answer. She stared at the stove, the circle of blue flame buzzing beneath the pot. She turned the black knob; the flame went out and the water calmed. This was unlike Gloria, not telling Victoria where she had gone, when she would be back. Not that there was anywhere to go around here, only the vast expanse of the plains on every side. She had no idea whether there was a town ten or a hundred miles away. Gloria had taken care of all the navigation, but she did point out the signs to Victoria as they drove along: Wawa, Sudbury, Manitoulin Island, Dryden, Winnipeg. Victoria especially remembered Manitoulin Island because her father, a physician, had worked there one summer when Victoria was four or five. She remembered the sweet taste of the maple sugar the Indians brought to her father as payment for his help. And the haw berry jam her mother made. The red haw berries tasted like overripe apples. Victoria liked the jam better when her mother combined the haw berries with blueberries. They lived near a river, and when her father wasn't working they'd go fishing in the wooden rowboat that she'd helped her father paint green. Almost every time they went out they'd catch something, perch mostly.

Manitoulin Island was the first place Victoria had seen Indians. She'd asked her father who they were and why they looked so sad. Her father took a long time to answer. He said a lot of them were sick, not well. When she asked why that was, he said he didn't know.

The wind was blowing harder now. Beyond the highway and fields, churning slate-grey clouds and dark panels of cloud — rain? — extended to the ground. A paper cup clattered and tumbled end over end across the parking area. They needed to pack up. Where was Gloria? A burst of wind swept Victoria's hair across her face. The waxed paper from her sandwich flew off like a bird. Fingers of wind slipped under the tablecloth, and it billowed up off the table. The trees swayed and swooshed.

Victoria hurried to return the plates and napkins, sandwiches, and raspberries to the basket. She hated to toss the hot water but didn't see what else she could do. She walked to the edge of the picnic site to look beyond the line of trees. She called

Gloria again, asked her to please come. Drops of rain grazed her arms and face. The mass of dark cloud, like an angry monster in a children's book, loomed closer and larger.

She rolled up the tablecloth, tossed the hot water, and closed up the stove. Pushing against the wind as if she was walking uphill, she started for the car. She kept her head down, trying to protect her eyes from the bits of dirt, grass, and leaves that swirled about. She tripped over a clod of earth and almost lost her balance. She dumped the tablecloth and stove onto the back seat, returned for the cooler. It was so heavy and bulky, she had to drag it a few feet at a time. She could feel the wetness across her shoulders, down her arms, specks of rain on her face. The massive cloud bank was almost overhead. As much as she loved the fresh scent of rain, that sense of cleansing that was brought to the hot air and the dry earth, she didn't fancy getting drenched.

She left the cooler and dashed to the car.

It took all her might to get the car door open, so strong had the wind gotten. Within seconds of the door closing, the sky unleashed itself. A torrent rushed over the windows, clattered on the roof like snare drums in a marching band. Not rain. Hail. Tiny white balls bouncing off the car, jumping up from the ground. A blanket of white appeared within a few minutes. Victoria could barely see beyond the hood of the car, but she caught a glimpse of Gloria running, then stopping to pick up the cooler, striding in the downpour.

The trunk of the Chevy banged shut, then Gloria was in the driver's seat, water dripping off her nose, chin, hair, her clothing soaked through.

Victoria fumbled in her purse and passed a handkerchief to Gloria. "Don't think this will help much."

Gloria gasped thanks and pressed her face into the purple pansies embroidered on the white handkerchief. She patted her

260 — *Lynda A. Archer*

arms and neck, said as soon as things let up she'd get a change of clothes out of her suitcase.

"Do you mind me asking where you got to?" Victoria said. "I was worried."

"I'm sorry," Gloria said. "When we pulled in here, I suddenly felt sick."

"You should have said something."

"I know. I don't know what it was, maybe the single picnic table. It looked so alone. Those clumps of wildflowers. The solitary outhouse. Everything single. I thought about Glenna, and the sadness just gushed over me. I had to be alone." She pointed to the left of the picnic table. "If you go through that clump of trees to the other side, there's a road, just a couple of dusty ruts in the middle of the field, I suppose the farmer uses them. I started walking, crying, remembering Glenny, how it had always been the two of us, right from the very start, inside my mother's womb, the two of us. Except when we were born. Glenna led the way; I came out six or eight minutes later. We did everything together. " She laughed. "Like two humps on a camel. Until the middle of high school, we were always together. In the last few years we started to do things separately, but we talked every day. She had her friends, I had mine. But we were still each other's best friend."

She returned Victoria's handkerchief, shoved her hand in the breast pocket of her blouse. "I found this on that dirt road. It's so perfect."

Victoria drew her finger over the mouth cavity, around the tiny orbs that had once been eyes. In its entirety, the skull was about the size of a walnut, perhaps a little bigger.

Glenna had had a fascination with bones; Gloria did not. Glenna said people took bones for granted, but without bones nobody would be walking about. We'd all be slithering around like snakes and salamanders, slugs and worms. Glenna saved chicken, beef, fish, and pork bones. She had been ecstatic the day they'd come upon a cow's skull in a field. She liked to impress upon people that without bones, we'd have no idea what dinosaurs were like.

Victoria had never given any thought to bones. Like most people, she took them for granted. She was sorry for Gloria's distress.

The patter on the car roof had begun to slow; a patch of blue appeared in the dark sky.

Victoria closed her eyes, clasped her hands in her lap. She realized how frightened she'd been about Gloria, how worried she'd been that she'd not get to Elinor.

Gloria put her hand on Victoria's. "We're almost there. Soon you'll see her. Are you excited?"

Victoria smiled. She said she felt like a kid who'd been given a new bicycle. She was excited but also scared. Would she be able to ride it? Would she wreck it? How was one supposed to feel, she said, at meeting the person who has given you life? But you have spent your entire life having had no contact with her. "Sometimes I need to pinch myself that this is happening. Are we really going to get there? Will the car break down? When you disappeared, I worried something had happened to you and I'd be stranded. I'd get there too late. She'd have died."

34

A t the stream's edge, a muskrat, its plump, wet body shiny in the sunlight, scurried along the bank then slithered into the water. From the walking trail that overlooked the stream, Elinor waited on a bench for John. She welcomed the warmth of the mid-morning sun on her shoulders and neck. A child's voice, exuberant and chirpy, drew her attention. The girl, her blond hair in pigtails that stuck out from the side of her head, pedalled a red tricycle. Her mother followed a few feet behind. Elinor smiled. When the two came abreast of Elinor, the girl climbed off her trike and sat beside Elinor. Her mother said, "Emily, don't bother the lady," but Elinor said it was no problem.

Elinor asked Emily how old she was and the girl held up five fingers. Her mother laughed and said she was only three, almost four. Elinor drew her hand over Emily's head, relishing the fine silkiness of her hair.

Emily asked Elinor how old she was. Her mother told her she shouldn't ask such things. Elinor chuckled and said she didn't mind; she often asked herself the same question. She turned to Emily, held up her hands, and opened and closed her fingers several times.

"I'm very, very, very old," Elinor said.

Emily's eyes opened wide; a solemnity came over her face. "Are you going to die soon?"

Emily's mother gasped.

Elinor smiled. "Very soon."

Emily patted Elinor's hand, told her to be careful of the mosquitoes because they made bad bites, then hopped on her trike. Elinor's heart throbbed and her throat tightened. So precious. Children were so precious. She wanted to tell the mother to watch over her child, to keep her close. Elinor urged her body up from the bench and she shuffled along the path. A young couple, holding hands, walking briskly, veered around her.

If asked what her life had become, Elinor would say she lived in a dream state. Sometimes everything was clear, colourful and bold. Other times she was confused and lost. She yearned to wake up, even as she knew that dreams were to be cherished for the wisdom they brought. Like the web of a spider, she was strong yet fragile, able to break apart at any moment.

John came alongside her, said he'd had to go farther than he thought for her Coke and asked where she was going. She told him she was keeping the blood moving through her heart; she feared if she stayed still too long it would thicken and come to a halt. John suggested they walk to the next bench and she could have a swig of her Coke; that would keep her ticker going a little longer.

With Elinor gripping John's arm, they crept along to the next bench. The Coke was cold. She coughed and sputtered as it slipped down her throat, but it gave her a jolt. John told her he'd planted the potatoes and beans; the spinach was up in the cold frame. Elinor said she hated spinach. John said it was good for her. Elinor grunted. She asked him to tell her about his school. John said there wasn't much new to tell. She asked him about the boy who'd sawed off his fingers in shop. What did they do with the fingers? John laughed and said it was a good question. He didn't know what became of the fingers. Shortly after the incident, the family moved to another school and he had to confess he was glad of it. Elinor wanted to say that at least they had the freedom of choosing another school.

"Why do you think Dickens wrote that book? There's that young fellow, Pip, he's an orphan, hardly a penny. He gets involved with these rich folks. And then he gets this inheritance. He acts like he was never poor, wants nothing to do with the people and places he came from. Even the family that was good to him. I don't understand how people can do that." She slapped John on the thigh. "You've never tried to forget where you came from. Not like my daughter. So much of her life spent putting distance between herself and her roots. Not healthy. Where would all the plants be if they gave up their roots?"

"Dead, I expect," John said.

"Exactly. Do you think it's stupid of me, that I keep reading the Dickens book?"

"People read the Bible over and over, don't they? And if you get something from it, what does it matter?"

Elinor nodded. "I suppose. But the Bible's different from a storybook, a novel." She unbuttoned her sweater, stood up, and they continued on the path.

"I wouldn't say this to my students, but they're both stories, aren't they? Stories about people getting themselves into messes — jealousy, fear, greed, love, and lust. Theft and killing, too. And sometimes there is justice and resolution."

"I wonder why I keep reading the thing." She stopped walking, ran her tongue over her lips, then turned to John. "I've felt like an orphan, homeless in a way. Lots of our people feel that way. I guess Pip gives me hope. He strayed a long way away, but he finally came home. That's it. It's the coming home."

When they reached the car, John asked if she had enough energy to go to her house. Without hesitation, she said yes.

As soon as they were out of the city, beneath the canopy of the prairie sky, the flat expanse of the land all around her, she sighed, knowing that was what she had needed. She thought she might weep when the road dipped into the valley, and she saw its tawny, soft flanks, the curve of the dark river at its base. They drove along the valley floor, past the garden centre, the white chip wagon, past black cattle grazing, a couple of abandoned sheds, rusted green and red chunks of farm machinery. They crossed over a bridge of wooden planks that spanned a marsh, then through a village of a few houses, a hotel, bakery, and Co-op store. Another ten minutes and they pulled into her driveway. She'd not been to her house since the incident that had landed her in hospital. It wasn't much, the turquoise cottage with porch across the front, outhouse behind, and garden plot that had been totally taken over by weeds. At least the windows were all intact and it seemed no one had bothered the place.

They strolled through the property, stopping from time to time for Elinor to contemplate the tiny berries that had just set on the saskatoon bush, the rusted shovel that had been left out all winter, a six-inch hole dug near the corner of the house — a badger's work, she suspected. She laughed as she stood outside the fence of the garden area. The fence did nothing to fend off the weeds, which were easily a foot and a half high. She squatted and tugged at a few of them with little success. John asked if she had any seeds in the house. She said she wasn't sure. John continued to pull weeds while Elinor rested in her wicker chair, sucking in the scent of the earth, basking in the sun like a snake on a rock.

"Look at this," John said.

"What is it?"

"Tulips." In the area that he'd cleared of weeds, a couple of tulip plants had sprouted.

"The ones Alice and I planted last fall. Victoria will enjoy those. She's a gardener, it seems. In the photograph, she's holding roses and clippers. Never cared for roses myself. They need too much attention and you can't eat them. And they're not too happy about you cutting them, either, all those thorns."

John suggested they go inside. Elinor told him the spare key was beneath the porch to the left of the top step. She shuffled behind him, the tall grasses and weeds rustling against her skirt and socks.

John pulled open the screen door then wiggled the key into place.

Elinor stepped inside. Alice had taken some of her things to Louise's, so everything was not exactly as she'd left it. Her lumpy navy blue couch with blankets and squishy pillows remained, as did the little pine table covered with magazines, ashtray, arrowheads, and dried tiger lily flowers near the window. She snatched up her box of roll-your-owns. Still six inside, now crisp as late-summer grass. Such a waste. The kitchen counters were covered in mouse droppings. She pulled open a drawer and found a bundle of straw, strips of cloth, shells and husks of seeds and nuts: a mouse's home for the winter months.

John opened windows and propped open the door. He found the broom and swept the kitchen. Elinor chuckled to herself; she had so rarely swept, even when she was living in the house. She wandered down the hall to her bedroom. Alice must have made up the bed, something she, Elinor, rarely did.

She went to her trunk. If something had happened to the trunk, she wouldn't have the photograph, and finding her child might never have gotten off the ground. She thanked the Creator for that. She'd wondered who had slipped the photograph into her little cupboard, the one thing in that whole school, except for her bed, that she thought of as her own. It wasn't, of course.

Everything in that school belonged to the church. Even the children. They were like a bunch of ants living in a colony, crawling over one another. Ants probably had more sense of direction and purpose than any of the children in that school.

She sat on the edge of the bed and sniffled.

Bright Eyes was the only good that came out of that school.

She rolled onto the bed and closed her eyes. The swish, swish of the broom scratching over the floors washed over her. Like the little waves on the lake in the early morning, before the wind got up and set them churning and frothing. She slipped into the dream world, back to the time when she and Swift Eyes were sweeping the floors at the school. In the dream their brooms were huge; they grew larger with each sweep. They swept through doors, walls, and windows, sent stoves, desks, and chairs from their rooms. Lights, frying pans and pots, beds and outhouses went flying. Socks and aprons, sheets and towels, potatoes, onions, and carrots. Nothing was spared. Not even the nuns and priests. They were swept onto the prairies, far into the distance, back, back into another time.

The light was thin. The window in her bedroom was covered by saskatoon berry bushes that had grown as high as her house.

She didn't know how long she slept. She knew she had dreamt but remembered very little of it. She figured it must have been a good dream because she felt happy and rested. She didn't get up. Eventually, John came to check on her and she pointed at her trunk, said she wanted to get into it.

John pushed back the lid. Elinor pulled out sweaters and socks, blankets and hats. When she got to Joseph's old jean jacket with the hawk embroidered on the shoulder and his ochre deerskin vest with panels of red, yellow, and blue beading, she stopped. She clung on to the garments, brought them to her nose. She smiled and chuckled, said she had never had them cleaned and she could still smell Joseph on them. Although she had tossed the other items into a pile on the bed, Joseph's clothes she laid carefully and separately away from the others.

"Is there something in particular you're looking for?"

"Moccasins," Elinor said. "My mother's." She asked John to search; the trunk was too deep for her to reach to the bottom.

John pulled out more blankets and sweaters, pillows, a drum, a pair of snowshoes, and laid them on the bed. "What's this?" he asked, holding up two narrow boards with leather strapping across them.

"*Tihkinâkan.* A cradle board. I carried Louise in that. She hated the thing. Never liked to be tied down." She laughed. "I suppose I should have taken that as a clue."

John kneeled at the trunk and dug down to the bottom. "Are these them?" he asked. He held up a pair of flattened, stiff brown moccasins. The soles were black; only a few beads remained on the uppers. They gave off a distinctly smoky smell. Elinor took them from him, cradled the moccasins in the palms of her hands.

"It's all I have of her. Still Like Stone. That was my mother's name. She was so calm, so steady in all ways. Sometimes I wish I was more like her. She was a healer. Whenever one of the children got hurt, one of the elders was sick, my mother was called to them. Sometimes I'd go with her. People were calmer after my mother had been with them. A few days later, they'd say the pain was gone, they could walk better, their faces had a smile on them."

She turned one of the moccasins over, stroked her finger the length of the black bottom. "Oh my … the stories these slippers could tell, the places they have been. I want these for Victoria so that she can know of her roots." She turned to John. "When will she come? Any news?"

"I expect it will be any day now. As soon as tomorrow, maybe."

Elinor grinned and nodded. "Not any too soon."

35

A plane, loud, low in the sky, passed over the house as Elinor sat in the garden mid morning. The drone of the plane faded, replaced by children's voices, giggling and calling from the neighbour's yard. Such fresh sounds, like the sparkle of rushing water in springtime, like the joy when she first held Bright Eyes. A joy that was soon eclipsed by fear because her mother and aunties were not there to help her. Naively, oh so naively, she'd hoped and believed that Man Face would replace her own mother in that moment when she took the child, said she'd wash and clothe her. And the lies Elinor had been given for hours and days after that. That the birth needed to be registered ... that they must make sure Bright Eyes was healthy ... that they had to bathe her, get all the mucus and blood from her so she could breathe better. On and on it went. When finally Elinor knew her baby was not coming back to her, she didn't know she was able to be so angry.

For the first few days she refused to eat or get out of bed, saying her stomach ached, saying she was sore down there. That worked for a while, and the nuns and teachers let her alone. The young nun even brought her a piece of toffee, trying to entice her to eat, but Elinor refused. She tucked the candy away for another time. At night her friends brought her a hunk of bread, a piece of potato. As soon as the lights went out she'd whisper with them, hoping they had seen the baby, that they'd found out where she had gone.

But there was no news of her child. It was as if Elinor had never given birth.

A couple of her friends were bold. They asked the nuns where Elinor's baby had been taken. The nuns said there had been no baby; they should stop with their stories. Some got the strap, one swat for every time they said the word *baby*. A few weeks after she gave birth, Elinor dreamt of her father. Tall and straight, hair to his shoulders, he was standing at the edge of their camp, the circle of tipis behind him. He was watching a hawk circling and circling, plunging to the ground then rising up with a gopher in its talons. In the dream Elinor was young, four or five years old, she'd not yet been taken to that school. She wept for the gopher hanging limp in the bird's claws. Her father told her it was the way of the world. There were the strong and the not so strong. Even so, the gopher had its own strength. There were many more gophers than hawks, and they were skilled at tunnelling into the earth, hiding away from those who might hunt them.

The morning after the dream, Elinor woke early, before the others. In the dim morning light, she sat on the edge of her bed, looking over that room. Thirty or forty cots, every one the same, each with one pillow, each with one thick black or grey blanket. But no two girls were the same, even though the nuns strived for that. On her right, Mary Kathleen, her long arms flung off the bed, whimpered and jerked; she did that most nights. On Elinor's left, Helen slept curled in a ball, like a dog, at the foot of her bed. When Helen first came to the school she cried herself to sleep every night. The crying stopped when Elinor invited her to come into her bed. Elinor was happy to have Helen in her bed but the nuns soon put a stop to it.

In the autumnal morning air, shivering, Elinor crept over the cold hardwood, trying to step carefully, hoping to avoid the creaky boards, but almost every plank had something to say. The window (one of the many she'd cleaned over the years) overlooked the backyard and the gardens of the school. Of all the work she'd done at that school, and there was lots — ironing clothes, washing toilets and floors, hanging clothes out to dry, peeling potatoes and carrots, cleaning the chicken house — she'd most enjoyed the summer garden work — planting beans, carrots, potatoes, and onions, weeding, and harvesting.

Frost had sprinkled itself over the grass, the sidewalks, the roads. So beautiful, even though it meant winter was soon to follow. A hawk, shoulders hunched, its curled beak larger than she remembered, had perched itself on top of the flagpole. The raptor twisted its head in Elinor's direction. The black, beady eyes gripped her like she imagined its talons held on to a fish. The bird extended its wings, flapped once or twice, and then it was coming right for her as if she was a mouse or a sparrow. At the last second it swerved from the window, but not before grazing a wing on the glass. Elinor gasped and jumped back.

When she crept back to the window she located the hawk on the ground, still yet upright. Its beak was opening and closing as if it was gasping for air. She wanted to go to the bird but the doors to their dormitory were locked, as they were every night. Years later she'd hear of a fire in a residential school. Six children dead from smoke inhalation before the doors were unlocked.

The bird took a couple of steps, ruffled its feathers, preened its wings, then waddled a few more steps. It extended its wings half of the full distance it was capable of, flapped a couple of times, and then took off.

First in her dream and now at the school, Hawk had come to her. That morning she had decided she must be strong, take what she needed to keep herself that way. And she must find her daughter.

The child that a few minutes ago had been giggling in the neighbour's yard was now crying, screaming at the top of her lungs as if she had been hurt. As much as the sound pained her, Elinor had always marvelled at the strength in a child's crying, the ability to let it out, to flaunt it if need be, to ensure that she was not ignored. So many years she, Elinor, had spent holding in her hurt and tears. That's what they all learned to do at that school.

One sound she had never learned to abide at that school was the ringing of the bell.

Clang, clang, clang.

Clangclangclangclangclangclangclang.

Every event in the school started and ended with the clatter of the metal bell. Mornings were the worst. On and on until her head hurt; she cursed those of her classmates who were slow to get out of their beds, those who resisted, and even those who were ill. The priest stood next to their beds. *Clangclangclang.* Elinor wanted to smash the bell over the priest's head, break the thing into a hundred pieces.

One day one of her classmates managed to remove the clanger from inside the bell. Oh, the look on the priest's face when no sound came from the thing. He had shaken it again, but still nothing. At first her friends tried not to laugh. They stuck fingers in their ears, pretending the bell was still ringing. Giggling and tittering rippled through the room. The priest, the short, fat one, was furious, but he didn't let go. He never let loose. He made up for it with his cruel patience. She thought he was the worst of the lot. The tall, ugly priest with the crooked nose shouted and clapped his hands, slapped the nearest child or pinched his ears, then stomped away. No breakfast, or lunch, or trips to the bathroom, the fat priest said, until the person who removed the clanger had returned it to him. He sat on the edge of the nearest cot and asked all the children to kneel by their beds while they prayed.

He prayed aloud. In English, French, Latin. He asked forgiveness for the sinner in their midst. One of the youngest, Elinor noticed, had peed, a puddle growing between her feet and legs. Bells were ringing in the other rooms; the voices of boys and older girls in the halls. They were going to breakfast.

Elinor's stomach grumbled. She heard other stomachs churning. Still no one came forward. She had no idea who had done this. Usually it was the kind of thing the boys did, not the girls. And maybe it was one of the boys. Frank. Samuel. Jacob. Those three always seemed to get into trouble. Frank ran away often. Samuel started fires in the garage, in the woodshed. Jacob bit and kicked anybody who stood too close to him, took too much food, and sang too loudly in church on Sundays.

When she heard the next bells she knew breakfast was over. Time for chores. And still the priest, head bowed, hands clasped together, kept praying. She didn't know why she did it. She kept wondering how it would end. How could the father be stopped? And the next thing she knew, she was standing up. She was saying the words. "Father, I took the clanger."

The priest continued to pray. In English, French, and Latin. Just as she was thinking she would repeat herself, the priest stood up. He adjusted his collar, wiped the wrinkles from his apron. As he walked toward Elinor, another girl stood up and said no, she was the one who had done it. Another girl stood up and claimed it was her doing. Then another. Soon ten or twelve girls were standing by their beds, all in nightgowns, claiming to have stolen the clanger.

The priest's neck was apple red, his cheeks were throbbing. He told everyone to line up. Then he told them to hold out their hands. Four times he went down the line, three strikes of the strap to each hand of each child.

Elinor struck a match and brought the flame to the bowl of herbs. Languorously, the smoke curled upward. Elinor cupped the smoke over her head and down her body. She nodded toward the east, west, north, and south. She thanked the Creator for Victoria's safe passage and for her own journey through the last night. She sucked in the sweet scent and leaned back in her chair.

Fingers caressing her palms, Elinor strolled toward the pond. She eased her body onto the bench. She untied her laces, pulled off her shoes and socks. She stared at her stubby toes, wiggled and stretched them. She was missing the baby toe on her right foot; it had never been there. The soles of her feet were more tender now than in the days when she ran everywhere barefoot. At least she didn't have bunions like Louise.

She curled her toes into the dry, scratchy soil, rubbed the bottoms of her feet against each other. Soon her feet would be able to rest.

36

Elinor inched herself to the edge of the rocker. Her arms shook and trembled so badly when she tried to stand up that she decided to wait for Louise. Louise returned with towels and soap, a basin of warm water. She spread a towel on the bed. She slipped her arms behind her mother's back and pulled her from the rocker.

"What is going on with that business in the east of the city?" Elinor asked as Louise pulled the nightgown over her head.

"Which business?"

"That ... that business about building an amusement park on a burial site of our ancestors."

"It's stalled. It's not certain it's a burial site. But some Indians are digging in their heels until we know for sure."

Elinor grunted. "Good. That's as it should be. We need more people like that. People doing what Piapot and Poundmaker did a hundred years ago. They understood the lies, the injustices that were being heaped on our people."

Louise squeezed the washcloth into the water, lathered it with lemon-scented soap. She worked the washcloth around the fingers of Elinor's left hand, over her wrist, and up to her shoulder.

"I met him once," Elinor said.

"Who's that?"

"Piapot. He was a wily and fearless one. Even though he was short, he seemed tall."

Piapot, Elinor said, tried to interfere with Macdonald's plan to build a railway across the south of the province, through Indian hunting lands. He got braves to pitch tents in the railway's path. He wasn't in a hurry to sign Treaty Four. He wanted to wait until there was a better deal on the table. He finally had to give in because so many Indians were starving and the government had promised to give them food if they signed.

"Did you tell your children about those days?" Elinor asked.

"Probably not as much as you think I should have."

Elinor swatted at Louise's hand. She grabbed the washcloth and threw it across the room. She almost threw the basin of water at her daughter, but didn't want to risk her own things getting wet.

"You get me so mad," Elinor said. "Who do you think is going to look out for our people if we don't? Do you think governments and whites will do it?" Elinor pointed at the towel, told Louise to give it to her and to get out of the room.

"I'm not leaving," Louise said. "You've had your outburst and in another minute you'll be exhausted and falling over."

Elinor grunted, pressed her arms to her sides and shoved out her bottom lip.

"You're being stubborn," Louise said.

"And you're not?"

Louise said she'd bought Elinor a new blouse, skirt, and sweater; she asked if Elinor wanted to see them.

"You're trying to bribe me now?"

"No. Do you want to see them?"

"I'll take a look."

Louise took the basin of water, washcloth, and towel and left the room.

Elinor draped her gown over her shoulders. It was stupid arguing with Louise. Even though she was her mother, she did not understand her. There was something about Louise that she had never been able to put her finger on. And now she was running out of time to do that. She stretched out her legs. So many bruises. She ran her finger along the length of the long scar on her right calf and sighed. So many scars. Louise had scars, too; hers were on the inside.

"Here they are," Louise said. "What do you think?" She held up a pale yellow long-sleeved blouse, a navy blue skirt, and a black-and-blue sweater with purple and yellow flowers down the front panels.

Elinor stared at Louise, the clothes draped over her arms, the cautious smile on her face. For a fleeting moment she saw a young girl, ten years old, trying to please her mother. But she was hidden behind the clothing. That was it. She was hiding. Elinor's vision blurred. Her body was shaking inside. Louise had been hiding something all her life. That was the reason for her rigidity and stiffness, like the shell of a turtle. Elinor swallowed hard; she didn't want Louise to see her crying. How could she, Elinor, her mother, have not understood that? All this time pining after Bright Eyes, when it was the daughter standing in front of her who most needed her help.

Elinor smiled and said the clothes were lovely. She slid from the bed, rested her hand on Louise's shoulder, and stepped into the skirt. Louise drew the blouse around Elinor, did up the buttons, and stepped back to look at her mother. Elinor rubbed her hands over the soft fabric of the shirt, then down the folds of the skirt.

"They're lovely. You can bury me in them."

"Don't say that."

"I've been thinking these past few minutes," Elinor said. "I hate that it has taken me so long to see it. Yes, we need to protect the graves of our ancestors. Even more important, we must care for the living." She patted her daughter's cheek. "You're afraid of something, Louise. I think you've been afraid for most of your life." Elinor shuffled to her rocker while Louise fluffed the pillows on the bed, wiped crumbs from the sheets.

"Everybody has things they're afraid of," Louise said. She was bent over Elinor's bed, pulling the blanket over the pillows.

"Yes, but your fear is different from that of most people."

Louise turned to Elinor. "I have no idea what you're talking about."

Elinor fingered the buttons on her new sweater. She didn't believe her daughter. Lawyers were trained in bluffing. After a while they didn't even know they were doing it.

"It's a lovely sweater," she said.

As Louise closed the fridge door, one of the eggs slipped from her grasp and splattered onto the floor. Bright yellow goop flecked with brown shell. She cursed the slithery resistance of the egg white as she tried to wipe it up. She was irritated; she hated when her mother thought she knew Louise better than Louise knew herself. Of course she was fearful and worried, more so in the past few days. Who wouldn't be? She feared Elinor would die before Victoria arrived. Or that Victoria might have a heart attack en route and never get to Saskatchewan. And she had doubts that Victoria was who she claimed to be. She knew too well from her work how slippery and deceptive people could be. How they could prey on those who were weakened, those with deep and grave yearnings.

There were always fears brought on by her work. Certain judges were scarier than others, the ones who thought women should be in the kitchen, not the courtroom. They tried to hide their sentiments, but they leaked out in little ways — a scowl, a turning away, a comment about her attire (never anything said about what her male colleagues were wearing). But she knew these were not the fears her mother was thinking of.

Her mother sensed Louise's other fear, the one she'd lived with most of her life. Like a cowlick, a limp, a stammer, much of the time she barely noticed the thing. So deeply buried was that fear, she sometimes wondered if the event that spawned it had occurred at all.

Elinor chuckled. "I don't think Victoria will care whether or not the floors are clean."

Louise, squatting on the floor, wrestling with the egg white, said she wasn't doing it for Victoria. She kept her eyes on the floor when she asked her mother what fear she had been speaking of.

"Not for me to say. Just a sense I have. Whatever it is, you've done well with hiding it all your life."

Louise dropped bread into the toaster, took the egg from the hot water. She tapped the shell of the egg with a knife, scraped the blade through to the other side and scooped out the contents. She placed the bowl in front of her mother, along with butter, salt, and pepper.

Elinor dropped a large gob of butter on the egg, sprinkled it vigorously with salt and pepper. She chased bits of egg around in the bowl and seemed prepared to do it for some time until Louise gave her a spoon instead of the fork.

Elinor ate slowly, eyes closed as she chewed. She nibbled at the end of a strip of bacon. For a time, head drooped to her chest, she ate nothing.

"Don't you want to be free of it? Don't you want me to go to my grave in peace?" Elinor asked. She stuck out her tongue, grabbed the chunk of bacon off of it, and wiped it on the plate.

She's not going to let go of this one, Louise thought.

"How's that friend of yours?" Elinor asked. "What's her name? That one who worked in the café with you?"

"Mary? You mean Mary."

"Yes."

"Not so good."

"Sorry to hear that."

Louise flipped through the pages of a recipe book.

"I'll bet *she* knows what you're scared of."

Louise wanted to shout at her mother to let it go. She didn't see how telling her mother the secret she and Mary shared, had shared for forty years, would send Elinor to her grave in peace.

Louise turned to her mother. "I'm sorry I left you," Louise said. "I shouldn't have done that."

Elinor shrugged her shoulders. "That's in the past. As much as I have yearned to meet Victoria, I can see that what is most important before I die is for you to be free of what you have been hiding for so long. Why do you not want to tell it to me? If Mary knows, why can't your own mother know?"

Louise stared at the mixing bowl and the cup of white flour that she was readying to spill into the bowl. So pure and fine. So simple. She yearned for simplicity. She dumped the flour into the bowl and turned to her mother.

"You may be right about this. I do want to honour your request. Except it's not a nice thing. It's a horrid thing. Nothing to be proud of. However much time you have left, I want it to be good — happy and easy. Let me give you that. So much time has been lost, wasted, between us. I see that now."

Elinor extended her fingers, picked at the nail of her left thumb, then looked into her palms for a long time.

"You're forgetting who I am, Rose Louise. I have survived residential school, the theft of my first-born, the loss of babies, the murder of my husband. It doesn't get much worse than that." She pushed her chair from the table and her body swayed as she attempted to move from sitting to standing.

Louise rushed to her side.

"After Victoria leaves, you will tell me. I want that for you. And I'm still your mother."

Louise slipped an arm under her mother's. "I'll think about it."

Elinor slapped Louise's hand. "No. You will plan how and when you are going to tell me. And you'll hope I don't die before you get to it."

They shuffled from the kitchen to Louise's study, where Louise had set up a cot for her mother.

Louise drew a blanket over her mother, tucked it beneath her legs, over her shoulders.

"Maybe when I wake up she'll be here," Elinor said.

"Let's hope," Louise said. Mostly, she hoped her mother would wake up from this sleep. "She did say she was trying for today."

Louise grabbed the foot-high weed at its base and tugged. With one yank, the plant's six-inch white root let go. She pulled a couple of others of the same kind, tossed them onto the pile. The weeds whose foliage spread flat to the earth rather than standing upright were less co-operative. She wiggled her fingers under the crown of the plant to find something to grab on to. She yanked hard, then harder. The head of the plant tore away but the weed stayed rooted amongst the red and purple zinnia plants.

She stood up to straighten the stiffness in her knees and back. Weeds were like humans. Some were agreeable and easily extracted. Others, prickly and thorny, were entrenched and stubborn. Like her mother.

That was unfair. *Tenacious* was a better word to describe her mother. Even so, she could not see what was to be gained by telling her mother what she and Mary had done. It was so long ago. Did it matter anymore? She rarely even thought of it. But when she did … when she did she was immediately agitated and worked hard to expel the thoughts from her head.

As much as she hated to admit it, her mother was right. What if she, Louise, as a mother, suspected one of her children had a secret, something that needed telling? Would she encourage Andrew or Catherine, Alice to tell her? Of her three children, she thought Alice was most likely to be the one with something to hide.

She pushed the shovel into the earth, leaned back, and uprooted the weed. This weed, unlike the others that came out so easily, had a multitude of shorter roots. She swatted the weed against the shovel, shook the clumps of earth from it, and dropped it on the pile.

She didn't hear the car pull into the driveway. Her thoughts had moved on from weeds to a client who was proving difficult, refusing to accept her counsel about being more conciliatory in his divorce proceedings or risk losing much more. Nor did she hear the car doors close. Or the few words exchanged between the two women. Some moneyed men could be so stubborn. Rarely did it serve them well. She shifted her position and, at last, saw the two women moving toward the house.

She didn't choose or will it, but her mind seemed to switch into slow motion as she watched Victoria drift toward the house — a tall woman taking short steps. Each step a decade in her life. Each step a distance of two, three, five hundred miles. Stately and elegant, there was softness in Victoria's face. If Louise had been closer, she'd have seen brightness in Victoria's eyes, even as the fatigue in her body was palpable.

Victoria was swaying, her knees giving way. Gloria leapt forward. Louise rushed to the two of them.

"Oh my," Victoria said. "I was so excited. I got out of the car too quickly." She sucked in a breath, looked directly at Louise. "And you must be Louise."

She settled herself, with Gloria's help, onto the front steps. She stretched out her legs, leaned back on her hands, and sighed. She told Louise she had fallen in love with the prairie, the golden flatness of the land, the enormity of the sky. She laughed and spoke of how she had been entertained by the gophers, the way they darted and scurried, tails wagging, into their holes, how they sat on their haunches surveying their world like little generals.

"Mother will not want to miss another word," Louise said. "Let me tell her you're here. She's having a nap."

"Don't wake her," Victoria said.

"She'd never forgive me if I didn't," Louise said. "Come on into the house whenever you're ready."

Louise paused at the door of her study.

A fan of sunlight spilled over Elinor. Hands clasped on her chest, ankles crossed, she looked peaceful. Elinor said she liked the blouse Louise had bought for her, but Louise could now see it was too big around her neck, too long in the sleeves.

Elinor didn't stir as Louise moved over the carpet toward her. She knelt beside Elinor, squeezed her arm, and whispered, "Mother, Mother." Elinor didn't stir. Louise spoke louder. "She's here. Victoria is here."

"Why didn't you tell me that at the start?" Elinor said, lifting her head, bending her knees. "That was the only thing that was going to wake me." She stretched out her arms; Louise pulled her up to a sitting position.

"How is she? How does she look? Is she all right?"

"She's tired, but she seems fine. She's anxious to meet you."

An onlooker might have remarked that she'd never seen Elinor smile so widely. But it was short-lived. Suddenly, Elinor rolled away from Louise, curled into a fetal position, and pulled the blanket over her head.

Louise hesitated. In these kinds of situations, it never worked to try to convince her mother of something.

"I'll come back in a few minutes. I'll get Victoria settled."

Elinor flung the blanket from her head and rolled onto her back. There were tears in her eyes. "I'm scared. What if it isn't her? What if she doesn't like me?" She patted her hair, asked if she needed to comb it. "Help me up," she said.

Louise settled her mother on the couch in the living room, draped a blanket over her legs. She sat beside her, asked if she needed anything. Elinor grasped Louise's hand. "Thank you for all that you've done. I am happier than a hen with young chicks." Then her eyes narrowed and sternness flashed over her face. "And I will be even happier when you trust me enough to share your burden."

Louise patted her mother's arm, told her she was thinking about it. As she leaned forward to stand up, Elinor grabbed her arm. "Did you tell Victoria about her father?"

"No."

"Good." Elinor clasped her hands together. "We'll tackle that gopher when we get to him." She waved her hands at Louise. "Go. Go."

Gloria, seated on the steps next to Victoria, was pointing at something in the sky. Louise wished John was home. He'd know better than Louise how to make Victoria comfortable. If it didn't go well … She shoved that thought from her mind.

She opened the door, stepped onto the porch. Victoria and Gloria turned to her.

"She's bursting to meet you," Louise said.

"That makes two of us." Victoria glanced at Gloria. "Will she mind if Gloria stays for a bit?"

"Not at all," Louise said. She held open the door.

Her mother wouldn't have wanted it, but Louise wished she'd taken pictures, pictures of the first few seconds. It had been months since Louise had seen such joy, such rapture in her mother. It was the kind of thing poets wrote about. Louise was no poet, but she imagined ... a toddler's delight with her first steps ... a six-year-old's joy achieving independence on his bicycle ... crocuses, fuzzy and tender, opening to a spring sun ... a mother exhausted from labour, cradling her newborn ... John's pleasure at the first rose to bloom in June.

Elinor insisted Victoria sit next to her on the couch.

For a full moment, Elinor did nothing but look at Victoria. "Do you mind?" she asked. "Can I touch you?"

Victoria, eyes moist, whispered yes.

With the faintest touch from her fingertips, Elinor slid her hands down Victoria's cheeks, then up again. She squeezed Victoria's shoulders and arms, fingers. She placed both hands on top of Victoria's head, where she remained for a long time while she hummed a tune that Louise did not recognize.

Finally, Elinor squeezed Victoria's hands and said *tatawaw*. Welcome.

"Thank you," Victoria said.

"Pardon me for all the touching," Elinor said. "It is the first thing that mothers do with their babies, isn't it? Stroke them, nurse them, count their fingers and toes, rub their backs, squeeze their arms, wipe their bottoms." She laughed. "Don't worry, I'm not planning to do all that."

Elinor shoved her hand in her pocket and pulled out a black-and-white photograph. Three corners were curling, the fourth was gone. "This was you," she said, "hours after you came into the world. It is a miracle that we are finally back together. We must chatter fast now, like a couple of squirrels, because my time is coming to an end."

Elinor asked Victoria to tell her everything; she was thirsting to know it all. Victoria said she didn't know where to start.

Elinor patted her hand and said it was like visiting a new country. Everything was new; everything was interesting.

Victoria said when she saw Elinor's picture on television, she didn't make much of it at first. She'd come home from a neighbour's; they'd been playing bridge. The house was cold. She'd cranked up the heat, wrapped herself in a blanket, and sat down with a cup of tea to watch a show about the Badlands in Alberta. The news ran again. And there was Elinor's picture again. Seeing it the second time, she had a jolt. Something about the eyes, the cheeks. But it was so fast. She hurried to make dinner, watching the news report three more times, studying the photograph, waiting with pencil in hand to write down the phone number.

"Did you win at your bridge game?" Elinor asked.

"I don't remember. I'm not very good at it, so probably not."

"I've always enjoyed bingo. Do you play?"

"When I was a child, my mother took me every week to the bingo nights at the church. I won a box of popcorn once. What about you? Did you ever win anything?"

Elinor smiled. "Lots of things, most of them pretty useless — a pair of skates, a couple of lamps, some cushions, six cans of jam — all orange marmalade, which I hate. Once I won a radio, a cheap thing, but funny, it still works. Probably it's playing right now in my little cottage."

Victoria laughed, said she loved radio, more than television. But if it hadn't been for television, she might not have found Elinor.

While Louise longed to stay, she left the two women alone. Gloria went sightseeing.

The time drifted by. Louise swept the kitchen floor, cleaned out the birds' cage, dusted the windowsills, collected the mail. She filled the kettle with water, took cups from the cupboard. She tried not to hover, even as her curiosity was chomping at the bit. She caught snatches of conversation: Her mother telling Victoria about the Qu'Appelle Valley where she was born. Victoria speaking about her son, her husband's work with the bank, her childhood spent on Manitoulin Island. Victoria laughed, and Louise enjoyed the robustness of the sound. It was harder to hear what Elinor was saying; her voice had grown weaker.

Louise poured the boiling water and covered the pot with a tea cozy. She rummaged into the back of a cupboard and found a wooden platter to hold plates, napkins, and spoons, cream and sugar. Standing at the kitchen window, waiting for the tea to steep, she watched a sparrow flit about, then a robin jab its beak into the grass and extract an earthworm. This never ceased to amaze her — that something as hidden as an earthworm could be found by a robin.

John had been the robin in Louise's life, ferreting out the guilt and shame, her lies. She'd lied to him at first, saying she was orphaned, her parents dead from influenza. Over time John caught the inconsistencies in her story, small things that he kept track of. One time she told him the orphanage was in Regina, another time in Saskatoon. Once she said she was adopted at eight, another time at eleven. He wondered why she never wanted to see her adoptive parents. After she told him where she had come from, who her parents were, she expected he'd be gone the next day. For years she wondered what he saw in her, and she expected he'd leave one day. She kept her worries from him, worries about her mother and father, cousins and aunts on the reserve. And she refused to tell him about the remarks by lawyer colleagues: their challenges that an Indian couldn't know anything about white people's justice; the taunting questions about why she wasn't on the reserve breeding more dark-skinned babies. More than once she'd been propositioned by senior lawyers wanting her to show them how an Indian had sex, promising her quicker advancement if she complied.

She remembered the moment she started to think differently. It was the day after a judge had propositioned her, promising to rule in her favour if she did as he asked. She and John had gone to the park with Catherine, who was almost a year old and beginning to walk. Catherine had thick, dark hair, round brown eyes, sturdy legs. She was always smiling. It was 1935, another year of crop failures for the farmers. The city was full of transients, hungry and dirty, hoping for work. As they walked, they passed a young couple with two children, four or five years of age. Everything about the family was grey — their clothing, their skin, the looks on their faces. The thin arms and legs of the children, the scabs on their faces, sickened Louise. She picked up Catherine just as the man stepped forward and asked John if he could spare some change. John, always the kind one, shoved his hand in his pocket and pulled out a couple of nickels. The man thanked John, then reached over and shook Catherine's hand, said she was lucky to have the parents that she did, parents who seemed to be doing okay for themselves even when others couldn't buy nice clothes for their kids, only had enough food for one meal a day. Louise squeezed Catherine closer; she wanted to get going but the man was standing right in front of them, blocking their way. He tugged at Catherine's dress, said he wished his daughter had something just as nice. Then he turned to John, as if Louise wasn't there. "Indian, ain't she? Don't seem fair that she's all dolled up and my wife ain't."

Without a drop of anger in his voice, John said, "She's a human being just like you and me. Sorry that things have been hard for you." He shoved his hand in his pocket again, slapped a coin in the man's hand and suggested he buy his kids an ice cream. "Now, if you'll excuse us."

When they were well away from the man, Louise said she was tired of being told she was Indian, as if she didn't know it, had to be constantly reminded. Indians didn't go up to white people and ask if they were white. And then she told him about the judge. John was furious, said the man should be made to step down.

They stopped at the pond. Catherine grabbed handfuls of sand and threw them in the water.

"Does it get to you?" John asked. "This being asked ... *told* that you're Indian?"

"Of course," Louise said. "Every day. I feel like an imposter. Like I'm living in someone else's world. Like I don't belong here; I should go back to the reserve, be with my people. Make some more of those dark-skinned babies, so eventually there will be enough of us to rise up and send you all back to where you came from."

John squeezed her hand, drew her toward him. "Every time something like that thing with the judge happens, I want you to tell me. So I can tell you it's not right, that you are a human being deserving the same rights as everyone else."

"I'll try," Louise said.

"I don't want you to just try. I want you to do it. You know why?"

"Not really."

"Because I want our children to be able to go anywhere and be proud of their mother. But they won't carry that pride if you don't show it to them first."

Elinor and Victoria were holding hands when Louise brought out the sandwiches. Elinor was in the middle of telling her about the time she and Joseph had taken the train through the Rocky Mountains, how Joseph had charmed a bear when a group had gotten off the train to take a hike. Five minutes into the hike, a bear appeared on the trail. Joseph told everyone to turn around slowly and go back to the train; he'd distract the bear. Elinor said she was so worried; he was always doing something like that, rescuing animals, people in trouble.

"Got him killed in the end. I went with the others; there were ten or twelve of us. We got back to the train. Twenty minutes later Joseph wasn't back, and the train was ready to depart. We waited another hour."

Elinor sucked in a deep breath, leaned back on the couch for a moment then sat up again. She said she was sure the bear had dragged Joseph off. Or that he'd come running out of the woods covered in blood, the bear at his heels. Another fifteen minutes went by. The engineer came; he had a shotgun. She didn't want the bear to get killed and she was getting mad at Joseph for taking him on. Just as the guy was shoving bullets into the gun, Joseph came strolling down the path, calm as could be, grinning.

He was in his glory, Elinor said, for the rest of the trip, spinning this long yarn about how he sat down on the path, hung his head, and waited for the bear to leave. The bear came up to him, sniffed his face and neck, arms, then he sat down next to Joseph. He smacked his lips and Joseph thought he was going to be lunch. Then the bear sprawled out and went to sleep. Joseph didn't want to move in case he startled the bear; for sure, he would attack. So Joseph waited. He thanked the Creator for bringing the bear to him; he asked the Creator to give each of them safe passage through this predicament. And he didn't move until the bear woke.

"Was Joseph my father?" Victoria asked.

"I wish he had been," Elinor said. "I'm sorry to tell you that your father was not a nice man. I don't like talking about him."

"Of course," Victoria said. "But you do know who he is?"

"In some sense," Elinor said. "And he has long since left this Earth. That's a conversation for another time."

Elinor waved her hands, said Victoria and Louise were sisters and they should talk for a time; she'd listen.

Louise showed Victoria photographs of Alice, Andrew, and Catherine, and Catherine's daughter, Mariah. Alice, she said, was keen to meet Victoria; the others lived out of town. Victoria showed her pictures of her parents, her house and garden, her son, Robert, a slight, tall man who appeared to be a few years older than Louise.

Elinor kept her eyes closed. She didn't look at the pictures of Victoria's son or house, but she did ask to see the photograph of Victoria's parents. Victoria's father, in suit, vest, and tie, stood behind Victoria's mother, who was seated on a chair; she wore a dark suit and white shirt and was holding a single rose.

"What were their names?" Elinor asked.

"Jack and Kathleen."

Elinor grunted. "Did they love you well enough?"

"Yes. Yes, I believe they did," Victoria said.

"Louise," Elinor said.

"Yes, Mother."

"When I'm gone, you must tell Victoria everything, to know who her family is, where she came from."

Another time Elinor would have told Louise to stop fussing around her — folding her clothes, fluffing the pillow, asking if she needed a drink — but she was too tired even to bring her lips together, shift the position of her tongue. But the fatigue was only part of it; she didn't want to dispel the good mood between the two of them. It had been her plan to let herself sink away after meeting Victoria, tell Joseph she was coming. Now she had to hold on just a little longer. She had to bring this daughter, the one tucking the blanket around her shoulders, in from the wilderness of her fear and shame.

Joseph would wait. He'd understand.

37

Stones and gravel, dry grass and weeds crunching beneath their feet, Louise and Mary strolled along the grid road for a quarter of a mile. The mustard crop on their right was a swath of bright yellow; the wheat on their left a buff gold. Mary said she loved the smell of a truckload of wheat kernels. She'd had a friend once who worked in a grain elevator. A dusty place, bad for his lungs, but the scent of the grain was intoxicating. At the end of the workday, he took the scent home with him, on his overalls and shirt, in his hair, inside his belly button.

Where the crops ended and the prairie began, they passed a small, weathered storage building that leaned so far to one side Louise imagined that the next deer or steer that rubbed against it would send the thing to the ground. They hooked onto a narrow trail that had seen more hooves than shoes. Mary had been keen to go walking when Louise suggested it, although they both knew she might not get far. Mary said she'd be tired, but it would be a good tiredness, not the dull lethargy of sitting around her house.

"She came," Louise said.

"Your mother was super happy, yes?"

"Over the moon."

The trail, now inclining upward gradually, passed through a clump of chokecherry and silver-bush shrubs. They walked in single file, Mary first, her pace slowing. Another twenty steps and she stopped to suck in a deep breath. Then she was hacking so hard and for so long Louise expected to see blood. Louise asked if they needed to go back, should she get the car, but Mary was quick to shake her head and croak out a no. She wiped the wet from her eyes, took a long swallow of water. She said she was curious how it had been for Louise to meet the woman who was supposedly her half-sister.

"It's an odd thing," Louise said. "I remind myself that we both started in the same place, came from the same womb. I want to have warm feelings, I think I should, but I've had nothing to create those feelings. I'm not like Mom. I haven't spent my life yearning to meet this person who had been taken from me."

"Did you like her?" Mary asked.

Louise kicked at a stone, sent it skittering over the ground. "I didn't *not* like her. She wasn't rude or demanding. She was interested in hearing about her mother's life, where she had come from. But it was always in the back of my mind how she had come to be. What my mother had endured."

"That needn't make Victoria any less lovable. It wasn't her fault. She didn't ask for it."

"True. It seems she had a far easier life than my mother, father, LeRoy, me … you."

"How so?"

"She lived in the white world. Very separate from the Indian world."

"You make it sound so simple. White is good; Indian is harsh and dirty."

"Have you been living under a rock? It's a fact. If you could choose to be white or Indian in this country, which would you rather be?"

"Do you really want me to answer that?" Mary said. "I was mostly interested in your mother. She can die in peace now."

Almost, Louise said to herself. She'd been working up to talking to Mary about the past, what the two of them had done.

They came out of the clump of shrubs, pushed on a little farther until they were near the top of the rise. Mary stopped again and crouched down. Louise suggested they go back. Mary said they were almost there and that this might be the last time she'd get to the valley. She said she wanted to feel the wind on her face one more time. She hummed a song Louise knew and hadn't heard in years.

"Down in the valley, the valley so low, hang your head over, hear the wind blow ..."

They strolled the final distance. A memory fragment slipped into Louise's awareness — dry summer heat, flies buzzing, swallows darting, she and her brothers and father at the lake. Le Roy was always scared to swim, but Louise and Charlie rushed in. Her father would dive underwater, pinch their toes, and ask them if they had all ten; the fish were hungry that day.

Mary took hold of Louise's hand as they drew close to the viewpoint.

"You've been a good friend," Mary said.

"No better than you have been to me," Louise said, squeezing Mary's hand, gently, careful not to put too much pressure on her lumpy, arthritic knuckles.

"She wants to know about it, Mary. She says she'll not die in peace unless she knows that I am free of it." Louise wished it was that simple. Even with telling her mother, she would never be free of it.

"Of course she does," Mary said.

Carved by ice-age erosion, the gentle slopes, curves, and coulees of the valley walls gave no suggestion of its harsh genesis. At the valley floor, a serpentine stream; overhead, an endless sky. In both directions they could see for miles. It was every bit as breathtaking as the snow-capped mountains of the Rockies.

And the wind blew.

Mary turned her head into it, angling it upward like a dog lifting its snout to a scent. She stayed still for a long time in that one place, allowing the long curves of the valley walls, the breeze, the wafts of grass scents and dry soil to curl around her, to work their magic.

"It's up to you," Mary said. "I don't think I'd want to deny my mother her last wish. But then, I never knew what my mother's last wish was."

Mary turned from the valley.

Louise thought her friend looked younger, her stride longer and stronger, as they started back.

38

The meeting room of the Indian Friendship Centre, a place that Louise had never been, was three-quarters full, possibly forty or fifty people staring at the five-by-five cards filled with rows of numbers. Most people were dark-skinned, black-haired, Indian, but there were a few with lighter skin and hair. Louise had one card, but her mother, a look of great concentration on her face, was playing four. Elinor said in her heyday she'd played eight or ten cards; most times she played, she won.

The caller rotated the drum full of numbered white balls.

"Under the *O*, sixty-five."

"Under the *B*, thirteen."

"Under the *B*, seven."

Louise could not understand the appeal of bingo. It wasn't like poker, bridge, or horseracing, all of which involved a little skill, some logical reasoning and knowledge. Bingo was simple, a child could play it. In fact, Catherine, Andrew, and Alice had loved the game. For a time, the whole family played on Saturday afternoons during the winter. Maybe that was the point of the game, its simplicity. And the camaraderie. The players against the caller and his numbered balls. Elinor had already struck up a conversation with the woman sitting next to her.

Louise placed a token over the number seven, then put tokens on numbers twenty-three and fifty-six as they were called. Elinor glanced at Louise's card and told her she needed just one more and she would be a winner. One of Elinor's cards also needed just one more number for her to win.

Two more numbers were called and a man across the room shouted "Bingo!"

A hush of disappointment swept over the room.

"Damn," Elinor said. But when she saw the prize — a plastic pink flamingo — she decided it was better that she hadn't won.

Elinor spilled the red plastic tokens from her cards back into the container, placed a token in the free space in the centre of each card, and waited for the next game to begin. She waved at an overweight grey-haired man with a black patch over one eye sitting across the room.

"That's Jerry," she said. "Haven't seen him in a long time, but then, I haven't been to bingo in a long time."

"Under the *I*, twenty-six."

"Under the *B*, twelve."

"I think you'll be a winner this time," Elinor whispered to Louise.

"How can you tell?"

"I've made a study of it. After hundreds of bingo games, I've noticed that if you start a game and the first two numbers are under letters that are beside each other like 'B' and 'I', 'G' and 'O', and you have both of them, like you just did, you have a good chance of winning."

"That makes no sense," Louise said as she placed another token, making for three places in a row covered.

"Just because it makes no sense doesn't mean it can't be true," Elinor said. "It made no sense that so many of our people died at the turn of the century, but it was true. That's why I've played bingo so much. At least you get a little prize from time to time for so little effort."

Life, Elinor said, wasn't much different from a game of bingo. She placed three more tokens on her cards. Louise placed another. Life, Elinor said, like bingo, has its winners and losers. She nodded at Louise's card.

"See there. You just need one more."

The man calling out the numbers called out two more. Louise placed another token; she had a full row.

"See. What did I tell you?" Elinor said. "Shout it out. You're a winner."

Louise called out bingo, but not loud enough, and the caller continued pulling out white balls from his drum. Elinor waved an arm at the caller and pointed at Louise. "We've got a winner here." An assistant, a tall, stocky woman about Louise's age, checked Louise's numbers with those that had been called, confirming that Louise was a winner.

Elinor beamed, said she was happier than if she'd won herself.

Louise's prize was a set of six coasters with scenes from across Canada — a prairie grain elevator, white-capped mountains, Niagara Falls.

Elinor stacked her cards, said she was ready to go home.

Louise teased her mother, said she was on a roll, maybe they should keep playing.

Elinor pushed her chair from the table, said she'd let others win. She patted the shoulder of the woman next to her, waved at Jerry, and turned toward the door.

Within minutes of getting into the car, Elinor was asleep and snoring.

They drove by the train station, a grand sandstone edifice. In years to come it would be sold and converted to a casino. Louise would remark that if her mother was alive she would have been one of the first in the door.

Louise had been on edge for the past week, rehearsing what she'd tell her mother. There was no one with whom she could practise. Not even John. She would wake in the middle of the night, wander around the house, check on her mother, determine that she was still breathing, and tell herself she must do it the next day. The next day would come and go. Through some quirk in her reasoning, she'd decided that she held the power to her mother's continuance, that once she told her mother what she and Mary had done, her mother would die. At the same time, she was terrified her mother would die before she had honoured her final request.

Louise pulled into a park at the perimeter of the city. Across the road the prairie ran without interruption as far as the eye could see; in the near distance the airport, and beyond that a grain elevator. She turned off the car and switched to a radio station that played classical music. She was enjoying Vivaldi's *Four Seasons*, the "Spring" movement, and watching a red-haired three- or four-year-old boy chase after a puppy when Elinor awoke. She asked if Louise had won yet, where were her bingo cards. Then she righted herself and said the flowers were lovely. She said she remembered a time when there had been no airport, just a few buildings and no trees. She took hold of Louise's hand and asked if she was ready to tell her. Louise squeezed her mother's hand, pointed to the bench near the flower garden, and suggested they sit there.

"You might have to carry me." Elinor chuckled. "Keeping track of all those numbers and letters hasn't left me with much energy. I'd like to be near the flowers, near beauty, while I'm hearing something ugly. I'm assuming what you want to tell me isn't pretty."

Louise shook her head. "Not very pretty."

In the short distance between the car and the bench, her mother's feather-light body squeezed against her own, the scent of tobacco, the tickle of her mother's hair against her cheek. Louise's legs claimed their own authority, refusing to move quickly, creeping over the asphalt like oil or molasses. With each step the bench seemed to shrink from her. Each step took her farther, not closer. Despite her mother's insubstantial weight, Louise's arms were burdened and stiff. She settled her mother on the bench and returned to the car for a blanket. She tucked it around Elinor's legs and over her feet. She wished she'd brought a Thermos of tea and some cookies. She sat on her mother's left.

"Bring me one of those gladiolus," Elinor said.

"They're not supposed to be picked," Louise said. "If everyone picks one there will be none left."

"Do you think I don't know that?" Elinor said.

Louise looked around; she didn't see anyone. "What colour do you want?"

"Red, of course."

Louise chose a stalk with several red flowers still in bloom. She bent the stalk, twisted it one way and then the other, but it didn't break away. The stem was at least a half-inch thick; she needed a knife. Her mother seemed oblivious to her struggles. Louise scanned the area for other visitors, then bent over and bit through the stalk. It was stringy and woody, bitter tasting. She spit out the pith and took the flower to her mother.

"Thank you," Elinor said. She drew a finger around the thin edge of a petal and did the same with the flower beneath it. She poked at the stamens, rubbed the dark dust between her fingers. She shoved the flower at Louise, told her it was time for truth-telling.

"You can't tell anyone," Louise whispered.

"Where I'm going, everyone knows everything and everyone is speechless," Elinor said.

Louise leaned close to Elinor. She told her about the Scotts, the young children, and the wife who was pregnant. She spoke about how hard she worked from morning until night, washing and mending clothes, hauling water, cooking meals, feeding the chickens, weeding the gardens. The chores were endless. During a trip to town with the family, she had met Mary and the two became fast friends. Mary, Louise said, had more freedom than her and came to the farm when she could.

Louise twirled the gladiolus in her hand. She was aware of the tension across her chest, in her belly. The next part of the story was less easy to speak of.

"In the last weeks of the pregnancy, when Mrs. Scott became sickly, Mr. Scott started paying more attention to me," Louise said. She ran her tongue over her lips, stretched out her legs. "Do you really need to know all this?"

"It's not that I need to know any of it," Elinor said. "You need to speak of it. That's what is important."

Louise cleared her throat.

"So ... he'd stroke my hair ... rub my chest." She paused. "My breasts." There were prickles on the back of her neck at the thought of it. "He'd come to my bed most nights. I wasn't getting any sleep and the work never let up. In the midst of all this, Mary arrived. Somehow, I think because I was exhausted and frantic, I managed to tell her what was going on. That I'd propped a shovel against the door to keep him out, slept with a knife under my pillow. Mary said he wouldn't give up. White men thought Indian women were theirs for the taking; that I would be the next one to get pregnant.

"I was terrified," Louise said. "I didn't want a baby. Not then, not with him. Mary said the only way he'd leave me alone was if I ran away ... or killed him."

Grasping the edge of a blossom between the tips of two fingers, Louise rubbed her fingers incrementally back and forth over the flower's thin flesh. The satiny texture was momentarily soothing.

"Some choices," Elinor said. "Better odds with bingo."

"Mary said if I ran away he'd come after me. It would be worse; I'd never be free."

Elinor pulled the blanket up to her chin. "Freedom is good. We all long for that. Freedom from something. Freedom from someone. Freedom to do something. Freedom from ourselves. There was always some kid running away from that school. A few made it. We all cheered for them."

A tour bus pulled up across from them. Passengers disembarked. Some headed toward the gardens, swarming over the trails and down to the stream. Others lingered at the bus, waiting for the driver to open the luggage compartment.

Louise squeezed her fingers into her knees. One of the bus passengers was shouting, waving a fist, pacing up and down the road while the driver rummaged in the luggage compartment. Louise shifted her body so she didn't see what was going on.

"I prayed Mr. Scott would lose interest in me, find some other woman. I thought about telling Mrs. Scott, but she was in no shape to hear anything like that. I was so tired I couldn't think straight. I thought maybe it wouldn't be so bad if he had his way with me. Then I remembered what Mary said; I didn't want a baby. I talked to Mary some more. I can't believe I did what I did. I was desperate. Mary said she had some herbs. She said they were powerful; they would work quickly. I put the herbs in his lunch the day he was going out to mend fences. A neighbour found him the next day. That was forty-six years ago. July eighth, 1923. I felt horrible leaving Mrs. Scott pregnant, and with the two little ones, but I couldn't stay on after he died. I was afraid I'd tell her what I had done."

Elinor took the gladiolus stalk from Louise. She stared at it quietly for a long time. An elderly couple settled on a bench near them. He took her out of her wheelchair, laid a blanket across their laps. They were holding hands and laughing. An ant crawled onto the toe of Louise's right shoe, wiggled its antennae, turned around, and went back the way it had come.

Louise glanced at her mother.

Elinor patted Louise's hand. "I am sorry. It is a terrible thing to take another's life. I should tell you to go to the police. That would be the proper thing. You know that yourself. But I don't know what good it would do anyone now. Not speaking the truth is also a terrible thing. It always corrupts. It's like a worm burrowing in a tree, making things rotten in the core." She steepled her fingers, brought them to her lips, and closed her eyes.

"I thought a lot about telling Father," Louise said.

"It would have caused a big argument between us. He would have wanted you to go to the police. I wouldn't have been able to bear that, even though I would have agreed he was right. They would have hanged you. Poundmaker tried to make peace, gave himself up. What good did it do him? They sent him to jail, in Manitoba, away from his family. He got so sick in there they let him out, so it wouldn't be on them that he'd died in their jail. There's no justice for Indians in the white man's system."

Elinor shuffled her shoes over the ground.

"Did you ever see the wife, the children after that? The children must still be alive."

"Never saw them. Actually, that's not true. I saw them in town once. After she had the baby. I ran so fast the other way. I have thought about finding out where they live now, what they turned into. It wasn't their fault their father was who he was." She shook her head. "It was such a horrid time. I couldn't bear to have anything to do with them."

"Did the police talk to you? What did they say about why, how he died?"

304 — *Lynda A. Archer*

"They didn't talk to me. I was certain they would. I stayed in the kitchen, outside with the chickens, in the garden, when they came to the house. Maybe they figured I was a dumb Indian. Now, with all the fancy police methods, they'd probably find something in his stomach, figure out he'd ingested a poison."

"What did his wife say?"

"Nothing to me. But her sister came and I heard them talking. The sister said Mrs. Scott — her name was Rebecca — was better off without him. He was a brute. Are you upset?" Louise asked.

Elinor shoved out her bottom lip. "Too late for that. I am glad that the gulf between us is smaller. How have you lived with it?"

"With what?"

"You killed a man."

Louise glanced around her. "You don't have to say it so loudly."

"I should shout it."

"Mom ..."

"All right, all right. I want to know, how does someone live with that? I've never known a person who has done what you did."

Louise pressed her lips together and sucked in a breath. There was a commotion near the tour bus, someone shouting. A woman angry with the bus driver about her luggage. She was waving a two-by-four. Louise wondered if she should help, but saw others intervening.

"How does a person live with that? How did you?"

"In terror and fear for years. In the belief that I was a horrible person. That it would have been better to let the man rape me. Even get pregnant."

"Does John know?"

Louise shook her head.

"Probably just as well," Elinor said. She flung off the blanket, started to stand up, and turned to Louise. "Maybe one day whites and Indians will stop killing each other. You are your mother's daughter whether you like it or not. If I could have gotten away with it, I would have killed that nun. Not the man who raped me; at least something good came of that. But that nun, the one who stole my child, I have never forgiven her." Elinor patted Louise's hands, smiled into her face. "Let's go home, have some tea."

"Yes, let's do that." Louise folded the blanket, slipped her arm into her mother's.

"You've been very quiet tonight," John said, dropping his glasses on the newspaper. "Everything all right?"

"Everything's fine," Louise said. She lowered her law journal to her lap. "We played bingo this afternoon."

"How was that?"

"Enjoyable."

"Win anything?"

"A set of coasters."

"I see. We already have several sets, don't we?"

"We do. After bingo we sat in the park near the airport."

"Did Elinor like that?"

"I think she did. I think she was content."

"So, it was good all around."

"It was. Mind you, for a moment it was a bit chaotic." Louise slid the journal onto the side table, swung her legs from the footstool.

"What happened?"

"A tour bus pulled up while we were in the gardens. One of the passengers, a woman, went after the bus driver with a two-by-four. The police came pretty quickly, took her away."

"Strange. You don't expect that kind of thing from a woman. Wonder what her problem was? What did Elinor say?"

"She didn't see it. And I didn't tell her."

John nodded and grunted. He switched off his reading lamp, said he had an early morning. He asked if Louise was coming to bed; she said she had more reading to get through for the next day. He kissed her on the forehead and shuffled from the room. *His knees are bothering him again*, Louise thought.

Louise leaned back into her chair and closed her eyes. She could never tell John what she had done. As much as she hated keeping things from him, she didn't see what good it would do. Maybe she was making excuses for herself. Maybe she feared his anger. Or she wanted to spare him. John being John, he would be deeply upset with and for her. Her deepest regret was that Ian Scott's children grew up fatherless. Perhaps Sarah had remarried. And Ian Scott being the man who he was, maybe Sarah and the children were better off without him.

In the early years of her law practice, every time she had a new client with the name Scott she'd get nervous, wonder if they were related, if the death of Ian Scott would come out somehow. Her mind circled round to John's comment about the woman with the two-by-four, that such things weren't expected from women. She chuckled, picked up her law journal. The things people didn't allow for women.

There's talk, I heard them the other day, of a renovation.

Upgrading, making things more modern.

I didn't like the way the man, a young fellow, looked in my direction.

As if I wouldn't be necessary in the new museum.

As if I was little more than a mangy, extinct creature.

Another time I might have been upset, but this being stuffed in a museum for years, it's like a second dying. The only thing that made it bearable were the visits from the old Indian woman.

And she'll not be back.

39

In the valley the snow had receded, except in deep crotches where wolf willow and silverbush grew. Winter had come early and stayed late. So thickly and persistently had the snow fallen, birds didn't fly, schools and highways were closed, and roofs collapsed from the weight of the snow. Creatures unable to forage through the deep drifts starved. For weeks, bitter cold clenched the thermometer like a fist, keeping the mercury at the bottom of the glass tube. No town, village, hamlet, field, lake, or stream in the province was spared.

Meteorologists said it had been the worst winter in decades.

Louise and Alice strode in silence up the side of the low, grassy hill. The past few months, they'd taken to walking together; no formal arrangement, just a tacit agreement that each honoured.

Within days of Louise's disclosure about Ian Scott, Elinor died. She went to sleep one night and didn't wake up. She'd been especially cheery that day. When Louise thought about it later, she figured her mother knew it was her last day.

Victoria had stayed for two weeks. When the initial excitement waned, it was awkward for a time. So many questions. Questions that stirred anger, sadness, and grief. Who was Victoria's father? Why had Elinor not searched for her child sooner? What did it mean for Victoria that she was half-Indian? What had her family told her about Indians? Alice took Victoria to Elinor's house in the valley. Alice had wondered if it made Victoria uncomfortable, to learn that she'd been rescued, spared such an impoverished existence. But Victoria remained gracious and grateful for all that she was offered. The last few days of the visit, Victoria and Elinor were with each other constantly; neither expressed a desire to do anything or go anywhere. They seemed content to linger in each other's presence, watching the fish swim back and forth across the pond, the yellow creeping around the edges of the leaves, a hairy caterpillar inching along the garden path. Louise and Alice marvelled that Bright Eyes had been found, that Elinor hadn't died before having the chance to meet her.

At the station, waiting for Victoria's train, Louise had seen the adoration in Elinor's eyes. And she saw Victoria's attentiveness to Elinor. Louise wondered if Victoria would have been the daughter Elinor had always wanted. Louise vowed to herself to be more attentive to her own children, to mend the rifts, to receive them for who they were.

Louise, hands clasped behind her back, turned to take in the view of where they had come from. Alice's truck was a miniature at the side of the road. Beyond the truck a tributary of the Qu'Appelle almost overflowed its banks. Ancient willows, their wispy leaves the fresh green of spring, flung their branches over the bursting waters.

They walked along the crest of the hill, the wind blowing into their faces, the scent of cow manure wafting toward them from a farm below. A tractor clawed over an open field; a car, a plume of dust behind it, climbed up and out of the valley.

A large white cloud mass blocked the sun. Louise pulled her jacket tighter around her body and did up the buttons. They tromped into a coulee, following a narrow path left by deer and coyote, then up the flank of the next hill, along the crest, down and up again. Here and there in quiet affirmation of the arrival of spring, patches of crocus had bloomed. Furry purple blossoms, low to the earth, keeping themselves out of the prairie winds.

When they came up against a fence with black-and-white cattle on the other side of it, they turned around, headed down, strode along the road for about a mile. The wind had picked up and it blew hard on Louise's face, into her ears. She covered her ears with her hands; she'd not brought a hat.

The wind whipped Alice's long hair across her mouth and into her eyes. She turned away from the blast and walked backwards, facing her mother. When she lost her balance and almost tripped, she twirled around and ran hard to the truck.

Louise picked up her pace and walked more briskly. She was warm enough and found the cold air invigorating after a long week in the courthouse. She had bumped into one of Alice's high-school friends; she had a babe in arms, a ring on her finger. The girl asked after Alice, told Louise to have Alice call her. When Louise told Alice about Marnie, Alice shrugged and was non-committal about whether she would call. Louise had observed that Alice spent much of her free time, vacations and weekends, with her friend Wanda; they seemed very close. She wondered if Alice would ever marry; she'd not had a boyfriend in a few years. She supposed that was all right; some women never did marry.

Alice started the truck, turned the fan on high to clear the frost from the windows. She rubbed her hands briskly together then shoved them under her thighs. The warm air crept up from the bottom of the windshield, sculpting long curves and arcs in the white frost. Her mother, hands over her ears, a half-block from the truck, was walking fast. Alice waved, but her mother didn't return the wave. Alice wondered if her mother missed Elinor.

For so much of their lives, the two had been irritated with each other. Since Victoria's visit, her mother seemed calmer, quieter, less argumentative. Maybe there'd come a time when she'd be able to tell her about Wanda. She reached across and opened the door.

Hands pressed around the small red plastic tumblers filled with hot tea, they stared forward, following the long run of the gravel road until it curved toward the valley and the river. The truck shook with a blast of wind. Louise chuckled. Alice turned to her mother, asked what was funny. Louise smiled, said she imagined that gust of wind had been Elinor, reminding them that she wasn't far away, that she'd always be with them.

Alice nodded and smiled. "I like that idea. Do you think of her much? Do you miss her?"

Louise peered into the black tea. "Oh yes. I'm surprised how often I think of her. I regret that we spent so many years apart." She fell silent for a time. "It's been good to walk with you."

"Yes, I agree." Alice swallowed the last of her tea, turned the mug on the top of the Thermos.

They drove for several miles over gravelled back roads, up and down low hills, past solitary farmhouses with caragana hedges, yards filled with trucks and trailers, rusted red farm machinery, green John Deere tractors ready to move into the fields in the next month. They drove in silence. From the radio, a Mozart flute concerto, then a Rachmaninoff sonata. Eventually, they came to the Trans-Canada Highway and turned west. Louise said it wasn't the way home and asked where they were going. Alice said she'd see soon enough.

Louise recalled her confession to her mother. The yellows, purples, and reds of the flowers — silent witnesses to her dastardly deed. She recalled the frailness, and the feistiness, of her mother. She understood, in a way she never had before, the requirement that those found guilty of a crime should stand before a judge and a court and confess their crime. Tell the world what they had done. No more denial, lying, or hiding. *I killed, I raped, I stole* ...

Alice thought of Wanda. She regretted she'd not told Elinor about her, that there had been only one brief meeting between the two. She lamented that the two people she adored had not been able to know each other. She hated that her affection and *amour* for Wanda made her uncomfortable, that she struggled with her desires, that she anticipated only disapproval and disdain from others. Love is never wrong. Her gran would have told her that.

Alice turned from the highway onto a dusty grid road.

Two or three miles ahead, buildings, as if they had pushed up out of the prairie like mushrooms, huddled on both sides of the road. They crawled through the village. The municipal roadway was the main and only street in the town. Within the space of two or three city blocks, passing the post office, the Co-op and hotel, general store, and ten or twelve homes, most two-storey and painted white, they had traversed from one end of the town to the other.

Alice pulled up in front of the last building before the prairie resumed, a squat white stucco structure with black trim.

"What's this?" Louise asked.

"You'll see."

Once through the door they were immediately in a single, brightly lit, white-walled room, large, but not overly so. In the centre of the room, two shiny pine benches, a rocking chair, blankets, and pillows. The walls were covered with paintings and drawings of various sizes and shapes. Most were the traditional rectangular form, but some were small squares, others circular.

Louise remained still for a moment before moving closer to the artwork. In silence, she examined one, then another and another. A pencil sketch of a deer at the edge of a coulee. An ink drawing of the valley. A perfect oil painting, six by eight inches, of the valley in summer, fluffy white clouds mirrored in the long lake. More drawings in pencil. Her father with the smile Louise knew so well. Louise, at eight or nine perhaps, hair halfway down her back, crouching by a boulder.

"Where did you get these?" Louise asked.

"Went through Gran's cottage. She had things stuffed everywhere. We should have done something sooner, so she could have seen them all."

Shifting slowly to her right, Louise studied the drawings and paintings.

"What gave you this idea?" Louise asked.

"When I took Victoria to the cottage, she was enthralled by Gran's work, said it should be hung somewhere. So I started to think about that."

Louise stepped closer to a sketch of a circle of tipis beside a stream, then stood back. She studied the work on the first wall, then the second and the third. After she had looked at the last painting, she went around again. Closer, then dropping back, close again. When finally she settled on one of the benches, Alice joined her. Together they viewed the largest painting in the collection. Done in oil, tones of buff, slate, and blue, with patches of yellow and burnt orange, it was a long view of the valley, a huge expanse of sky and the dark waters at the valley floor. Along the lower perimeter of the painting, if one looked closely, there were eyes, round and ovoid; ears, small, tall, and pointed; and snouts of varying dimensions. Near the water's edge a cluster of tipis, a few horses, and a wooden horse-drawn wagon with a man and young child inside.

Louise strolled around the room again. This had been her life.

Eventually, she stopped at the grouping of older sketches. Smudged and torn, they showed Louise's family — crouched at a fire, picking berries, sad old men, children, their faces filled with laughter.

"These ones were done on the reserve before I left. I remember Mother working at them. I remember ..."

Louise talked for a long while. Alice listened.

At the window of the tiny gallery, Elinor watched and smiled.

On the prairie, grasses were poking through the dark soil, earthworms were tunnelling.

And the wind blew.

ACKNOWLEDGEMENTS

Many people stayed the course with this book, and I am hugely grateful to them all. The students and faculty of the MFA Program in Writing at Spalding University, Kentucky, have been, and continue to be, nothing short of amazing in their support and nurturing of my literary efforts. Special thanks to Julie Brickman for her guidance in the novel workshop and for years of encouragement. Roy Hoffman, Mary Yukari Waters, Robin Lippincott, and Neela Vaswani, mentors extraordinaire, read early drafts and provided insightful feedback. Karen Mann did a comprehensive read of a later draft for which I am most appreciative.

Special recognition goes to Frances Hanna (1944–2011), literary agent, who believed in the book from the get-go. Bill Hanna continues in that capacity.

Thanks to Allison Hirst, my editor at Dundurn, for her thoroughness, and to the Dundurn design department for a beautiful cover.

Others who guided me along the long and winding road include Deirdre Gainor, Marie Schommer, Michelle Benjamin, Maria Tuchscherer, Debra Shogan, Gloria Filax, and Shirley Routliffe.

Many people, and sources, aided me in researching and writing this book. In particular, I wish to acknowledge the following:

The Online Cree Dictionary (www.creedictionary.com); *Our Grandmothers' Lives As Told in Their Own Words*, Freda Ahenakew and H.C. Wolfart; *Treaty Promises, Indian Reality*, Harold Lerat with Linda Ungar; *Plain Speaking: Essays on Aboriginal Peoples and the Prairie*, P. Douaud and Bruce Dawson; *A Recognition of Being: Reconstructing Native Womanhood*, Kim Anderson. And for my Big Brown character, Tom McHugh's *The Time of the Buffalo*.

Gratitude to the prairie skies and lands that nurture my soul and spirit. Gratitude to the First Nations people, who have taught, and continue to teach me.

And finally, for her equanimity and unfailing support, I thank my first and last reader, my partner, Carroll Hodge.

MORE GREAT FICTION FROM DUNDURN

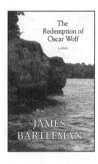

The Redemption of Oscar Wolfe
James Bartleman

In the early 1930s, Oscar Wolf, a thirteen-year-old Native from the Chippewas of Rama Indian Reserve, sets fire to the business section of his village north of Toronto in a fit of misguided rage against white society, inadvertently killing his grandfather and a young maid. Tortured by guilt, and fearful of divine retribution, Oscar sets out on a lifetime quest for redemption.

His journey takes him to California where he works as a fruit picker and prizefighter during the Great Depression, to the Second World War where he becomes a decorated soldier, to university where he excels as a student and athlete, and to the diplomatic service in the postwar era where he causes a stir at the United Nations in New York and in Colombia and Australia.

Beset by an all-too-human knack for making doubtful choices, Oscar discovers that peace of mind is indeed hard to find in this saga of mid-twentieth-century Aboriginal life in Canada and abroad that will appeal to readers of all backgrounds and ages.

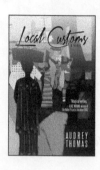

Local Customs
Audrey Thomas

Nominated for the 2014 Victoria Book Prize

Letitia Landon, "Letty" to her friends, is an intelligent, witty, successful writer, much sought after for dinner parties and soirées in the London of the 1830s. But, still single at thirty-six, she fears ending up as a wizened crone in a dilapidated country cottage, a cat her only companion.

Just as she is beginning to believe she will never marry, she meets George Maclean, home on leave from his position as the governor of Cape Coast Castle on the Gold Coast of West Africa. George and Letty marry quietly and set sail for Cape Coast. Eight weeks later she is dead — not from malaria or dysentery or any of the multitude of dangers in her new home, but by her own hand. Or so it would seem.

Local Customs examines, in poetic detail, a way of life that has faded into history. It was a time when religious and cultural assimilation in the British colonies gave rise to a new, strange social order. Letty speaks from beyond the grave to let the reader see the world through her eyes and explore the mystery of her death. Was she disturbed enough to kill herself, or was someone — or something — else involved?